"I...we have a problem."

Gideon swiveled in his seat to face Lupe, though he dreaded seeing the pain he would soon put in her eyes. "The call from the lawyer last week..."

"You said it was a matter of mistaken identity," Lupe reminded him.

"I figured it was." He inhaled deeply, exhaled and settled into his seat. "A friend was killed in a car crash a couple of weeks ago.... She had a baby girl. In her will she identified me as the father."

"So it *wasn't* a case of mistaken identity. You lied to me, Gideon!"

"I was afraid—"

"Where's your little girl now?"

"With her grandparents. She'll stay with them until this gets resolved."

"Resolved? What does that mean?"

"I have to decide if I'll take her or let her be adopted."

"You'd let somebody else raise your child?"

"I want you to be my wife," Gideon told her. "To have babies with you."

"Take me home, Gideon."

"Lupe..."

"Take me home Gideon. Now. You're not the man I thought you were."

Dear Reader,

We all make mistakes. After all, we're human. Sometimes our most troubling blunders are the ones we don't even know we're making—until the consequences come back to haunt us.

Gideon First, the youngest son of Adam First, former owner of one of the largest ranches in Texas, falls into this category. Gideon is a professor at the local university. He's a handsome, respected, popular and all-around nice guy, who conscientiously tries to do the right thing. He's also in love.

Then a crisis develops. One of his own making, though certainly not by design. And now he's faced with a dilemma. How should he handle it? Looking at the situation from the outside, perhaps the answer seems perfectly clear, but when you're emotionally involved— when you're in love—it isn't always that easy.

I hope you enjoy getting to know Gideon First and Lupe Amorado. They're both good people who have a lot of soul-searching to do before they can truly love each other. It's a journey we can take with them.

This is my third story in the FIRST FAMILY series. But stand by, there are more to come.

I enjoy hearing from readers. You can write me at Box 4062, San Angelo, TX 76902, or through my Web sites at www.superauthors.com or at www.outreachrwa.com.

K.N. *Casper*

Gideon's Baby

K.N. Casper

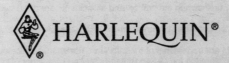

TORONTO • NEW YORK • LONDON
AMSTERDAM • PARIS • SYDNEY • HAMBURG
STOCKHOLM • ATHENS • TOKYO • MILAN • MADRID
PRAGUE • WARSAW • BUDAPEST • AUCKLAND

ISBN 0-373-71022-4

GIDEON'S BABY

Copyright © 2001 by K. Casper.

Visit us at www.eHarlequin.com

Printed in U.S.A.

To Jan Daugherty and Priscilla Keating,
for their kindness, friendship and wise counsel

CHAPTER ONE

GIDEON BOLTED to his feet, staggered forward and clenched his hands. Slowly he turned to face the attorney behind the big, shiny desk. "She said *I'm* the father?" Disbelief and panic had his chest pounding. "That's impossible, Mr. Pike. I can't be."

Unfazed by the outburst, Cavanaugh Pike went on in businesslike fashion. "She asks that you acknowledge the child, give her your name and see to her welfare."

Gideon couldn't stand still. He had to pace, had to regain his balance. He made a small circle, inhaled deeply and let the air out. The news that Becky Runyon, his former girlfriend, had been killed in a car accident was devastating enough, but this...

"You're not listening to me, Mr. Pike. I don't understand what's going on here, but I can assure you this child is not mine. I haven't seen Becky in nearly two years." That wasn't completely accurate. He'd seen her more recently, but that last time had been to have lunch, not to sleep with her.

The old man's face betrayed the stoic skepticism of one who'd heard it all before. "The child is fourteen months old."

Arithmetic. Gideon knew how to add and subtract.

Why wasn't he able to do it now? He squeezed his eyes shut and tried to visualize the numbers. Fourteen plus nine equals twenty-three. Almost two years. Damn. He sank into the armchair he'd just vacated.

"I tell you, this child is not mine, Mr. Pike." Anger and doubt were battling with fear and dread—and losing. "I have no intention of assuming responsibility for a kid that isn't mine." He thought of Lupe's children. Miguelito was nine and Teresita seven. He was going to be their stepfather. But that was different. He was also marrying their mother.

Why was Becky pinning this on him? Money? If she'd been a poor waif, it might have made sense. But she was from a comfortably well-off family. Her father was in oil, after all—not that the domestic petroleum market was exactly thriving. On the other hand, Becky herself was…had been…a successful commercial artist. Besides, if she was after money for her baby, it would have made more sense if she'd come to him while she was still alive, not wait until after she was dead. This whole affair was bizarre.

And the timing couldn't be worse. The woman of his dreams had just accepted his proposal of marriage. What would her reaction be if he presented her with his illegitimate child? Her religion and upbringing didn't permit premarital sex, so he didn't have to think twice. Never mind that his liaison with Becky had been before they'd met.

"Indeed, sir, I fully agree," Pike said. "You have no moral or legal obligation to accept responsibility for someone else's offspring." He smiled thinly. "Fortunately, these days paternity is easily enough proved—or disproved. It's a simple matter of a blood test.''

Gideon always used a condom. It was the safe and responsible thing to do. He wasn't reckless. Sure, the rubber could have failed. Nothing was perfect, but...

He didn't consider Becky to have been promiscuous, but he wasn't naive enough to think he was her sole sex partner, either. They were friends who enjoyed each other's company, but neither of them had been exclusive.

''If you'll agree voluntarily to take a blood test,'' Pike said, interrupting his thoughts, ''we can clear this matter up very quickly.''

''Voluntarily?''

The lawyer leaned back in his chair and laced his fingers across his round middle. ''I can obtain a court order, if you insist, Mr. First. Getting one won't be difficult under the circumstances.'' He pursed his lips. ''You claim this child isn't yours. Fine.'' He fixed his eyes unyieldingly on Gideon. ''Why not take the test and prove it?''

Gideon didn't like being boxed into a corner, but what real choice did he have? He needed to get this behind him. Then it hit him. They were talking about a human being, a helpless little baby. An orphan. ''What's the girl's name again?''

Pike's face softened into a grandfatherly smile. ''Janna.''

A pretty name. Gideon had the sudden image of Becky holding her in her arms and cooing at her. ''Where is she now?''

"Ms. Runyon was living with her parents in Dallas. Janna is still with them. She's well cared for."

At least she wasn't in some institution. This child wasn't his, but for some reason he couldn't explain, he felt an unexpected sense of protectiveness toward her.

"I'll take the blood test, Mr. Pike. Set it up for as soon as possible."

LUPE WASN'T making much headway in her school-work Monday morning. She'd gone to the university library early to catch up on the research she'd neglected over the weekend. For the past five years, her family and her studies had been the focus of her life. In a few short months, she'd be graduating from TUCS, Texas University at Coyote Springs, with a master's degree in physical therapy, the fulfillment of a dream. And then she'd be going into practice with Gideon. With her husband. On a sigh, she checked her watch. Noon, and she'd accomplished nothing. Ever since Gideon had proposed on Saturday, her brain had been scrambled, her concentration mush.

All she could think about was being with Gideon, making love with him, touching his body in ways she hadn't yet dared, having him touch her in ways she hadn't yet allowed. She reminisced about Miguel sometimes, too. About how she'd nestled in his arms early on a Sunday morning before they went to church—warm, content, cherished. She yearned to experience that bond again, the sensuous pleasure of sex and the inner joy of fulfillment that followed. Perhaps she should feel guilt, thinking of her late husband and wanting another man in her bed. She loved Miguel. She always would. But she loved Gideon, too.

She'd confessed this ambivalence to her priest. Almost smiling, he'd absolved her of lust and reminded her she was free to marry again with the blessings of the church. That had been important to her. A year after Miguel's murder in a drive-by shooting, at the conclusion of the traditional period of mourning, Lupe had moved her wedding ring from her left hand to her right. She wasn't trying to forget the man she'd married at eighteen and lived happily with for five years. But this small gesture was a quiet acknowledgment that she had entered into a new phase of her life.

Then she'd met Gideon.

It was her *suegra* Elena's approval of him that had given her the courage to remove the wedding band altogether and put it in her jewelry box.

Lupe gave up her vain attempt to assimilate the morphology of the human nervous system. Other body parts were getting in the way. She neatly gathered her incomprehensible notes, slipped them into a leather portfolio and made her way to the student union building. She wasn't particularly hungry, but she was ready for something to drink.

The cafeteria was crowded. She stood in line for several minutes, her mind flitting from one subject to another. There was so much to do—plans to make, details to coordinate. She felt like a kid in a candy store, not sure which mouthwatering piece to sample first, wanting them all at the same time.

She picked up a prewrapped tuna fish sandwich.

No sense standing in line for nothing more than a soft drink. Maybe she was hungry after all. She hadn't eaten much breakfast.

"Lupe, over here," a woman's voice called.

She searched the room. Karida Sommers, the dean's secretary, was waving to her from a table in the corner.

They tried to get together for lunch a few times a week. Until recently, Karida had spent all her time caring for her terminally ill mother at home, rather than put her in a nursing home. Mrs. Sommers passed away a month ago, leaving Karida grief-stricken and guilt-ridden with relief. She was only now beginning to rebuild a social life.

"Hi." Lupe deposited the sandwich and drink on the table and slipped her briefcase onto one of the two empty chairs.

"Wow!" Karida exclaimed. "Look at the size of that rock. Ooh, let me see."

Lupe felt like a queen, extending her left hand across the table. The ring sparkled even under the flat fluorescent light. Karida studied the diamond in its field of rubies.

"God, that's beautiful," she said, gushing. "It's the biggest engagement ring I've ever seen—up close and personal, that is." She released Lupe's hand and grinned. "But then what can you expect from a guy like Gideon? The soul of generosity."

The setting was beautiful, magnificent, beyond Lupe's wildest dreams.

"Congratulations are definitely in order, girl. I'm so happy for you," Karida continued effervescently as Lupe unwrapped her sandwich. "He's one good-looking stud. Hell, any woman would kill for that tall, blond hunk. And his family's ranch is one of the biggest in Texas. Yep, quite a catch." She raised her can of diet Coke in a toast. "You've done well, kid."

Lupe couldn't keep the grin off her face. It seemed to flow up from her heart. "It's a cliché," she said, "but I consider myself the luckiest girl in the world."

Karida returned the smile. "Do your kids like the idea of having a stepfather?"

"They're thrilled. They've already decided they want to call him Daddy."

Karida looked at her from under raised eyebrows. "And Elena. How does she feel about all this?"

"She's been wonderful, Karida. She even offered to sew my wedding dress if I can't find something I like."

"Having seen the outfits she'd already made for you," her friend noted in genuine admiration, "she'll do a great job. Be a lot cheaper, too. Not that you'll have to worry about money anymore." She forked through her salad and selected a ripe-red cherry tomato. "What about after you're married? Will she stay in the house you have now by herself?"

Lupe took a bite of her sandwich. "She's coming to live with us."

Karida's eyes widened. "Are you okay with that? I mean your ex-mother-in-law…"

"Actually, it was Gideon's idea." And another reason to love him. He had such a strong, caring sense of family. "He said we can buy a place with a mother-in-law house in back. Or build one. That way she'll be close to her grandchildren, and we'll still have our privacy.''

''Sounds like a plan,'' Karida said enthusiastically, though her distracted glance hinted at doubt that the setup was wise. ''The perfect solution.'' She speared a chunk of iceberg lettuce from her salad. ''Have you set the date?''

''In about three months, but we don't know exactly when yet.'' Lupe laughed. ''It'll take me that long to get used to the idea and organize everything.''

''Where will the wedding be?''

''At his father's ranch.''

''Oh, that'll be nice. I've never been out there. I hear it's beautiful.''

It was hard not to chuckle at the not-so-subtle hint. ''We'll be putting directions in the invitations on how to find the place. Don't worry, you won't get lost.''

Karida beamed, then laughed at herself. ''I guess I could just follow the crowd. No question about it. Your wedding will be the social event of the season. All those movers and shakers. I better brush up on my protocol.''

''Hey, they put their pants on like everybody else—one leg at a time,'' Lupe assured her.

Karida daydreamed. ''Hmm. I wonder how they take them off. Maybe I'll find Prince Charming.''

''Sorry,'' Lupe consoled her. ''I already got him.''

''Spoilsport.'' They both laughed. ''So about your dress. Do you have anything specific in mind?''

''I wish I did. This isn't my first marriage, so wearing the traditional white gown isn't appropriate.''

"These days," Karida observed, "no one seems to care."

"I do." She'd been a virgin when she married Miguel. Now, two kids later, she couldn't claim that apparently rare distinction.

After a couple of months of going together, Gideon confessed that he wanted to make love with her. Sex outside of marriage wasn't the way she'd been brought up. But she'd wanted him, too. Wanted him desperately. In fact, he probably would have been shocked if he'd known how much she fantasized about making love to him. She hadn't said no, but he must have sensed her ambivalence and apprehension, because he'd backed off. "When we make love," he'd said, kissing her sweetly, "I want it to be absolutely right—for both of us." She loved him all the more for not putting pressure on her and secretly wished he had.

"Elena and I will check the local dress shops this weekend," Lupe said. "Gideon's sister Julie is coming, too. Want to join us?"

"Wish I could. Should be fun," Karida observed. "But my uncle's arriving this weekend to help me clear up the last of my mother's affairs."

Lupe nodded sympathetically.

"Say," Karida went on, "I have a bunch of catalogs you might want to go through. If you don't find anything here in town and you decide to have Elena make your dress, maybe they'll give you some ideas. I'll bring them in tomorrow."

"Thanks," Lupe said sincerely. "That'll be a big help."

NICK SILER was compiling his notes from a staff meeting when he looked up from the desk and saw Gideon standing in the doorway. The somber expression on his face was both rare and ominous. "Hey, guy, what's up?"

"It's quitting time. Let's go for a few laps in the pool. You need to exercise those knees, and I need to talk to someone I can trust."

Hmm, this is serious. Nick checked his watch. A few minutes before four-thirty. "Okay. Give me a second to straighten up."

With a fleeting expression of impatience, Gideon parked himself in the chair next to the door and grabbed a magazine from the table next to it. He flipped pages, but Nick could tell he wasn't seeing them. Puzzled by his friend's unusual demeanor, he quickly returned several reports to their respective folders, filed them in the bottom drawer of his desk and turned off his computer. "Ready?"

Gideon tossed the magazine aside and rose to his feet. Nick locked the office, and they started down the corridor toward the side exit. Several people greeted them on the way. Nick hit the crash bar on the outside door and let Gideon pass. "You don't look particularly happy, Gid. Don't tell me you're getting cold feet already." Then with a wide grin, he added, "Or is she?"

A late-afternoon breeze buffeted them as they headed down the path to the indoor pool next to the gym.

"Lupe took a message for me Friday afternoon

from a lawyer by the name of Cavanaugh Pike,'' Gideon told him.

"Never a good sign."

They entered the back door of the gymnasium and turned left to the locker room reserved for male faculty and staff. Fortunately, no one was there, so they could talk freely.

"I tried to call him back—" Gideon opened his tall metal locker, sat down and removed his athletic shoes "—but he'd already gone home." He tossed his white socks in the bottom of his narrow compartment.

Nick draped his argyles on top of his soft-soled oxfords and placed them neatly in his own space.

Gideon pulled his white knit shirt over his head. "Lord protect us, we've had enough of lawyers to last a lifetime. There was that trouble a couple of years ago when my sister Kerry sold her share of the Number One to the bank, and Dad ended up losing control of the ranch."

Old history. Nick wondered why his friend was taking so long to get to the point.

"I considered the possibility that someone from the nursing home where I volunteer on weekends was suing me. I've signed an agreement with staff there that allows me to supervise exercises, but occasionally they think I'm prescribing therapy, and professional jealousies get in the way."

"But it wasn't that," Nick concluded as he pulled on his trunks and sat down to massage his right knee, the one that was giving him the most trouble. Within a year, probably sooner, he'd have to give in and get both joints replaced. He dreaded going under the knife. "Gid, you're telling me what this guy Pike didn't want. Stop beating around the bush and tell me what he did."

Gideon huffed. "You remember Becky Runyon?"

"Your old flame? Haven't seen her in a couple of years. Moved to Dallas, didn't she?" He quirked Gideon a playful smirk. "Don't tell me she's shown up and now you—"

"She'd dead. Killed in a car accident last week."

Nick ceased his kneading motion and studied his companion. "Gid, I'm sorry."

"This lawyer is handling her estate."

"Bummer. But why'd he get in touch with you? Did she leave you something in her will?"

"You could say that." Gideon shucked the rest of his clothes and put on his swimsuit. "A baby."

Nick lowered his leg and gaped at his friend. "A what?"

Gideon took a deep breath. "She had a baby a little over a year ago. After she left here." He slammed his locker door, the metallic clang reverberating off the concrete walls. "In her will she named me as the father."

Nick had suspected Gideon and Becky were sexually involved. Levering himself to his feet, he asked, "Are you?"

"It's remotely possible," Gideon acknowledged. He rose swiftly from the bench, grabbed a towel from the stack on a table at the end of the aisle and marched to the door. "Let's swim." Nick followed.

The pool area echoed with the sounds of voices and

splashing water. The clean smell of chlorine hung heavy in the warm damp air. They swam for twenty minutes, Gideon power-stroking twice as many laps as Nick. Finally, he pulled himself up on the edge of the pool beside his friend, who had resumed massaging his right knee.

"You'll have to do something about those knees pretty soon. You can't keep taking cortisone shots and popping pain pills."

"I'm aware of that." Nick had been a competition cross-country runner and had won several marathons. But a fall while mountain climbing three summers ago had jammed his knees and ruined his athletic career. Soon Mother Nature would have to give way to the wonderful world of plastic.

"After it's done, you'll kick yourself for not doing it sooner," Gideon assured him.

"I'll be that flexible, huh?"

"Yep." Gideon grinned for the first time.

"Why don't we hit the showers—" Nick climbed stiffly to his feet "—then you can tell me the rest of the story."

Ten minutes later, they were finished dressing. "Okay," Nick prompted, "start talking."

Hands braced on the edge of the bench, Gideon exhaled loudly through his nose and stared straight ahead. "The last night I spent with Becky was almost two years ago, twenty-three months to be exact." He sat motionless for a long moment. "She was an interesting person, Nick, talented and well read. We talked about everything—books, music, current events."

"You had a lot in common."

"Actually, we disagreed about almost everything, including religion and politics."

"But not sex."

Gideon smiled. "In that department, we got along real fine. Not that we were in love. I couldn't see myself spending the rest of my life with her, and she made it clear she wasn't interested in marriage. Not to me, at least."

Nick hadn't been all that well acquainted with Becky, certainly not as intimately as Gideon, but in his last conversation with her, Nick sensed a kind of restlessness, a searching and growing and perhaps a hint of frustration that Gideon wasn't searching and growing with her. "You didn't see the way she looked at you."

Gideon flexed his jaw, a familiar indication that he was uncomfortable. "We were friends, Nick. And we had great sex together," he added with a certain male pride. "But that was as far as it went."

Nick couldn't resist a taunt. "Yet she had your baby."

Gideon's temper erupted. "We don't know it's my baby. And what are you suggesting, anyway? That she intentionally got pregnant, then went off to have my love child as some sort of trophy?" He snorted, letting the heat dissipate. He never did stay angry very long. "Give me a break. She was dedicated to her career, not to raising a family. I suspect that's why she moved in with her parents rather than get a place on her own. I certainly don't recall her being very close to them. The few occasions I met the Runyons they didn't strike me as particularly warm people.''

"I doubt she got pregnant intentionally,'' Nick conceded, ''but that doesn't mean she wasn't in love with you—'' he held up his hands in surrender ''—or that the baby isn't yours. You said yourself it's possible.''

"I said it's *remotely* possible. Damn it, Nick, if she'd told me she was pregnant—'' he spread his hands in an imploring gesture ''—don't you think I would have asked if it was mine? I always used protection, but I'm not naive. Accidents happen.'' He grunted. ''Obviously.''

Nick checked the toiletries in his locker to see if any needed replenishing. ''So the last contact you had with her was two years ago?''

"That was the last time we had sex,'' Gideon clarified. ''I saw her about two months after that. She called me at work and invited me to lunch at the Old Mesquite Grill. To say goodbye. She'd been offered a good job as a graphic artist with a big advertising agency in Dallas and was moving there. I congratulated her, of course. By then, I'd met Lupe and we'd had our first date. I told Becky about her and she said she was glad I'd finally found someone special.''

Becky would, Nick concluded, especially if Gideon was rhapsodizing about Lupe the way he usually did. By then, Becky must have been aware of her condition. Maybe she'd planned to tell him, but seeing how happy he was with his new girlfriend, she'd decided not to.

They tossed their damp towels in a corner recep-

tacle and exited the locker room. In the parking lot,
Nick leaned against the fender of his two-year-old
truck and crossed his arms. "When are you telling
Lupe about this?"

Hands in his pockets, Gideon paced back and forth
for a minute, his head lowered. "I'm not. Not yet, at
least." At a tsk of annoyance, he glared at his friend.
"I don't even know if I'm the father," he said angrily. "Simply because Becky said I am doesn't make
it true."

Another tense minute went by. "Not telling her…is
that wise, Gid?"

"There's nothing to be gained by spilling the beans
about this. Not unless I have to," he replied, without
much conviction. "If the test is negative—and it will
be—there's no reason she ever has to know."

"Except she's going to be your wife. What happens if it's positive?"

Gideon took a deep breath. "Then…" He tightened his lips and shook his head. "It won't." It better
not.

GIDEON'S REGULAR Tuesday morning meeting with
the track coach took longer than he'd expected. It was
past eleven when he trekked back to his office and
found Lupe sitting at his desk, which she'd cleared
enough to set up her books. She often used his office
to study between classes when he wasn't there. It was
quiet and more convenient to her classes.

An uneasy smile spread across Gideon's face. This
was the woman he loved, the woman he wanted to
marry and spend the rest of his life with, the woman

he wanted to make babies with. He wished he could find a way to tell her how much he loved her. Maybe after they were wed, when finally they tore their clothes off and touched each other the way he'd been dreaming of doing, she would understand the depth of his feelings for her. Until then, he had to be content with looking and light touching.

"Don't you have a neurology lab this morning?" He glanced at the clock over the door. She was always scrupulous about attending even the most boring lectures. Labs were mandatory.

"They had to repair the light fixtures, something about one of the ballasts catching fire, so they're replacing them all."

Once he'd shut the door behind him, he moved closer to her. "And you decided to spend the time with me." He reached out, gathered her hands in his and pulled her gently to her feet. "If I'd known that, I would have been here sooner."

Unable to suppress a smile, she said, "What, disappoint Coach Davies?" She didn't object when he brushed his lips against hers.

"We could run our own muscle coordinating experiments here," he intimated, his mouth a scant fraction of an inch from hers.

"Special tutoring?" she whispered.

"Uh-huh." He kissed her more passionately this time. "Carefully controlled experiments."

He took her hand and gazed at the ring he'd put on her finger. Soon he would pair it with a gold band.

"I expected you to call last night," she said,

squirming pleasantly when he kissed her fingers, "to tell me what that lawyer wanted."

He'd deliberated calling her, but he knew she'd ask questions, and after his discussion with Nick, he wasn't sure how to answer them. He didn't like keeping secrets from her, but he was even more afraid of losing her. "Hmm?"

"Cavanaugh Pike," she reminded him, her head bent to one side. His response was to kiss her neck. On the tender skin below the ear. She had to remember to breathe. "You went to see him yesterday." She twisted under his lips. "What was it all about?"

"Oh, that." He released her hand and pulled back. "A case of mistaken identity." At least, he hoped it was.

The abrupt separation left her staggering. "Mistaken identity?" She moved to the front of the desk and peered at him.

To avoid meeting her eyes, he started sorting through the latest accumulation of papers. "Just one of those legal mix-ups."

She reached forward and cupped his chin so he had to look at her. "But he had your name."

He broke off contact almost immediately. "Yeah, but he'd been given some wrong information."

"I don't understand."

"A case of mistaken identity. I'm not the guy he was looking for after all." He touched the tip of her nose with a finger, eager to change the subject. "If you won't let me give you a private lab session, how about lunch? I hear the Peking Duck has a sushi bar now. Can you imagine? Sushi in Coyote Springs?"

Something was bothering him. Should she press him now or wait until he was ready to tell her?

"I can't," she finally said, and gathered her books. "I have to get over to the library and finish that paper. I've decided I hate kinesiology."

"Uh-huh." The twinkle was back in his baby blues. "How about kinesiologists?"

"Maybe them, too." But she was smiling when she said it.

Chuckling, he circled the desk and drew her into his arms. "Gee, I hope not."

The damned blood test better be negative.

CHAPTER TWO

THESE PAST FEW NIGHTS, Gideon had lain awake, rest-less, thinking about Becky, the relationship they'd had, and worrying about the baby she said was his.

Nick had been wrong—he and Becky didn't really have much in common. Not the way he and Lupe did. True, Becky had been fun to be with—in and out of bed. A good friend. A pleasant companion. But he'd never considered her as a possible life partner. She was too committed to her independence and driven by her career. Well, Lupe was, too, but in a different way. Lupe's primary dedication was to her family, whereas Becky hadn't shown the slightest interest in domestic matters. Had she really regarded him with the romantic interest Nick said he'd seen? Gideon doubted it.

What would he have done if she'd told him at their last meeting that she was pregnant with his child?

There was only one answer: offer to marry her. It would have been the right thing to do, the honorable thing. His father had told Gideon's sister Kerry that he didn't want any bastard kids in the family, then he'd forced her to marry the scum bucket who'd got-ten her pregnant. It had been a big mistake that had resulted in divorce three years later. The bitterness between father and daughter hadn't ended there, though. Two years ago, after their younger brother had been killed in a car accident, Kerry had sold controlling interest in the family ranch to a bank, destroying a heritage that went back nearly two centuries. Gideon didn't like to even contemplate what the old man's reaction would have been if he'd gone to him and told him he was about to have another illegitimately conceived grandchild.

Would Becky have accepted his proposal? He honestly didn't know. Could they have been happy together? That was an even bigger mystery. Maybe she would have turned into a devoted, nurturing mother. Her moving in with her parents suggested otherwise.

He remembered their last meeting. They'd laughed and joked the way they always had. He could recall rambling on through most of their meal about Lupe, singing praises to her beauty, her intelligence, the wonderful single parent she was, and how she, at least, liked to go fishing—something Becky jeered at as a totally boring waste of time.

He recollected, too, that there'd been a glimmer of adventure in her eyes when she told him she was picking up stakes and moving away—as if she'd reached a hard-fought decision that very moment. She'd taken his hand in an uncharacteristically sentimental gesture that had touched him, and wished him well. Pondering the glow that had emanated from her that day, he reckoned she must have realized she was pregnant. Perhaps she wasn't absolutely sure the baby was his, but she should have told him. Even if she wasn't interested in marrying him, he had the right to know he'd created a new life. It hurt to realize that, in spite of their closeness, she was more content to have the baby alone than involve him in their kid's life, in her life.

Whoa! It wasn't his kid. He had to remind himself of that. Obviously, she hadn't confided in him about her pregnancy because he wasn't the father.

Except…she'd named him the father in her will.

It didn't make sense.

Well, there was no point in losing sleep over it. He'd been up-front in his relations with her and had been prepared to meet his obligations toward her—or their baby, if there had been one. But she'd made her choices, and she hadn't given him any options under the circumstances.

The big question was what was the proper thing to do in this situation—if the kid turned out to be his? Of course he'd contribute to her support—if he was her father. But should he bring her up himself? Could he possibly ask Lupe to help him raise his illegitimate daughter? It would be asking a lot of any woman, and of course, Janna's presence would be a constant reminder that he'd made love with another woman. Knowing it intellectually was one thing, but having the evidence before you every day was quite another.

Nick was probably right; not telling Lupe had been a mistake. Especially if the baby did turn out to be his. But if Janna wasn't his…well, no harm was done.

"WHICH ONE would Gideon like best?" Lupe asked Julie and Elena. She held up a dusty rose midcalf dress that had a full skirt and a tight bodice.

''Not that one,'' Julie declared unconditionally. ''The color is wrong and the cut is too old-fashioned. It reminds me of a dance-party dress of the fifties.''

Lupe laughed. Gideon's sister was right. It would also make her look too short. At five feet four inches, she tried not to emphasize her diminutive stature.

Julie had come by the house bright and early and practically dragged the two women out to start their adventure. She was fun to be with, Lupe decided. Energetic and lighthearted. A bit blunt at times, but not unkind.

Lupe reviewed the gowns she'd seen so far. At the Wedding Salon, Elena had fallen in love with a pink lace, ankle-length dress with a mandarin collar and satin ribbons tipped with tiny silk roses hanging from the waist. It was beautiful but a bit too old for a woman of twenty-eight.

Julie favored a clinging silver lamé, knee-length number they'd found at Nuptial Nights. Another lovely choice—for someone else. Julie could have worn it easily and given it class and style. But Lupe wouldn't feel comfortable in something so flashy.

She was leaning toward a pale-lavender, full-length silk gown she'd found at Bridal Boutique, except that the V-neck wasn't quite right.

Julie brushed aside the notion of conferring with her brother. ''His opinion doesn't count. He's only the groom.'' Lupe's mind flirted with the image of tall, blond Gideon in a black tuxedo. A very stirring image. ''Besides, the lug wouldn't know a wedding gown from a cocktail dress. Given a choice, he'd probably prefer you in a miniskirt.''

"Be careful," Lupe warned with a wink and a chuckle, "you're talking about the lug I love."

Elena chimed in more seriously, "It is bad luck for the groom to see his bride in her gown before the wedding."

"I wouldn't let him see me in it," Lupe objected. "Maybe I could just ask him which color he prefers."

"He'll say blue," Julie insisted. "Men always say blue."

Lupe raised her brows in mock alarm. "Hmm. I would have thought red. I didn't realize you were such an expert on the male of the species." She grinned at Julie's suddenly sheepish expression. "But you're probably right. Blue is his favorite color."

"I can make you a dress like the one you picked out," Elena offered, "with the scoop neck you prefer. Let's go to Sophisticated Fabrics and see if we can find some material in the right shade."

"You're doing so much already," Lupe told Elena, pleased at the offer yet feeling guilty because it meant so much work. The gown was deliciously elegant in its simplicity, and Lupe knew from her feeble attempts at sewing that simplicity didn't mean easy or cheap.

"No more than I wish to do," the older woman said with a fond pat on her hand.

Julie, perhaps sensing Lupe's reservations, nudged her with an elbow. "Hey, this is for your wedding day, sister-in-law. A very special event. Let's make sure it's absolutely perfect."

Laughing, Lupe threw one arm around Elena's

waist and the other over Julie's shoulder. "You're right. So what are we waiting for, ladies? Let's go."

WHILE LUPE was shopping with Elena and Julie that Saturday, Gideon was inspecting vacant buildings in downtown Coyote Springs with Nick. There were plenty to choose from. Unfortunately, few of them came close to meeting their needs. Most property owners were willing to clean up long-vacant premises and make a few cosmetic changes, like painting walls and repairing flaws they'd have to correct no matter who occupied the space. But none of them would shell out significant amounts of money to customize the premises to larger specifications, like installing wheelchair lifts when the premises were on more than one level.

"That last place wasn't too bad," Gideon commented as they drove toward the university. "A little more space than we need, but that allows us room to expand. It's near the hospital, too, so the location is right."

Since Nick worked a regular forty-hour week as the registrar at TUCS and wasn't married, he often spent his evenings driving around town, scouting available commercial space. Gideon's schedule, while more flexible, was less predictable. In addition to teaching kinesiology in the physical therapy department and advising the athletic department's coaching staff on techniques for improving the performance of their competitors, he attended most of the university's sports events. Weekends were about the only time he could get together with Nick to check out the most promising prospects for their proposed physical therapy center.

"Forget it," Nick said. "If I'd realized beforehand it was one of Martin's properties, I wouldn't even have suggested looking at it."

"Why not?" They'd been planning on officially forming their partnership right after the end of the spring semester, after Lupe got her degree and credentials as a PT.

"Martin won't make the renovations we need," Nick explained.

"In that case," Gideon countered, "it seems to me it'd make a good bargaining chip in negotiations. The alterations we need couldn't cost that much, a few thousand dollars. We could pay for them in exchange for a reduction of the lease price." He turned west on San Jacinto Boulevard.

Nick shook his head. "Bad move. With almost anybody else, I'd probably agree. But I know Martin. He used to be on the city council. The guy's a shark. He'll let you improve his property, then he'll turn around and up the rent because it's more desirable."

"The guy who showed it to us said Martin would go with a five-year lease," Gideon responded. He turned south on Jefferson Drive. It would take them to the campus.

"Yeah, he says that now. When we get to actual negotiations, though, I'm willing to bet dollars to doughnuts he'll insist on a one-year agreement with *options* for follow-on years, claiming it's to protect us in case our venture doesn't work out. That way we won't be stuck with paying rent on a place we'll no longer be using.''

Gideon wrinkled his brow. ''What's so bad about that? Makes sense to me.''

Nick shook his head at his friend's innocence. ''The option will also allow him to raise the rent every year.''

''Hmm. Catch-22, huh? Would he really do that?''

Nick chuckled. ''Trust me, he's done it before. He tried to pull that stunt on Doug Carson last year.'' Doug ran a sign shop on South Travis.

''What happened? Did Doug have to pay?''

Nick smirked. ''Nope. He reminded Martin of the building code violations on the premises and that he hadn't bothered to get a permit when he added a shed to the back of the building. Martin decided to leave the rent as is. Doug's moving out at the end of the year.''

Gideon was frustrated. Nothing seemed to be going right lately. They'd been searching for a possible location for their PT center for over a month. Coyote Springs wasn't so big that finding something should take that long. He was also learning that he didn't know a damn thing about dealing in real estate. At least he had Nick to keep him straight on that score.

And, of course, there was the little matter of a blood test hanging over his head.

''We'll keep looking,'' Nick announced, clearly not happy with the situation, either.

''We'll build,'' Gideon declared.

''Build? Do you have any idea the kind of money you're talking about?''

"The lot on the southeast corner of North Travis and Second is perfect," Gideon reminded him, feeling very proud of himself, "and it's for sale."

"It is, but we can't afford to build."

"Why not?" Gideon asked with a shrug. "I can get the capital. Hey—" he tried to counter the scowl he saw on his friend's face "—this is our life's work. You, Lupe and me. If we build from scratch, we can be sure to get exactly what we require and we can design it to expand."

Nick ran his tongue across his teeth behind pinched lips. "This is a partnership, remember. I don't have the kind of money it would take to contribute to a building fund, and I'm sure Lupe doesn't."

Gideon's expression was one of complete confusion. "But I do, Nick. What's the sense of having money and connections if I can't use them?"

Frustration had Nick shaking his head. "It would be great if we could afford to pay back the loan, Gid, but we can't. I'm not asking for a gift. I want to be a full partner, not an employee."

"You would be a partner," Gideon insisted, clearly baffled by his friend's opposition.

Nick found himself confronting an old dilemma. Gideon had grown up on the renowned Number One Ranch, a huge tract of land larger than some states and a few countries. It was a world unto itself. His father, Adam First, had taught him discipline, hard work and generosity. Ironically, it was the generosity that was the problem. Gideon would give a person the shirt off his back—and then go and buy another one. Possessions really didn't mean much to him, and for that reason, he couldn't seem to understand that they did to other people.

"Thanks for the offer, Gid," he said, as they pulled up in front of the university pool where they would swim for half an hour or so, "but unless I can carry my share of the load, I'm not interested in the deal."

ELENA DREW HER NEEDLE expertly through a piece of combed linen fabric and peered over the top of her half glasses. "You are very quiet tonight."

They were sitting in the living room. It was late. The children had gone to bed. A wildlife program was playing on the television—its volume turned down low—but neither Lupe nor her mother-in-law was paying much attention to it.

Lupe chortled. "What you hear is exhaustion." She stretched her arms above her head. "The dress is beautiful, Mama. Are you sure you don't mind making it? It's so much work."

They'd found the perfect fabric, a shimmering powder-blue silk and rayon blend, and a pattern that was almost exactly like the one at Bridal Boutique. It came with an optional scoop-neck design.

"Mind?" Elena pulled back her chin, but there was a gleam in her dark brown eyes. "Don't be silly, child. I love doing it. It's nice to have something to contribute." She took several more stitches, then lowered the sewing. "I am so very happy for you, *mija*. He is a good man—Gideon." The name sounded more like Hideón, though Elena's accent in English was generally so mild as to be nearly imperceptible.

Lupe's fatigue of a few minutes earlier vanished.

"Oh, Mama, it's all so exciting." She grinned broadly. "I keep pinching myself. I can't believe we're really getting married."

The TV emitted the muted cry of a lonely animal. Both women ignored it. In a worried tone, Lupe added, "Sometimes it scares me, too."

Elena gave her a shrewd smile. What woman didn't have the jitters at an impending marriage?

"Mrs. Gideon First." She said the words experimentally and with a bit of reverence. "Me. Guadalupe Hernandez-Amorado. It's a little overwhelming."

Elena smiled to herself, pleased for the young woman she loved like her own daughter. Lupe had been a good and true wife to her son, Miguel. She'd made him happy. Elena tried not to think about how brief that happiness had been or the void it had left. Lupe was still young and alive, Elena reminded herself. She deserved to find happiness with a man again.

"It'll take some getting used to though," Lupe added. "I'm not accustomed to walking into shops and buying things merely because I like them, the way Gideon does."

That, apparently, was a family trait. Julie had refused to let them even see the prices on the fabrics they'd looked at, insisting cost wasn't a consideration. She'd put the entire bill for the material, pattern and accessories on the ranch credit card, reminding Lupe that before long she would have one of her own.

"He wants to make you happy," Elena reminded her daughter-in-law.

"I'm certainly not used to hobnobbing with judges and powerful politicians." Lupe rambled on.

Enjoying her daughter-in-law's euphoria, Elena noted, "At his father's birthday party, you met many people like that, and they were charmed by you." She caught Lupe's shy glance. The girl couldn't disguise the smile that came automatically to her lips. "They were all such nice people, and I heard as much Spanish spoken there as English. Your Gideon—he speaks Spanish very well, too."

Elena took several more stitches, knotted and clipped the thread, examined her work, then rested it on her lap. She gazed at the young woman sitting across from her.

"I am very proud of you, *mija*. You have done so much with your life." Her daughter-in-law's face radiated pleasure. "You have brought up Miguelito and Teresita to be good, respectful children, and soon now, you will graduate from college. The first in your family."

Lupe's glow faltered. "Because of Miguel," she said softly.

The old woman's lips quivered for the briefest of moments. Miguel. She'd brought him into the world, loved him, then laid him to eternal rest. The pain would never go away, nor would the pride she felt in knowing he'd been a good man.

The payment on his life insurance policy had allowed his grieving widow to go to college. Lupe had resisted at first, insisting the money should be put away for his children's education, but Elena had convinced her to use part of it for herself. After all, with higher job skills, she could earn more and provide better for the family. The children would see, too, how important learning was.

"No, *mija*. Because of you," Elena corrected her. "You are a good mother, an honor student and a strong woman. Miguel would be proud of you."

Impulsively, Lupe jumped up from her chair, ignored the magazines that tumbled to the floor and went to Elena's side. With glistening eyes, she bent and kissed her *suegra* affectionately on the cheek. "I wish—"

Swallowing her tears, the older woman said, "Do not wish for the past, child. You cannot change it. Work for the future. That is where you can make a difference."

With a tight voice, Lupe said, "I love you, Mama. And I'm so grateful to you for being so wise and understanding."

Elena snorted in self-deprecation, but the words warmed her greatly.

After another embrace, Lupe picked up the magazines from the floor and resumed her seat.

Elena sensed an uneasiness in the young woman. "Something is troubling you. What is it? Has Gideon said or done something to hurt you?"

Lupe's immediate impulse was to deny it. "Of course not. He'd been so positive and generous, Mama, so eager to please." She chuckled. "I have to be careful what I say. If we stop for an ice cream cone and I tell him pistachio is my favorite flavor, he's ready to order a gallon of it for me to take home." Yet, every once in a while, she glimpsed a faraway expression on his face that scared her.

Elena's lips curled in a happy grin as she resumed her sewing. "Ah, he's a man in love."

A warm feeling washed over Lupe. "Sometimes, though...I wonder if he's having second thoughts."

A snicker came from the old woman. "Of course he is. It is natural for a man to get nervous at the prospect of marriage. Even to the woman he loves." She took another stitch in the soft fabric. "Commitment isn't easy for a man, especially one who has lived a carefree and comfortable life."

"It hasn't all been easy for him, Mama," Lupe reminded her. "His mother died when he was thirteen, and his younger brother was killed in a car accident a few years ago right after graduating from college. Then his sister Kerry...she almost destroyed the family with her drinking."

"Yes, it is difficult when people die and when other people do things that hurt us." Elena snipped a lose thread. "But none of that was his fault, and there was nothing he could do about it. Marriage means commitment and responsibility. Other people's lives and happiness will depend on him now."

Lupe hadn't viewed it in that light, maybe because her background was so different from his. She hadn't grown up poor, exactly, but her parents did have to watch their spending. Still, Gideon wasn't completely reckless with money. He loved his family and wanted to start one of his own. Seeing the way he encouraged Miguelito and Teresita, she was certain he would make a good father—if he didn't spoil them. "So, it's just marriage that scares him?"

Elena nodded. "He loves you, *mija*. Everybody can see that."

They were beautiful words—*He loves you*. Even more beautiful was hearing him say *I love you*.

Her mother-in-law held up her work to examine it. Matching the two sides of a seam, she joined them with straight pins from the cushion at her elbow. Without raising her head, she asked in a quiet voice, "And you? Are you perhaps a little afraid of getting married again?"

"Afraid?" Lupe chuckled easily. "I love him, Mama. With all my heart." Then she added almost as an afterthought, "I'm not sure it'll be easy living with him, though."

Elena peered over her half glasses. "What do you mean?"

"He's good at his work. I can learn so much from him. But he's so disorganized it drives me crazy. You should see the desk in his office. It's always a jumble of files and letters. He doesn't even throw out the envelopes, even though the wastebasket is inches away." Unconsciously, she straightened the dust-cover on her easy chair. "And the town house where he lives—it's every bit as bad."

"So he's a slob?" Elena quipped with a smile.

Lupe pinched her lips together, though her eyes still glittered. "In a word, yes."

"Have you talked to him about this?"

Lupe snorted. "And helped him straighten things up. But the next day everything's right back the way it was."

Nostalgia softened Elena's features. "I know what

it is like to constantly pick up after a man. My Fernando, God rest his soul, left his clothes wherever he took them off. I would fight with him about it sometimes, but usually, I just did what had to be done. He was a man with virtues that made up for his vices.''

Lupe smiled sadly at the sweet memory of her late father-in-law. ''It's still very annoying,'' she contended, ''and not a good example for the children.''

''It is hard to teach an old dog new tricks,'' Elena rejoined, ''but I understand it can be done. Gideon is not so old that you cannot teach him a few things.''

Lupe laughed. Young and virile, if the impression he left on her from his embraces was any indication. And there were some tricks she was looking forward to. ''I'll give it a try.''

AFTER HIS FIRST lecture Monday morning, Gideon returned to his office to finish writing the Kinesiology 101 final exam for the end of the semester. He'd developed a bank of questions over the past few years that he could draw from, but he knew his prior-year students had passed most of them around, so he never gave the same test twice, and he always re-sorted the options on multiple-choice tests.

Lupe was hanging up the phone when he walked in. He'd forgotten she'd offered to help him write some new test items and reword the old ones. Yesterday, he and his sister Julie had taken her and the kids to the ranch to go horseback riding. Both Miguelito and Teresita warmed to the saddle without hesitation or fear. Julie had tutored the little girl in the preliminaries of neck-reining while Gideon coached the boy in barrel racing. Lupe, who had rarely ridden and wasn't particularly at ease with horses, had been content to sit and watch.

Later in the evening, when he and Lupe finally had a little privacy, there'd been a vague emotional chasm between them. At one time, he would have chalked it up to sexual tension—there was certainly plenty of that—but something else was holding them apart. He thought at first there might be some problem with the wedding plans—that she'd decided to have it at the church in town instead of at the ranch, or she was worried about the cost or the caterer. But when he asked her, she denied any difficulties. What he was really afraid of was that she might be rethinking marriage itself.

"Gideon, that lawyer called again," she announced as he entered the room.

His heart froze. He could hear concern in her voice. She knew or suspected something was wrong. But there was no point in jumping to conclusions. After all, the attorney might be calling to pass on the good news that the test had proved negative, that he was off the hook, that Janna Runyon wasn't his daughter.

He dumped his lecture notes on the corner of the desk, barely noticing that she'd reorganized his papers into neat stacks. "Did he say what he wanted?"

She kept staring at him, her eyes begging him to explain what was going on. "Only that he'd like you to stop by his office as soon as you can."

"I'll drop by this afternoon."

She didn't let up. "Gideon, what's this about? Why does this lawyer want to see you again?"

"I don't know, honey." He wrapped his arms around her slender waist and wished they were somewhere very private, in a place where he could painstakingly strip away the barriers of clothing between his hands and her skin. "We'll just have to wait and see." He nuzzled her neck, taking little nips with his mouth.

"But you said it was a case of mistaken identity." She squirmed away from his lips, apparently unmoved by his attention. "About what? I don't understand."

"I don't, either, sweetheart." He arched back, focusing on her luscious mouth rather than her eyes. "As soon as I find out, I'll tell you." He kissed her lightly on the lips. "Promise."

It didn't take more than a glance to see the worry on her face. The questions and doubt. He was holding something back from her, and she didn't like it. He felt like a fraud not telling her, but if Pike was going to say the test had come back negative, there was no reason to spill the beans.

"I've got a meeting with Coach Davies—" he checked the clock on the wall "—fifteen minutes ago." He winked at her. "As soon as I finish there, I'll go downtown and find out what this is all about." He released her. "If I don't get to see you again this afternoon, I'll pick you up at seven for dinner, all right?"

She hesitated for a split second, then perked up. Sticking a finger under his nose, she warned him with playful seriousness, "Don't you dare be late again."

"I wasn't late the other night," he declared haughtily. "You got the time mixed up."

When she pursed her lips, he kissed them. And he couldn't help but laugh when she contemplated him with half-closed eyes. "Okay, so *I* got the time mixed up. We're talking about a mere half hour."

She stroked her hand along his smooth cheek. "It's a woman's privilege to be late, Gideon, not a man's."

"Sexist."

With a taunting grin, she ran the tip of her index finger across his lips. "Just remember that."

He snapped at her finger, but she was too fast.

His lighthearted mood faded quickly after he left the office. The meeting with the head athletic coach and a runner he'd been helping recover from a broken tibia kept his mind diverted, but the moment it was over he jumped into his Explorer and hightailed it downtown. If he'd received the call from the lawyer personally, he could have asked for the results and this thing could have been over. It would have been so satisfying to hear the lawyer say, "You're off the hook. The blood test came back negative."

Since it was late in the afternoon, he found a parking spot in front of the building. His hands were sweaty as he rode the elevator to the sixth floor.

Pike rose in gentlemanly fashion from behind his desk and extended his hand. His bland expression gave nothing away.

"I assume the results are back." Gideon sat on the edge of the seat the attorney waved him to.

"Yes, Mr. First, they are." As if it were the most natural thing in the world to drag out suspense, he picked up a piece of paper from the top of his desk. Ordinary paper, but from the light slanting in through the window behind the lawyer, Gideon could see the shadow of the letterhead.

"I received the report this morning." He paused and regarded him from across the wide desktop. Gideon decided the man was some sort of sadist, dragging this out.

On a deep breath, Gideon asked, "And what does it say?"

Another brief pause. "It affirms Ms. Runyon's statement, Mr. First, that you are the father of her child. Janna Runyon is your daughter."

CHAPTER THREE

THERE SHOULD HAVE been a streak of lightning and a sharp crack of thunder. But there wasn't. Gideon should have felt something. But he didn't. He was numb except for the sinking feeling in the pit of his stomach. His world had irrevocably changed. And he knew it.

"I see," he mumbled.

Cavanaugh Pike, to his credit, said nothing. His gaze resting impassively on Gideon, he waited patiently for a further response. It took several minutes in coming.

"Is there any chance the results are wrong?"

"They're not," Pike said flatly. "The laboratory that does them is very thorough and reputable."

Gideon exhaled a burst of air. "What happens now, Mr. Pike?"

"That depends in part on you, Mr. First. Will you honor Ms. Runyon's requests?"

"To give the child my name and provide for her welfare?" Gideon asked rhetorically. "Of course. I won't abandon my child." The words echoed in his ears. *My child.* He looked at his hands. He was wringing them, something he couldn't recall ever doing before. Stilling them, he raised his head. "Exactly what do I have to do?"

"Papers will be filed in family court to officially transfer custody to you—assuming you want to take direct custody of her. If, for some reason, you feel disinclined to raise her yourself, you can put her up for adoption."

"Adoption?" The possibility hadn't even crossed Gideon's mind. "Then she wouldn't have my name," he objected.

"A mere technicality," Pike observed. "Ms. Runyon's request for her daughter to bear your family name is not legally binding. Or the name could be changed when you assume legal responsibility for her and changed again when she's adopted."

Damn it, having a child was supposed to be a joy, not a matter of legal maneuvering. "You make her sound like something to be bartered and sold."

"You asked what your options are, Mr. First. I'm telling you. If you'd prefer to confer with your own counsel—"

Gideon shook his head. "Please go on."

"You can also place her in the foster care system and agree to pay all expenses associated with her upbringing."

"No." He sprang from the chair and began pacing. "Not foster care. She has the right to a real home."

"Are you married?"

"No." But he wanted to be.

"At least you don't have to worry about explaining this to your wife, then."

Gideon tried to picture Lupe's face when he told her he had an illegitimate child. His heart sank.

Pike continued in his impersonal manner. "I assume you have no other children—"

Gideon spun around at what he considered an insult. "No, Mr. Pike, I don't," he stated coldly. The idea sent a new wave of adrenaline coursing through his veins. How could he be sure? If one condom failed, why not another? Would other women be coming forward claiming he was the father of their children? He ran a shaky hand down his face.

"Then adoption may be your best alternative." The lawyer went on undaunted. "I am authorized to inform you that Sylvia and Albert Runyon, Rebecca's parents, are prepared to legally adopt their granddaughter. It would appear to be the ideal solution under the circumstances. No disruption in Janna's life. She stays in familiar surroundings with people who love her. And I should also mention that the Runyons are a family of means. I'm sure they would be willing to waive child support."

"I don't care about the money," Gideon said.

Pike ignored the disclaimer. "Perhaps you would like to discuss this with members of your family, a clergyman or a social worker. I can give you the names—"

"That won't be necessary," Gideon said more sharply than he intended. He placed his sweaty hands on the arms of the chair, took a deep breath and climbed to his feet. His legs were stiff from tension, the muscles cramped. He needed to run or swim or do something before he developed charley horses. "I'll be in touch with you in a few days, Mr. Pike."

Pike rose, as well, and circled the side of the desk. "If I can be of any further assistance, please don't hesitate to call me."

For a second, Gideon suspected the old man was being sarcastic, because he sure hadn't been any help thus far, but the sincerity in his gray eyes stifled any retort. They shook hands somberly, and Gideon left.

How was he going to tell Lupe? And what would her reaction be?

"HE PROMISED to be punctual tonight," Lupe assured her mother-in-law as she helped put the food on the table for the children. She hadn't eaten since lunch, her stomach was beginning to grumble, and the spicy aroma of Elena's chicken enchiladas was making her mouth water. Gideon better show up pretty soon or she'd be forced to sample a small portion, a taste— though not enough to ruin her appetite for dinner at the Outback. She loved their onion blossoms.

"If running a little late is his worst vice—" Elena opened the oven door and used two hot pads to remove the bubbling casserole "—you are one lucky woman. My Fernando was always forgetting birthdays and anniversaries, and he hated shopping. Every year when we decorated the tree on Christmas Eve he'd suddenly remember he was supposed to buy me a present."

Lupe chuckled. "Bet that made for some interesting gifts."

Fond memories softened Elena's features. She

laughed. "One year it was an iron he bought at the corner drugstore. Another year it was a set of horseshoe coasters. I didn't even ask him where he got those."

"It must have been a terrible disappointment, not getting anything personal or from the heart."

Gideon was always offering her little presents. A charm for the silver bracelet she occasionally wore, an insulated mug for her car, a wind chime to go on the back porch. Once he'd given her a set of designer erasers and she'd teased him about accusing her of making a lot of mistakes. The corners of his eyes had crinkled when he told her women didn't make mistakes. They just changed their minds.

"There was nothing wrong with his heart, Lupe," Elena said, referring to her late husband. "He made up for his forgetfulness in other ways. Besides, during the sales after Christmas, he always let me buy whatever I wanted." The older woman went dreamy for a moment. Lupe remembered her father-in-law fondly. He hadn't been handsome or well educated, but he'd been an intelligent man who loved his family and shared his happiness with everyone he met.

On a sigh she probably didn't realize she'd made, Elena placed the hot dish on a trivet in the middle of the kitchen table. "Miguelito, Teresita," she called into the next room, where the children were watching a television show, "go wash your hands. Supper is ready."

"That smells so good," Lupe commented.

"Have a little," her mother-in-law coaxed her. "He won't be here for another half hour and then it will probably be another hour before you get to eat. The restaurant is always so crowded.''

Lupe relented. ''Maybe a half of one.''

Gideon was ten minutes late. For him, that was practically early. Still, she couldn't resist chiding him about it. ''Going to be prompt, huh?'' She awarded him a crooked smile.

''Sorry,'' he said without giving her his usual smart come back. ''I tried to be, but a couple of guys on the swim team showed up when Nick and I were finishing at the pool, and they asked me for advice on how to improve their kicks.''

''And their kicks are more important than your fiancée?'' Elena asked under knit brows.

''Not more important,'' he replied without taking apparent offense. ''I just lost track of time.''

''A big alarm wristwatch for his birthday.'' Elena shot Lupe a playful glance. ''One that gongs.''

''Or hits him over the head,'' Lupe quipped.

''You don't want to hurt his head,'' her mother-in-law objected. ''It's too pretty.''

Lupe caught the first sign of emotion on Gideon's face—annoyance. With his blond hair, golden tan and sky-blue eyes, he was incredibly handsome. He especially disliked being referred to as pretty or beautiful.

The children bounded into the room. Teresita leaped into his arms. ''Are you eating supper with us tonight?''

''It's not Friday,'' Miguelito reminded her with big-brother superiority. ''They've got a date. See, only three places at the table. And Mama is wearing a dress.''

Gideon ruffled the boy's straight black hair. ''Smart kid.''

''Can we go with you?'' Teresita begged.

''It's a school night,'' their mother reminded her.

Gideon disentangled the girl's arms from around him and put her down. ''Maybe next time.'' Teresita shrugged off her disappointment and took her place at the table.

''We won't be too late, Mama.'' Lupe picked up her purse from the end of the counter and turned to Gideon. The preoccupied expression was back on his face. Something was wrong. ''Shall we?''

He stared blankly at her for a second before answering. ''Yeah, sure. Let's go.''

Elena peered at her daughter-in-law, clearly aware something was amiss.

They drove in silence to the restaurant while a CD played an orchestral version of Bach's *Toccata and Fugue in D Minor.* Definitely not a good sign. Gideon's tastes in music ran the gamut from Japanese koto to hard rock. Classical music was what he used for contemplation. Lupe was becoming more concerned as the minutes slipped by. She was about to ask the crucial question, when he turned into the parking lot.

''Crowded,'' he said dully. Usually, he enjoyed crowds. ''You still want to go here or try somewhere else?''

''Not as bad as a Friday night,'' she reminded him,

trying to lighten the mood, "when there's no football game."

"You're probably right," he said without humor. A car pulled out ahead of them.

His uncharacteristically somber mood was scaring her. "What's wrong, Gideon?" He maneuvered into the vacant spot without answering. "Something is bothering you. Please tell me what it is."

"We'd better get our name on the list, then we can have a drink in the bar while we wait." Before she could object, he got out of the car, walked around to her side and opened her door.

She began to tremble as panic swept through her. Gideon was never like this. Whatever the problem, it was serious. She accepted his hand, then stood by while he closed the door. Cupping her elbow, he escorted her to the front door of the crowded steak house.

Even on this off night, the crowd inside was loud and jovial. Gideon added his name to the reservation list and, cradling Lupe's back, swept her into the bar area, which was even more noisy and boisterous. Coming here was a mistake, he concluded. He should have found a quieter place, one without distractions.

He felt disoriented and exhausted. After leaving Pike's office, he'd gone to the university pool. Nick had joined him there, but today both the locker room and the pool were packed, so they didn't get a chance to talk privately. When a couple of competition swimmers asked Gideon for his advice on improving their butterfly strokes, Nick had excused himself. He couldn't hang around because he had a date for the evening. Gideon hadn't even had a chance to ask him with whom.

Disappointed in not being able to unburden himself to his best friend, Gideon had devoted himself to helping the swimmers. What he hadn't told Lupe was that he'd used their questions as an excuse to linger, to put off the inevitable. But the inevitable had waited patiently, and here it was.

Lupe requested her usual frozen daiquiri. Gideon called for a draft beer, then suggested they take them onto the patio. His first bit of good luck was spying a couple vacating a wrought-iron table in a far corner.

"The place is packed," he commented, trying to sound nonchalant and failing miserably.

"Perhaps we should go somewhere else," she remarked.

He hated feeling so indecisive. "Do you mind?" he asked. "I need to talk to you about something, and this isn't the place to do it."

"Then let's go." Lupe pushed back the chair she'd just taken and stood.

He escorted her to the car, opened the door and handed her in. From behind the wheel, he said, "You must be starving."

"Let's talk first. Afterward we can either pick up something or come back here. By then the crowd should have dwindled."

A woman of wisdom. One of the many reasons he loved her.

He drove them to the lake and parked near a vacant boat ramp. Lights from the surrounding houses twinkled on the placid water. They'd been here before.

He'd wrapped his arms around her, luxuriating in the warmth and scent of her body against his. They'd talked and kissed, and he'd tortured himself with fantasies of what other sensations he craved to explore. He wondered now if he'd ever experience them.

She released her seat belt and turned in his direction. "Now, what's this all about?"

"I...we have a problem." He swiveled in his seat to face her, though he dreaded seeing the pain he'd soon put in her eyes. "The call from the lawyer last week..." He trailed off.

"You said it was a matter of mistaken identity," she reminded him.

"I figured it was. I hoped it was." He inhaled deeply, exhaled and settled into his seat. "A friend of mine, Becky Runyon, was killed in a car crash a couple of weeks ago."

"An old girlfriend?" Apprehension made her question tentative, as if she wasn't sure of its significance.

"It turns out she had a baby girl." He took a deep, fortifying breath. "In her will, she identified me as the father."

There was a long, dry silence. Finally, Lupe said quietly, "That's why the lawyer called you."

"I agreed to take a paternity test." He tried to read her. Surely, she'd figured out the results. He expected an outburst, cold anger or even boiling rage. What he found resembled disappointment.

"So it wasn't a case of mistaken identity, like you said. You lied to me, Gideon." Her voice was a whisper, with a razor-sharp edge. "Why?"

"I didn't lie." His reply was perfunctory, and another lie. "I told you what I hoped was the truth."

"You told me you didn't know what the attorney wanted. But you did. Why couldn't you be honest with me?"

"I was afraid—"

"You didn't trust me," she accused.

"It wasn't a matter of not trusting you, sweetheart. I didn't want to spoil things." He turned away from her piercing stare, unable to bear the hurt and anger in it. "I just didn't think you'd..." The words hung suspended because he didn't know what he could say that would convince her he never intended to hurt her.

She let the silence linger for several long, torturous heartbeats. "What's her name?"

His little girl. His baby. "Janna. She's fourteen months old."

"Where is she now?"

"With Becky's parents. She'll stay with them until this gets resolved."

"Resolved?" Her voice hitched and rose in an indictment. "What does that mean?"

"I have to decide if I'll take her or let her be adopted."

Even in the dim light of the car he could see her dark eyes go wide. "Adopted?" Shock sharpened the single word. "You'll put your baby up for adoption?"

"It's not like you think." He snapped the words out, then softened his voice in a plea for understanding. "Cavanaugh Pike says Becky's parents want to keep her, legally adopt her. I haven't decided yet, but it's an option I have to consider. That's all. They're comfortably well off, so Janna will have a good home. And I can set up a trust fund for her, for her education—''

''You'd let somebody else raise your child.'' It was a statement delivered in a dull, nonjudgmental tone. Did that mean she agreed with the idea, that it was the best way to ensure she wouldn't be constantly reminded he'd made love to another woman?

''I love you, Lupe,'' he murmured across the dark void that separated them. More than anything at the moment, he needed to reach over and touch her, feel her warm skin under his hand, draw her to him and rest her head on his shoulder while he stroked her back.

''I want you to be my wife,'' he reminded her, ''to be a father to your children and have babies with you. I realize I have no right to ask you to take this child.'' Tears glistened in her eyes, and for a euphoric moment he thought she understood and agreed with him.

''Take me home, Gideon.''

''Lupe…sweetheart…'' He extended his hand toward her, but she recoiled before he could touch her.

''Please take me home,'' she insisted.

He studied her a moment and felt despair, then he switched the key in the ignition. The engine started, but he didn't put it into gear. He turned again to face her. ''Lupe…''

She raised a hand, and he could see it shaking. She bit her lip and shut her eyes. ''Take me home, Gideon. Now.'' There was aching pain and tempered steel in the quiet words.

He knew better than to try to argue with her when

she was in this state. As if there were a defense he could raise. He'd calculated and lost. In her eyes, he'd disgraced himself. In his eyes, too. There was no justification for lying to her. The question was whether she would ever forgive him.

"I'm sorry," he mumbled. It was a pathetic statement. He would have said more if he could have conjured up any words that might melt the wall of ice that had formed. Diligently, he released the brake and backed out onto the road.

A few minutes later, he entered her driveway and turned off the engine. Hands still on the wheel, he dropped his head and took a shallow breath. "Lupe, I know all this comes as a terrible shock. I'm sorry. I hope—"

"You lied to me, Gideon. I asked you about the lawyer, and you said it was a matter of mistaken identity."

"What I meant was…I really didn't think I was the father of Becky's child. I figured it had to be a mistake, that the baby was somebody else's."

"But that's not what you told me." She peered at him and blinked back another tear. "You weren't going to tell me about this at all, were you? You planned to keep it a secret from me."

"There wouldn't have been a secret to keep if I wasn't the father," he said, rationalizing.

"You knew you could have been."

He felt defeated. "My affair with Becky happened before I met you," he insisted. "There's never been anyone since our first date." She didn't believe him.

He could see it in her glance. Recrimination. Humiliation. "I swear it."

"Your little girl," she went on. "You'll leave her with her grandparents, for them to bring up, but you'll make sure she's well provided for."

"Of course." It was his turn to be offended. "What kind of man do you take me for?"

She bit her lower lip as fresh tears ran down her cheeks. "All I know," she said thickly, "is that you're not the man I thought you were."

Silence hung between them for several seconds.

"Lupe, I love you. I—"

She shook her head and signaled with a brusque wave of her hand for him to be quiet. Finally, she took a deep breath. Her eyes were red, like the rubies around the diamond on her finger, his ring. He started to reach out for her, but she turned away and grabbed the door handle before he had a chance. She swung open the door, fled from the car and disappeared into the house.

Gideon sat for several minutes, his head down, then leaned over, shut the car door, restarted the engine and slowly drove away.

LUPE RAN through the living room and down the short, narrow hall to her bedroom. Elena, who had been halfheartedly watching an evening soap opera on the Spanish station, looked up from her sewing in time to see her daughter-in-law run past. Lupe's door closed more forcefully than necessary.

"I was afraid something was wrong," Elena muttered. She rose from the deep cushion of her easy chair and went to the bedroom door. "Lupe, may I come in?"

Receiving no response, she turned the knob and inched the door open. Lupe was stretched out face-down across the bed, her body heaving as she sobbed. Elena sat beside her. "What is it, *mija?* What's wrong?"

Lupe turned onto her side, her pretty face ravaged with tears. "Oh, Mama. He lied to me."

Elena stroked her arm, feeling the muscles tremble. "About what? Maybe you misunderstood—"

"No." The response was muffled. "I didn't misunderstand. He flat-out lied to me."

Soothing her with a gentle touch, Elena said, "Why don't you tell me what's happened. Maybe it will help—"

"There's nothing you can do." Lupe flung herself down in another fit of sobbing.

"I can listen." Elena waited patiently for her daughter-in-law to regain control of herself.

"He has a child, Mama." She rubbed her eyes and succeeded only in making them water more. "A little girl...with a woman who was killed in a car crash in Dallas."

Elena sucked air between her teeth and slowly shook her head. "Oh, *mija,* I'm so sorry. Gideon...he doesn't seem like a man who would be unfaithful. He was still seeing this woman after he started courting you?"

Lupe reached for a tissue from the box on her nightstand. She blew her nose. "He says he stopped seeing her after we had our first date."

"Do you believe him?"

She gave a shuddering sigh. "I guess so. Maybe."

"He has been aware of this baby all along and didn't tell you? Has he been supporting her?"

"No," Lupe said on a hiccup. "I mean, the woman, Becky, never told him. He didn't find out until a lawyer called him last week and informed him he was the father."

"But why would this Becky not tell him he was a father? Was she afraid of him?"

Lupe's eyes grew wide. Clearly, the notion had never entered her mind. Why should it have? He was so gentle, and Elena couldn't imagine Lupe tolerating a man who wasn't. Miguel had been gentle and sweet...and so young.

Perhaps there was another side to Gideon none of them had yet seen, but Elena didn't believe it. Instinct told her he was a good man—if sometimes foolish.

"He had to take a blood test. But, Mama, after he first went to the lawyer I asked why the lawyer wanted to see him, and that's when he lied to me. He said the man wasn't really looking for him but for someone else."

Elena reckoned she understood his motivation even if she didn't condone his action. "He hoped the child was someone else's," she concluded. "What man would desire to confess to his *novia* that he has created a *bastarda*. He was ashamed."

"He should be," Lupe blurted angrily.

"If he were not a good man, my daughter-in-law, he would have no shame. It is a sign that he understands he has done wrong that he kept this from you."

"Oh, Mama, that's no consolation."

Elena had to agree. "We all have secrets, child, thoughts and actions we don't want to share with other people. He slept with this woman before he met you. I cannot say whether he had feelings for her. Perhaps he did, but they were not strong enough to keep them together." She studied her dead son's widow and ached for the pain and sorrow she beheld. "It is not pleasant when a woman finds out her man has been with other women, but this was before the two of you were acquainted. Are you afraid there are other women now?"

"No," Lupe said quietly.

"But you are afraid there will be?"

Lupe shook her head. "I don't think so." But the doubt was unmistakable.

"Then why not forgive him?"

"The lawyer says the mother of his child asked him to take the baby, but he wants to give her away."

Elena drew back, not completely sure she understood what she'd been told. "He does not desire to keep his baby?"

"Becky's parents want to adopt her, he says. He will make sure she has money, but he won't keep her."

Elena's lips tightened in horror. "Gideon would do that?"

Lupe nodded and started sniffling. "I can excuse him for the baby, Mama, because it was before we met. And if he promises he will never be with another woman…I would believe him. But to abandon his own flesh and blood? No. For that, I cannot forgive him.''

''What will you do?''

''How can I marry a man who would reject his own baby, Mama?'' Biting her lips, she slipped the glittering ring off her finger.

Elena wrapped her arms around her daughter-in-law and hugged her. ''I am so sorry, child.''

CHAPTER FOUR

"SO THE KID is yours after all," Nick observed. They were sitting in his office on campus. He'd found a place at the corner of Jacinto and First that looked perfect. The building wasn't new, but it was in good condition, had potential for expansion and the owner was willing to share the cost of remodeling. Gideon had been pleased, though in a notably detached way. His announcement that Becky's baby was indeed his explained his preoccupation.

"Her name is Janna," Gideon informed him.

Nick leaned back in his chair, his arms crossed over his chest. "What are you going to do?"

"I'm not sure yet. Pike listed several options, keeping her myself and putting her up for adoption among them."

"Adoption?" Nick's brows rose precipitously. "Are you seriously considering that?"

Gideon shrugged uncertainly. "The lawyer for Becky's folks says they want to formally adopt her. They're Janna's family. It doesn't seem right taking her away from them. Besides, Lupe isn't interested in raising her, and I wouldn't be any good as a single father. What do I know about bringing up a little girl?"

"Lupe doesn't want her?" Nick was surprised at that. "Is that what she said?"

"She sent back the ring. That's pretty clear to me."

Nick regarded his friend. "It means she's angry and hurt, Gid."

"You were right," Gideon admitted. "I should have told her what was going on from the beginning."

"Women don't like to be lied to, especially by the men they love."

"I didn't lie to her." Gideon defended himself. "I avoided telling her about something I didn't think was true. That's different from lying."

Nick shook his head. "That's crap, Gideon, and you know it. When she asked you what Pike wanted, you didn't tell her the truth. Politicians might not call that lying, but us ordinary mortals do."

Gideon squirmed. "I figured it was a matter of mistaken identity."

"Because you didn't want to believe it," Nick persisted.

"Why are you being so hostile?" Gideon snapped.

Nick studied him for a long minute. "I'm not being hostile. I'm being honest and trying to get you to be. You screwed up, buddy. Now you've got to own up."

Gideon said nothing, but Nick could feel the negative tension emanating from him. Nick didn't often challenge his friend.

"Becky Runyon was head over heels in love with you, Gideon, and you didn't have a clue, so she left here and had your baby without you. Cavanaugh Pike tells you you're the father of her child, and your immediate reaction is to deny it. Okay, I guess I can understand that, but you knew it was possible. But then you compound the problem by deceiving the woman you love. Now you find out you really are the father of the child and you're trying to take the easy way out, give her to her grandparents to raise, pay someone else to do your job.''

Gideon was stunned. He'd expected sympathy from his lifelong friend, not this reasoned indictment.

''Maybe it's time for you to grow up, Gideon,'' Nick continued. ''You've lived a charmed life, my friend, where things always seemed to go your way. And if they didn't, you simply moved on. Well, you can't move away from this one. You have a responsibility to your daughter—''

''And I'll meet that responsibility,'' Gideon answered in a loud voice. ''What's best for Janna? To live in a two-parent family or be brought up by a single father who knows diddly about child rearing? I am thinking about her, damn it. If Lupe had accepted her, I wouldn't be having this dilemma.''

Nick shook his head sadly. ''Don't shift the blame to Lupe, Gid.''

''I'm not.'' Gideon was practically shouting. ''I'm just saying, if she'd hadn't broken off the engagement, if we were still getting married, Janna wouldn't be a problem.''

Nick gathered the papers spread before him and put them neatly into a folder. ''I don't think Janna's the problem, and neither is Lupe. You're the problem.'' Stiff-armed, he passed the file across the desk. ''This isn't a good idea right now, Gideon.''

Another blow. "You don't want to open the PT center?"

"Sure I do, but this isn't the right time to be making decisions about it," Nick explained patiently. "The three of us are supposed to be equal partners. That takes a lot of trust, and at the moment I don't think Lupe has a whole lot of confidence in your judgment. So let's put things on hold for a while. It's probably just as well this happened now. To be frank, I've had a few doubts of my own since you proposed building the center with your own money."

"Nick, don't do this. Please. We've been talking about this center, planning it, for months. I'm sorry if I offended you by offering to build on my own when it looked like we weren't going to find anything. Frankly, I expected you'd be pleased, but—" he waved the concept aside. "It's moot now. You've found us a perfect location, good facilities, great terms. Don't throw this away. Let me talk to Lupe. Maybe I can convince her—"

"I hope you do. But this place isn't going anywhere for a while. I wouldn't try to rush it, if I were you. Give her some time to calm down, because if she opts out, so do I."

CONSIDERING THE FUSS Karida Sommers had made over Gideon's ring, Lupe shouldn't have been surprised when her friend noticed immediately that it was missing. They'd run into each other in front of the student union after Lupe finished her morning class on medical and exercise issues in disabling conditions.

"We decided to wait a little longer," she replied to Karida's question.

"Come on, Lupe, level with me," Karida reproved her. "You hadn't even set a firm date. So what did you argue about? It must have been pretty important for you to give back a rock that size." Karida smiled sympathetically. "Another woman?"

"Why would you think that?"

Karida grinned. "He's a hunk, that's why. You're not the only female around here that drools over him. And he's certainly not immune to feminine charms. I had serious designs on him myself a couple of years ago—until my mother took sick."

"You were interested in him?" Lupe shouldn't have been surprised, but she was.

"You needn't act so shocked," Karida commented with a humorous chuckle. "I was out of circulation, but I wasn't dead."

"I didn't mean—"

"Forget it. I was interested in Gideon when I imagined I had a chance. Since you came along, he seems to be immune to other women's charms." Karida scanned the clear blue sky. "It's a beautiful day. Come on, kid. I'll buy you a cup of coffee, and we can sit outside and talk."

"I need to get over to the library," Lupe objected, and tried to keep walking.

Karida placed a hand on Lupe's forearm. "Oh, no, you don't. Whatever it is can wait. Besides, judging from the look on your face, you won't get much accomplished there, anyway."

Karida was right, of course. Lupe hadn't been able

to concentrate since last night. Crying on Elena's shoulder had felt good. She tried to tell herself she didn't need to talk about her breakup with Gideon anymore, but that wasn't true. The urge to unburden herself was still there, and apparently it showed.

With a heavy heart, Lupe accompanied Karida into the bustling student union cafeteria, where they bought a couple of lattes and took them outside. The sky was clear and brilliantly blue—like Gideon's eyes. The sun felt toasty warm on her back. The weather was all wrong. In Lupe's heart, it was gray and drizzling.

"The two of you had a fight," Karida said sympathetically. "That's clear enough. And it had to be a serious one for you to give him back his ring. So what happened?"

They arrived at the gazebo in a quiet corner of a small rose garden between the student union and administration buildings. Students rarely wandered in this part of the campus.

"Gideon got a call from a lawyer the week before last," Lupe began, "about Becky Runyon."

"Becky? Oh, I remember her. He brought her to a couple of faculty parties. She had the most beautiful green eyes. When I first saw them I assumed she was wearing contacts. Almost kelly green. Very striking. What does this lawyer have to do with her?"

"Becky was killed in an automobile accident in Dallas a few weeks ago, and the lawyer is involved in settling her estate."

"I'm sorry to hear that. It must have been quite a

shock to Gideon. Did she leave him one of her paintings in her will?''

When Lupe hesitated, Karida squeezed her hand and told her to go on.

"Not a painting. His fourteen-month-old baby.''

Karida gasped. ''You're kidding. He never said a word. So that's why she left town.''

"He didn't know anything about the baby, and at first, he denied it was his. But then he took a paternity test, and it's true.''

"Ah, honey. I'm sorry.'' She stroked Lupe's hand for a minute. "Fourteen months old,'' she continued pensively. "That means he was with her after—''

"After he met me," Lupe finished, "but before we started dating. It's not like we were engaged. I certainly had no claim on him. If he was interested in seeing other women—''

"Don't tell me it was all right." Karida snapped the words out. "Because it wasn't.''

"It doesn't matter," Lupe insisted. "He hadn't made any promises, or proposed.''

"You're a lot more generous than most women would be. Than I would be," Karida added. They sat in silence for another minute. "What's he planning to do with the baby? Has he asked you to raise it with your kids? Is that why you broke up with him?'' She didn't wait for an answer. "I don't blame you.''

Lupe shook her head. "He says he'll put her up for adoption.''

"Adoption? Oh, so he's not going to keep her.'' The notion didn't seem to bother Karida.

Lupe stared at her coffee cup.

"Uh-oh. That's what you're so upset about, isn't it? It's not that he slept with another woman. It's that he's giving his baby away."

"How can he do that?" Lupe pleaded, yielding to the tears that had been gathering all day.

"Men," Karida snorted. "It can't be that he doesn't like kids. You've told me how good he is with yours."

"He's been wonderful. I haven't broken the news to them yet…that we're not getting married. They'll be so disappointed."

"Had the two of you talked about having more children?"

"Several times," Lupe acknowledged. "He always said he wanted a house full of them."

"Then why not this child?"

Lupe considered the question, as she had all night, going over and over it in her mind. Why wouldn't Gideon keep his baby? He loved children. She was sure of it. Ultimately, she'd reached only one conclusion. If they got married and kept the child, Janna would always be a reminder that he'd loved someone else. "It's pretty hard bringing up someone else's children," she said.

"Especially," Karida added in an undertone, "when they're your husband's illegitimate kids."

Lupe nodded, consoled that her friend understood.

They sipped their coffees, which were barely warm. Finally, Karida said, "Maybe this is for the best, honey. At least you aren't married yet. If he has this kid that he didn't tell you about, how can you be sure there aren't more? Let's face it. He's a good-looking guy with a truckload of charm and personality.''

Lupe gaped. ''He's not like that.''

''I'm not saying he is. I'm merely saying you don't know if there are other babies out there. He claims he wasn't aware of this one, and maybe he's telling the truth. So how can he—how can you—be certain there aren't others? I can't imagine Becky was the only woman he ever slept with.''

Lupe ought to be arguing with her friend, but what Karida said was true in so many ways. Lupe knew he'd had sex with other women before he met her. It wasn't something she dwelled on. He also said there hadn't been any other women since he met her. But how could she be sure? She'd believed him in the past, but things were different now. He'd lied to her about the lawyer. Wouldn't he have even more reason to lie about other women? And now there was his baby. Why couldn't there be others, as well?

Karida was right. Better to find these things out now than after they were married. But God, how it hurt. In spite of everything, she still loved him, still wanted him.

As if realizing what was going through Lupe's mind, Karida said, ''I know how disappointed you are now, how much this must hurt, but you'll get over him. Give yourself time. There are other men. You'll find someone better.''

Because it would make her sound weak, Lupe didn't say she wasn't interested in someone else. She couldn't imagine feeling about another man what she'd felt about Gideon, what she still felt for him.

But her friend was probably right. After a while the pain would subside, just as it had after Miguel had been killed. Except the pain hadn't really gone away. She'd simply learned to live with it. Is that the way it would be with losing Gideon, too? Life would go back to normal? Normal being alone. No, not completely alone. She still had her children. The family was incomplete, but she still had one. That love would have to be enough.

TELLING HIS FATHER and the rest of the family of his newly discovered paternity wouldn't be easy. Gideon was not quite eleven years old when his sister Kerry had gone to their father and told him she was pregnant by a high school dropout and petty criminal. Adam First had been furious. Now Gideon was about to inform him he had an illegitimate granddaughter.

On weekends, Gideon frequently went to the ranch with Lupe and her children. He loved to watch the innocent delight they took in all the animals—horses, cattle, sheep and goats. The fact that the kids usually ended up doing what he considered chores didn't seem to bother them in the least. For them, the novelty was as exciting as being in an amusement park. They would gladly have paid for the privilege of filling horse cribs with grain and hay, cleaning tack or even mucking out stalls. Happiness, his father had often told him when he was growing up, was doing the work you loved. Gideon agreed—to a point. The other essential element was sharing it with a woman, one who got your blood pumping and your hands itching.

"Lupe and the kids not with you?" Sheila asked when he let himself in the kitchen door of the Home Place. Gideon's stepmother was a trim woman in her early fifties with a ready smile and intelligent blue eyes.

"Not this weekend." He wondered if Lupe would ever be out here with him again. "Something smells good. Chicken and dumplings?"

Sheila chuckled. "Living proof that the way to a man's heart is through his stomach. You are definitely your father's son."

He might not agree after he hears what I have to tell him. "I'm glad Lupe's a good cook." When Gideon didn't respond, she gazed at him. "Everything all right?"

He'd come out here today with the specific intention of telling her and the rest of the family about the situation he found himself in, but it would have been nice if he could have hidden it for more than thirty seconds. "I'll tell y'all about it at dinner." Meaning the noon meal. Supper was what they ate in the evening. "Are Michael and his clan coming over?"

"Should be here in a few minutes." Sheila regarded him with concern.

"Where's Dad?"

Still watching him out of the corner of her eye, she added milk to the dry dumpling ingredients in a big crockery bowl. "Fixing a leaky faucet in the guest house. We expected Lupe and the children to be here this weekend."

With a noncommittal sound, Gideon left to find his father.

Adam was on his back under the sink in the guest bathroom of the six-bedroom bungalow they'd built for visitors after restoring the century-old ranch house.

He must have recognized Gideon's boots. Without poking his head out from under the sink, he said, "Hi, son. Tell Lupe I'll be out of here in a few minutes."

"No hurry, Dad. She's not with me."

Adam shuffled to look at his second-born son. "Nobody's sick, I hope."

"Everybody's fine."

"Jaime Rivera sent over his little gray mare for Teresita. Savannah's twelve hands, about the right size for the tyke and real gentle."

Gideon steeled himself. "Dad, I need to talk to you about something."

"Be with you in a second." Adam applied measured pressure to the pipe wrench in his hand, removed it and struggled to sit up. "I'm getting too old for this contortionist stuff."

Gideon forced himself to laugh. "You have hands around here who could do that for you."

The years had been kind to his father, but he was getting close to sixty, an age when a lot of men contemplated slowing down. Not Adam First.

"Then you can get yourself a rocking chair and sit on the porch and jaw about the good old days, when you used to walk barefoot to school in the snow, uphill both ways."

His reply was a muffled, "Smart-ass. No respect. That's the problem with the younger generation."

At the moment, Gideon didn't feel young. He felt ancient. Old but not at all wise.

After rolling onto his side, then his knees, and finally standing upright, Adam tucked his blue-denim work shirt into his worn jeans. "Now, what's up?" He smiled at his son, then squinted mischievously. "Uh-oh. You and Lupe have a fight already?"

Gideon inhaled through his nose and snorted. Had he always been so transparent? "You could say that."

Adam stopped brushing his shirt and peered at his son. "Must be serious."

Gideon helped his father pack up the tools scattered on the floor. The two men didn't speak until they were outside.

"Now, tell me what's turned your smile upside down," Adam prompted as he settled a bit stiffly on the middle step of the stoop.

Gideon paced in front of him. "You won't like it."

"I've already figured out that much, son. Why don't you say it and get it over with."

Except it won't be over with, not easily, not quickly. "Do you remember Becky Runyon?" At his father's nod, he went on, "She was killed in a car accident several weeks ago."

"I'm sorry," Adam replied thoughtfully. After a brief silence, he shook his head sadly. "When Stu died," he said, confirming they were both thinking along the same lines, "it was pretty rough. But at least I still had the rest of you. Becky, as I recall, was an only child, wasn't she?"

"Yes, but there's another problem. Becky had a fourteen-month-old baby."

Adam's brows drew together. The silence between the two men probably didn't last more than a few heartbeats, but they were painful seconds. Before Gideon said the words "my baby" he realized his father had already figured it out.

"I see." The soft utterance wasn't filled with recrimination so much as disappointment.

"I didn't know anything about it," Gideon hastened to add, "until the Runyons' lawyer here in town called me. I couldn't believe it at first. Becky never even told me she was pregnant. But I took a paternity test, and it's true. Janna is my daughter."

Adam rose and stretched his neck but didn't go anywhere. "Where is she now?"

It was Gideon's turn to sit on the steps. "With her grandparents in Dallas."

Adam remained silent as he studied his son.

"She's well provided for, Dad. Becky's folks are financially comfortable. Albert Runyon's in oil and gas. They're interested in adopting her formally."

Adam closed his eyes, then slowly opened them. "Have you talked to Lupe about this?"

"She doesn't want to have anything to do with Janna or me."

An expression of incredulity creased Adam's face. "Are you sure?"

"She gave me back the ring, Dad. That's pretty plain, even to a dunderhead like me."

Adam didn't dispute the dunderhead part. "Let me explain something to you, Gideon, which in your vast education you may have missed. People don't always say and do what they mean. Women especially, or at least we men don't understand what they mean. Lupe's upset with you, and why not? If roles were reversed, I bet you'd be annoyed with her, too.''

Feeling defensive, Gideon countered, ''Women know when they have kids. And unless they're...well, promiscuous, they can name the father. Becky never told me about Janna. She had to get killed before I found out.''

''And if she had informed you?''

''I would have asked her to marry me.''

''Because you loved her?''

That question coming from his father surprised him. Marriage in this case was a matter of honor and duty, not love. With hope, with time, love would have developed. ''Because a child deserves two parents.''

Adam worked his jaw. ''That's what I reckoned, too. But it all depends on who the parents are.''

Gideon understood that his father was thinking of Kerry's forced marriage. It had been abusive. Adam had driven his son-in-law off the ranch at the point of a shotgun. ''I like to imagine that if you and Becky had gotten married, it would have worked out. Apparently, though, she decided otherwise. I'm sorry for that. I assume Lupe is aware that you would have married Becky.''

''I have no idea, Dad. She didn't ask, and it didn't occur to me to volunteer the information.''

''She knows you pretty well, son. Or she thought she did. I don't imagine she would have agreed to marry you if she couldn't count on you to do what's best for any children you might have—in or out of marriage.''

"Then why'd she break up the engagement?"

"Did you ask her?"

It was such an obvious query. But at the moment the answer had seemed perfectly clear. She didn't want to have anything to do with a man who'd fathered an illegitimate child. "I haven't had a chance," he responded.

His father looked straight at him, the disappointment of a little while ago back. "Maybe you ought to make a chance." It sounded very much like *take a chance*.

Is that what Gideon was afraid of? If he received an answer he didn't like, he'd have to live with it. Maybe Nick was right, that he'd always sought the safe course instead of the better course.

Michael's Suburban pulled around the back of the main house and disgorged chatty children and laughing adults. Gideon heard something about a trip to Six Flags.

Breaking the news to the rest of the family wasn't much easier than telling Adam, but Gideon managed to sit through the stares and dropped jaws without lowering his head.

"Are you serious about letting the Runyons legally adopt her?" Clare asked, disapproval ringing loud and clear in her tone.

"What about Becky's request that you give Janna your name?" Michael objected. "If the Runyons adopt her, she'll keep their name, won't she?"

"I stopped by and talked to Nelson Spooner yesterday," Gideon answered. Spooner was the attorney his father had gone to when he arranged Kerry's divorce and later when her son, Brian, got into trouble with the law. "He says the court will require me to pay child support, but Becky's request about the name is not binding. If the Runyons want permanent custody, I could also make her taking my name a condition of the agreement. They'd probably agree out of respect for their daughter's wishes. It's not as if they'll try to present themselves as the child's parents."

"How old are they?" Julie asked. She'd arrived with Michael and his family.

"I met them twice. They had Becky fairly late in life, when Mrs. Runyon was close to forty. Her husband is at least ten years her senior."

"Which means they're in their sixties and seventies. That's pretty old to be bringing up a kid. If you're serious about putting Janna up for adoption, maybe you ought to consider a younger couple."

Sheila gasped. Adam grumbled, and Michael and Clare stared at Julie and then at Gideon.

"Give the child away?" Clare asked.

Michael looked as appalled as Clare sounded.

"All I'm saying," Julie explained a little defensively, "is that Gideon's a bachelor. What does he know about raising a little girl? He has a full-time job, which means the kid would spend her formative years in day care or with sitters, so maybe it would be better if she were in an intact family. And if he does that, he ought to see to it that she gets a good home with people who are young enough to at least see her through high school."

They sat and discussed that point of view long after

Sheila had served pecan pie topped with vanilla ice cream.

The dishes had been cleared and the group was breaking up when Michael and Clare approached Gideon in the parking area in front of the old house.

"Are you really considering putting Janna up for adoption?" his brother asked, sounding worried.

Gideon frowned. "I want to do what's best for my daughter. Julie's right. I have no expertise in raising a child. I could quit my job, I suppose, but...staying home all the time so I can baby-sit... I don't know. If I were marrying Lupe, it would be different."

"Would you expect her to give up her job so she could stay home and take care of the child?" Clare inquired.

The dilemma was one he hadn't reconciled in his own mind. Lupe was a trained physical therapist. What a waste to not use her talents, and of course, they were planning on opening their own PT center.

"Lupe said that when we had our own kids, she'd stay home with them until they started school. With Elena there, she might be able to work part-time, but as far as Lupe's concerned, her first obligation is to her children, not to clients. It's not as if we'd need the money."

Clare had chosen the same route. She'd been a schoolteacher when she and Michael got married. She'd quit before Davie was born and went back as a substitute teacher only after Beth-Ann, their youngest, started school a few years ago.

"Michael and I have been talking," she said. "If you decide you don't want to raise Janna by yourself, we'll raise her for you. She can live with us and be part of our family.''

"She'll still be your daughter, Gid,'' Michael explained. ''We're not suggesting that we pretend to be her parents. You'll still be her dad. We'll be who we are, her aunt and uncle. But she'll be in an established family environment with her cousins.''

"That's very generous of you.''

"This isn't about generosity, Gideon,'' Michael reminded him. ''It's about family.''

CHAPTER FIVE

GIDEON DROVE the long cobblestone driveway to the front door of the two-story, white stucco house. Its many gables were covered with slightly irregular orange Spanish tiles, giving it a well-established appearance, though he doubted the building was more than five years old. Irrationally, he wondered why poor people wanted things to look new, and rich people designed them to appear old.

An arched portico shaded a heavy oaken doorway with beveled glass side panels. Large ceramic containers of blooming dwarf mountain laurel stood sentinel beside them. Once he'd shut off the ignition, Gideon climbed from his car and pressed the bell button on the right. He turned to take in the well-groomed front yard. Neat and manicured, it was bordered by beds of colorful flowers and disciplined shrubs.

The door opened behind him. "May I help you?"

He spun around to see a middle-aged woman in a tan-and-white dress. "I'm Gideon First, here to see Mr. and Mrs. Runyon."

"Yes, Mr. First. Please come in." She stepped aside for him to enter. "I'm Vanessa Cramer, Mrs. Runyon's sister." She shook his hand, then led him down a wide hall to a room on the left. "Syl," she called ahead of her, "Mr. First is here."

The room was large and airy, decorated in pastels and creams. Directly in front of him sat a fine-featured woman of perhaps sixty-five, with sharp eyes that were a deep, dark blue. She extended a bejeweled hand. "Hello, Gideon."

He could remember meeting the Runyons on two occasions. Once at Becky's apartment, they were just leaving when he arrived. The other was at a charity exhibition of local artists, to which Becky had contributed two of her oil landscapes. The paintings had sold for good prices, considering she was a relative unknown. Both encounters with the senior Runyons had been brief and friendly and hadn't gone beyond preliminary social amenities.

"Please be seated." She motioned him to the highback couch a few feet away.

"May I get you something, Mr. First? Coffee or perhaps tea?" Vanessa asked.

"No, thank you, Mrs. Cramer. Please call me Gideon."

"It's miss actually, but Vanessa is fine."

"Bring us coffee," Sylvia instructed.

Vanessa nodded, smiled at Gideon and left the room.

He turned to the grandmother of his child. "Please accept my deepest condolences, Mrs. Runyon. I didn't find out about Becky's death until after her funeral, or I would have been here. I'm very sorry for your loss."

"Thank you." Gideon had the impression the

words didn't come easily. "You're not here to discuss my daughter, though, but yours."

My daughter. The words had a strange effect on him, one he couldn't identify. "Where is Janna?"

He noted that there were no toys lying around. There'd been blocks and dolls and all sorts of rattles strewn throughout Michael and Clare's house when their kids were toddlers. Lupe's home, even now, was clearly a place where children lived. Games crowded tables and shelves, and occasionally chairs, in the living room, while magnets held schedules and school notices to the refrigerator door in the kitchen. Gideon bet there wasn't a single magnet on the fridge in this house's kitchen. The living room of the Runyon house was almost sterile in its neatness, more a set piece than a place where people lived and breathed.

"I sent her to the park with her nanny," Sylvia Runyon informed him. "I felt it would be better for us to speak in private first." She twirled one of her diamond-encrusted rings. "Mr. Pike tells me you were unaware that Rebecca had even had a child, much less that it was yours."

Had mother and daughter never spoken frankly? Surely, one of the first questions a parent would ask an unmarried daughter returning home in the family way would be who the father was and what role he would play in the child's life. The Runyons were older than Gideon's father, born and raised in a period when illegitimacy was a moral failing and a social disgrace.

"Both pieces of information came as complete surprises," he told her. "The last time I saw Becky, just before she moved here from Coyote Springs, she didn't say anything about being pregnant. She certainly didn't mention that the child might have been mine.''

The old woman's mouth tightened in what Gideon interpreted as disapproval. Whether it was at the implication that her daughter might have been sleeping with other men or the notion that she was pregnant out of wedlock wasn't clear. What was apparent was that Sylvia Runyon didn't approve of the situation her daughter had gotten herself in. But then, who would?

''Now that you know you are the father,'' she said in a tone that seemed to strain at being civil, ''what are your intentions?''

Gideon rested an elbow on the arm of the sofa. ''Becky wanted me to give Janna my name and ensure her care. I'll do both.'' He looked the stiff-backed woman squarely in the eye. ''You should know, Mrs. Runyon, that if she'd told me she was pregnant with my child, I would have offered her marriage.'' The woman seemed unimpressed. ''Not solely to give our child my name, but because I was very fond of Becky. I have no idea if she would have accepted—'' he didn't mention the obvious, that if she'd wanted to marry him, she would have told him about their child ''—but if she had, I would have done everything in my power to make it a good marriage. If she had refused me, I would still have met my obligations to support my daughter.''

''Janna doesn't need your support, Mr. First. We're quite capable of seeing to her needs.''

So it was Mr. First now. Clearly, his paean of honorable intentions toward her daughter hadn't impressed the woman.

"I'm not questioning your capabilities or willingness to provide for her, Mrs. Runyon, but Janna is my daughter. I'm simply explaining that I will meet all my obligations toward her."

The tension between them was broken by the arrival of Vanessa, pushing a tea cart through the wide doorway. "How do you like your coffee, Gideon?" she asked. Gideon pegged her at not much over fifty, if that, which meant she had to be at least fifteen years younger than her married sister. He wondered what her role in the family was. Did she live here or was she visiting to lend moral support? If the two sisters were close, it wasn't apparent.

"Black is fine. Thanks."

Expertly she poured the rich aromatic brew from a heavy silver pot, then passed the bone-china cup and saucer to him with a steady hand and a pleasant smile. She didn't seem to share her sister's hostility. "I understand your family owns the Number One Ranch," she said by way of polite conversation.

"Yes." He should say more but was at a rare loss for words.

"Are you a big family?"

"I have a brother and two sisters. I had a younger brother, Stuart, but he was killed in a car accident several years ago."

Sylvia gave him a tight-lipped glare, as if his mentioning this was in poor taste.

"I'm so sorry," Vanessa said. "You're familiar then with the pain of loss."

The statement didn't require a response. Gratefully, he sipped his coffee, which was hot and somewhat bitter.

"Oh, I almost forgot," Vanessa said to her sister. "Albert called while I was in the kitchen. He's delayed in traffic but said he'll be here in a few minutes."

"He shouldn't have gone in to the office at all," Sylvia replied curtly.

Vanessa seemed unfazed by the haughty tone as she plied Gideon with unobtrusive inquiries about the ranch. "I've been reading about the drought you're having in West Texas. Water rationing and all that."

"It'll probably last another two years, if the seven-year cycle holds true to form."

The sound of a key in a lock and the opening and closing of the front door interrupted their conversation. In walked a tall, scrawny man with thin streaks of gray hair stretched across a shiny pate.

Gideon placed his cup and saucer on the coffee table and rose to his feet.

"You're Gideon First," the man said as he approached, his large bony hand extended. "Yes, I remember you now. I'm Albert Runyon."

Gideon shook his hand.

Albert noticed the service cart. "Coffee. Good. I could use a cup."

Vanessa was already pouring him some.

He was considerably older than Gideon remembered him from their meetings three or four years earlier, at least ten years older than his wife. Which would put him in his late seventies. Despite his rail thinness, he appeared to be in good health, with ruddy cheeks and intelligent eyes. Still active in business, too, it would seem.

"Please accept my sincere condolences on the loss of your daughter, Mr. Runyon."

The friendly expression turned momentarily somber. "Thank you." He took the proffered beverage from his sister-in-law and sat on the other end of the couch farthest from his wife but facing her.

"I was telling your wife that I'm fully prepared to accept my responsibility toward my daughter."

Albert sipped, balanced the cup and saucer on his knee and studied his visitor. "In what way?" Before Gideon could respond, he pressed on. "I understand you're single. Do you propose raising Janna by yourself?"

Gideon wished with all his heart he could say he was about to get married and that Janna would have a completely normal home life. "I'm not sure yet."

"You don't know?" Sylvia demanded with a raised brow.

"There are several options I have to consider," he explained. "Bring her up by myself or put her up for adoption by an intact two-parent family."

Vanessa, sitting in an easy chair on the other side of the coffee table, regarded him curiously but without apparent emotion.

Sylvia made a startled sound. "Put her up for adoption? You don't mean...you're not considering letting someone else adopt her?"

"I—"

Albert immediately rescued him, perhaps sensing

his discomfort, perhaps realizing he had the initiative. "I believe Mr. First is just using the term in its general sense." He addressed Gideon. "I'm sure Mr. Pike informed you that we are interested in formally adopting Janna. She is, after all, our granddaughter, our only grandchild, and I'm sure our keeping her will make life easier for you." Abandoning the coffee he'd seemed so eager to drink, Albert rose from his seat and moved behind his wife's chair, his big-knuckled hands on its back inches from her shoulders. "I understand you're about to be married. Congratulations."

So the Runyons had been checking up on him. It was irritating, but in all fairness, he couldn't blame them. Their information wasn't as up-to-date as it could be, though. "It's on hold at the moment."

Sylvia snorted, while Vanessa sipped her coffee.

"I see," Albert Runyon said quietly, but in a way that left no doubt he recognized Janna was the obstacle to their engagement. "I'm sure you're anxious then to get this resolved. I can have my attorney draw up the necessary papers and courier them to you. We should be able to get this settled in a matter of days."

Everything was happening too fast. Gideon considered himself to be a decisive man of action, but he didn't want to be rushed into something this important too quickly. He hadn't even seen his daughter yet, and these people were pressing him to give her up. Still, if roles were reversed, he'd probably employ the same tactic.

"I have to consider Janna's best interests."

"What do you mean by that?" Sylvia asked, clearly fighting her impatience.

"Raising a young child can't be easy for you," he said, trying to be diplomatic. From the sour expression on Mrs. Runyon's face, he hadn't succeeded.

"She's our granddaughter, Mr. First. We will do whatever it takes to ensure her welfare."

Gideon was tempted to comment that no one had yet said anything about loving the child. But rather than further alienate them, he chose another approach.

"I don't doubt it for a minute," he conceded. "And I respect that—"

"Let's make sure we understand each other, Mr. First," Albert Runyon interrupted, his tone not nearly as friendly as it had been a minute before. "We are the only family this child has ever known. We are ready, willing and able to care for and support her. If you try to put her up for adoption by strangers, we'll fight you."

"I said it was an option I have to take into account. I didn't say it's what I was planning to do."

"But you implied it," Sylvia stated, her stormy midnight-blue eyes drilling into him. "One doesn't consider options one has no intention of pursuing."

She was right. He'd rejected foster care out of hand and never given it another thought. Of course, if Janna went to live with Clare and Michael, no formal adoption would be necessary.

"Allow me to start over again," he proposed. "I am Janna's father. In that capacity, I have primary responsibility for her well-being."

"But if she's adopted by strangers, we may never

see her again.'' Sylvia bunched her hands into fists and rested them on the ends of her chair. ''I won't allow it,'' she said adamantly. ''Do you hear me? I will not allow you to steal our grandchild from us. We are not without means or influence, Mr. First. We will spend whatever money is required to fight you on this. I will not have my granddaughter taken from her family. She's lost her mother and apparently her father doesn't give a damn about her—''

''Now, Sylvia,'' Albert said as he stroked his wife's sharp-boned shoulder. ''Don't upset yourself. We'll get this resolved.''

''And Gideon hasn't said he'll take Janna away, Syl,'' Vanessa added.

The older woman was breathing heavily, enough to raise Gideon's concern about her.

''Mrs. Runyon, family is very important to me, too.''

They were interrupted by the front door again opening. A younger woman walked in, holding the hand of a child.

The toddler was wearing pale-green shorts with little pink-and-yellow flowers printed on them, straps over her shoulders and buttons on the side of the pants. He caught a glimpse of the white plastic of her diaper. Her legs were chubby and dimpled at the knees. Beautiful dimples. He'd never realized how cute chubby legs could be.

But it was her face that captivated him. A little bit pink from the sun. Did they put sunscreen on her? Could you put sunscreen on a fourteen-month-old? Her eyes were a brilliant blue. Not her grandmother's shade. Those were dark and forbidding. Becky's had been green. Then Gideon realized what he was seeing. His own. First eyes. There could be no doubt. Janna was his daughter.

His daughter…and she terrified him. This perfect little creature…and he was her father. He was responsible for her welfare and happiness. Except he was a complete stranger to her. She was his little girl, and she didn't know him.

Vanessa opened her arms. "Come here, sweetheart." Gideon couldn't miss the genuine tenderness in the younger sister's voice. But his attention was glued to the child, who wobbled toward the outstretched hands. Like a Renaissance urchin with glowing, fiery red hair.

The child exhibited no hesitation in climbing into her great-aunt's lap and sitting there. Janna placed her hand on the woman's breast, and for the flash of a second, Gideon saw the most intimate maternal expression melt the spinster's face.

"Did you have fun at the park?" Vanessa asked.

Janna nodded happily.

"Tell Aunt Vanessa what you saw in the park," the young woman instructed her.

"Birds. Woof," she said proudly.

"Did you see birds and a dog? Were they pretty birds?" Vanessa asked.

"Big woof." Janna stretched her arms to demonstrate how big the dog was.

"And a big dog?"

"Tell Auntie Nessie what you did with the dog,"

the nanny coaxed the child. Sylvia's lips tightened, apparently at the nickname.

"I pet him." She stroked Vanessa's arm in simulation.

"That's very nice. What color was the dog?"

The child seemed momentarily confused, then decided she'd figured it out. "Big."

Vanessa chuckled, and Gideon was surprised to find it such a pleasant sound. "Well, we'll work on the difference between size and color later."

"Mr. First," Albert said, "this is Kim Rice. She helps out with baby-sitting."

The pert young woman, probably not much past her teens, had long straight brown hair and expressive amber eyes.

"Ms. Rice." Gideon went over and extended his hand, which she accepted politely. "You seem to have a very happy charge."

"She's an angel. Well, mostly," she added with a twinkle.

"Kim, why don't you take her to the nursery," Vanessa said. "It's close to her nap time. I'll be there in a minute."

"She's beautiful." Gideon couldn't keep himself from commenting.

"We love her very much," Vanessa said softly.

It was the first he'd heard the word *love* spoken. He had no doubt this woman did love her, too. He wondered, though, about the grandparents. Neither had made any overtures toward the child, nor had either of them declared or shown any affection for her. Janna had virtually ignored them.

"If you'll excuse me," Vanessa said, consulting her wristwatch and rising from her chair. "Kim will be leaving in a few minutes. I'd better help out with Janna."

"May I go with you?" Gideon asked. "I'd like to see her room."

Vanessa awarded him an approving smile. "Of course. Follow me."

With a nod to the two senior people, Gideon rose from the coach and followed Miss Cramer from the room. They mounted a wide, white-banistered staircase.

"Has Kim been with you long?" he asked.

"A few months. Strictly part-time."

At the top of the stairs, Vanessa led him down a short hall to the back of the house.

"Who usually takes care of Janna?" He suspected the answer even before he posed the question.

"I fill in when I can." He imagined she did more than that. "Syl...my sister is very active on several prestigious committees, and of course Albert works long hours. He also has to take frequent trips out of town."

"He's in oil, as I recall," Gideon noted.

"He's been expanding into alternative fuels, as well. With the energy crisis, he's been more busy than ever."

"I can believe that."

Vanessa led him through an open door at the back of the house. The room was big and sunny. The wallpaper had a nursery theme, ducks and teddy bears, rag dolls and crayon drawings of houses with gray smoke curling out of square chimneys.

"She's all changed," Kim announced with a glance over her shoulder from the crib along the far wall. "Aren't you, sweet thing?" She tickled the little girl under the chin. Janna giggled. "Got to run. Tomorrow again?" she asked Vanessa.

"Yes, but call beforehand to make sure."

"Okay. Nice to meet you, Mr. First." With a wave of her hand, she was out the door.

"You ready for your nap?" Vanessa gathered the child in her arms.

Janna shook her head, her attention focused on Gideon.

"Would you like to hold her?" Vanessa smiled uncertainly at him.

"Can I?" How ridiculous for him to feel anxious at the prospect of holding his baby. He'd held his nieces and nephews when they were little plenty of times. But they had been someone else's children. This one was his. That made her very special.

"Would you like to go to Daddy?" She nodded encouragingly to Janna.

The girl wasn't quite sure, but she didn't shrink away.

"This is your daddy," the great-aunt told her.

Janna hesitated, studying him. "You Daddy?"

Gideon felt a lump forming in his throat. "Yes, baby. I'm your daddy." Quietly, feeling strangely humble, he extended his arms. "Will you come to Daddy?"

After another second's hesitation, Janna leaned toward him.

The moment he held her in his arms and felt her soft body cuddle against him, he knew he couldn't possibly give this child up. Not to the Runyons. Not to strangers. Not even to his brother and sister-in-law. This was his child. His baby. His daughter, and an instinct, born millions of years ago in the human psyche, burgeoned forth.

He pressed her to his chest, inhaled the clean, delicate scent of baby skin and talcum powder, felt the warmth of smooth flesh and the unconditional trust of her tiny fist grasping his shirt—and the hair under it. He kissed the top of her head and glanced at the woman standing a few feet away. Tears were welling in her eyes.

A silent message communicated itself between them. He was taking this child away. He knew without a doubt that this woman was the one who cared for Janna, saw to her needs and gloried in her presence. He remembered Becky telling him her parents hadn't been very involved in her upbringing, either. Maybe it was because Becky had come so late in their life, or maybe she'd come so late in their life because they'd never really wanted to have children to begin with. Either way, the close bond of parent and child had never truly developed between them. Which made it all the more strange that Becky had chosen to move in with them when she became pregnant.

Janna gave him a weak, uncoordinated slap on the cheek. He gently pulled her tiny hand away and kissed her on the forehead. "Was Becky very involved with Janna?'' He had to know what kind of mother she had been.

Vanessa nodded, but behind the fleeting purse of her lips, he sensed disapproval. "She was a strong believer in quality time. She spent an hour or two with Janna almost every evening, reading to her, playing games with her, and when she was home, she always kissed Janna good-night."

Almost and *when she was home*. Not very positive phrases.

So Becky hadn't doted on her daughter, his daughter. That bit of information bothered him. "That's all? Only an hour or two a day?"

Vanessa cupped her hand behind Janna's frizzy head. "She worked a lot and put in a fair amount of overtime. Then there were the business trips. She was making very good money and received an offer to move to one of the major national advertising agencies in New York."

Janna had decided to examine Gideon's nose in detail. He moved his head to distract her from sticking her finger up his nostril, but otherwise let her explore. "Was she going to accept it?"

"She was giving it serious consideration. Would you like me to take her?"

"No, we're fine." More than fine. He'd told Lupe he wanted to be a father, and he'd certainly enjoyed the role of pseudodad with her children, but he had no idea fatherhood could feel like this.

Vanessa retreated a step or two and leaned against the crib. "Albert says Becky was at the point of negotiating terms."

The fast track in the Big Apple. Not a very good environment for a single mother to raise a small child. "Would she have taken Janna with her?" He closed his eyes just before Janna stuck her finger in one of them.

He opened them to see tension crease the bridge of Vanessa's nose. "We didn't actually discuss it, but my impression was that she was planning on leaving her here temporarily."

It was disappointing to hear, and yet Gideon wasn't really surprised. Becky obviously hadn't been moved by parenthood the way he was. At least she'd chosen to have the baby. But given the comfortable arrangement Becky had with her parents and aunt, Gideon wondered why she had wanted him to have their child in the case of her death. He could only speculate, of course, but he had the impression the relationship between Sylvia Runyon and Vanessa Cramer wasn't a wholly congenial one. If Janna had remained in this house, Vanessa might well have been driven out, leaving Janna prey to aged and cold grandparents.

Nick said Becky had been in love with Gideon, but it wasn't true. Or maybe instinctively she understood they weren't compatible—except in bed. He'd been truthful with Nick when he said they disagreed about most subjects. Had they ever discussed parenting, they would have disagreed about it, as well. If they had gotten married, Gideon realized, it wouldn't have worked. They were too far apart on the most essential level. Some differences simply didn't lend themselves to compromise.

"She would have been well provided for, Gideon.

Between Becky and her folks, Janna has had the best of everything—the finest clothes, the newest toys.''

Gideon remembered a Saturday afternoon when he'd stopped at Lupe's house to help her install some shelves in Teresita's room for her dolls. A woman friend had dropped by for a chat, bringing her two-year-old girl with her. Lupe didn't have any toys appropriate for a child that age, so she'd opened the bottom drawer of a kitchen cabinet and invited the munchkin to dump out all the Tupperware stored there onto the floor to play with. The toddler had been completely content with the impromptu playthings, and Lupe pointed out she could bang them to her heart's content without fear of getting hurt. Cardboard boxes, she claimed, worked equally well. From what Vanessa was saying, it sounded like Janna was living the life of a poor little rich girl.

''Except babies don't read designer labels or keep up with fads.'' He spun around, taking in the cherry-finished crib and changing table, the matching rocker and playpen, as well as the thick carpet on the floor.

''This is a beautiful room,'' he said. ''I bet you had something to do with decorating it.''

He wasn't sure why he said that, but he sensed it was true. She tried not to show her pride, but he saw it. ''Have you always lived with your sister and her husband?''

She practically choked. ''Good heavens, no.'' The very notion seemed to appall her. ''I happened to be visiting soon after Janna was born and was sort of at loose ends. I'd been a broker with a large investment company based in Chicago but had grown tired of the madhouse and resigned. My sister asked me to help her out for a few weeks, and since I had time on my hands, I agreed. Maybe it was a mistake. My being here, taking up the slack, so to speak, probably made things too easy for Becky. I figured she'd be staying home with her baby, so I decided I'd lend a hand until she regained her strength. I didn't realize how important her career was to her.''

Janna had grown bored with his facial features and hair and had rested her head on his shoulder, thumb in mouth. In the framed mirror on the closet door, he could see her eyes were still open, but the golden-lashed lids were getting heavy. Eventually, he might grow weary of holding her, but for now, the sweet warmth of her small body cradled against his chest was pure heaven.

"You know I'm keeping her," he said softly to the woman standing a few feet away.

She smiled, a sad understanding smile and, if he was reading her right, without recrimination.

"I think you'll make a very good daddy," she murmured. "Janna's a lucky little girl."

A brave front, Gideon realized. This woman's heart was breaking. "You're the one who'll miss her the most. I'm sorry."

She smiled again, and he could see she was fighting back tears. "I always knew she was mine only temporarily and that someday she'd be leaving." She bit her lip, then put out her arms. "I'll take her now." Janna's eyes had closed, her breathing slowed, her body gone nearly limp. "Come on, little lady. Time for your nap." She extended her hands to relieve him of his burden, then stopped. "Care to put her in her crib?"

He was totally amazed at how possessive he felt about this child, at how much he didn't want to give her up. He laid her gently on her back.

"Why don't you go downstairs," Vanessa whispered. "I'll join you there in a few minutes."

He suspected she needed the time to compose herself, to say goodbye, though he wouldn't be taking Janna back on this trip. There were still details to work out. He nodded to his daughter's great-aunt and stifled the urge to run his hands along his daughter's arms, fearful of waking her. As he walked down the hall toward the stairs, he heard Vanessa crooning a lullaby.

The Runyons were still in the living room when he returned.

"Thank you for providing so well for my little girl," Gideon said. They seemed to regard his gratitude as an insult. He let it pass. "And thank you for your offer to adopt her, but as soon as I can make arrangements, I'm taking her home."

"Her place is here," Sylvia said archly. "This is her home." She pulled a tissue from the box on the end table beside her and dabbed at her eyes. It was the first show of emotion, other than disdain and anger, that Gideon had seen her display.

"Mr. First, we've lost our daughter," she reminded him. "Please don't rob us of our granddaughter, too."

"We can fight you on this, you know," Albert said.

"But you won't," Vanessa said as she walked into the room. "Janna's place is with her father. If you try to contest his assuming full custody, I'll testify on his behalf.''

''Vanessa, what are you talking about?'' her elder sister protested. ''You of all people—''

''I'll be leaving as soon as Janna does. You have your committees, Syl, and Albert has his work. Now it's time for me to be moving on, too.''

CHAPTER SIX

HIS FIRST STOP when he returned to Coyote Springs late that afternoon was the office of Nelson Spooner. Gideon had telephoned him from Dallas immediately after leaving the Runyons and told him of his plans to assume full custody; now he found the attorney waiting for him, though it was after office hours. Even with his Italian suit coat off and his shirt sleeves rolled up above his wrists, the bachelor looked like something out of a fashion magazine.

"They're not wasting any time," Spooner informed him. "I received a call from Cavanaugh Pike about an hour after you and I talked. They're ready to sign the papers."

"That was fast. No quibbling?"

Spooner combed his fingers through brown hair that was beginning to thin on top. "Albert Runyon apparently made some noises about opposing the legal change of custody, but with a little prompting from me, Pike was able to convince him the effort would be futile and counterproductive. The provisions of their daughter's will, the positive paternity test and the Runyons' ages finally convinced the old man he couldn't win."

Vanessa's stand undoubtedly put additional pressure on them. Without her, the Runyons would be in a bind. Gideon could only imagine the conversation among them that had followed his departure earlier in the day.

"I also reminded Pike," Spooner added, "that alienating you might prevent them from ever getting to see their granddaughter again."

"So when can I go and get her?"

"Figure a few days to file the paperwork with the court, but without a challenge it's a matter of form. You can probably plan on getting your child a week from Sunday." This was Friday. A little more than a week away. "I'll coordinate with Pike during the week and let you know for sure. There'll be documents for you to sign, of course."

Less than ten days and he'd be bringing his daughter home. Realization was doing crazy things to his nervous system. Euphoria one moment, anxiety the next. How would he take care of her? What about clothes, food, furniture? He'd have to hire a full-time baby-sitter.

From Spooner's office, Gideon started to drive to Lupe's house. He couldn't wait to tell her about his little girl. About her flaming red hair and sparkling blue eyes. About her liking to pet a big woof. *Should I get her a dog?* Kids loved puppies.

Surely now that he'd decided to keep Janna, Lupe would forgive him for his distrusting her with the truth in the beginning. It would all work out in the end. He'd promise never to hold back the truth from her again, to always make her a part of every important decision. He'd beg her to put his ring back on her finger and to marry him.

He grabbed a CD from the console and stuck it in the slot. Dixieland. Happy, hopeful, liberated Dixieland. He turned up the volume.

But Lupe's car wasn't in the driveway, and the house was dark. Of course. Friday evening. Miguelito had soccer practice and Elena went with Teresita to her gymnastics class.

Deflated, Gideon proceeded, instead, to the Number One. His mood was up again when he arrived.

"Well, don't you look like the cat that ate the canary," Michael said with a laugh when he found Gideon at the back door of the ranch house.

"I'm bringing her home a week from Sunday," he announced as he breezed into the kitchen.

"Congratulations, Daddy." Clare came over and gave him a big hug, something she didn't do very often. "You're in luck. Just in time for your favorite meal. Leftovers."

"So you won't let the Runyons adopt her?" Michael resumed chopping onions on the butcher-block island.

"Nope." Gideon went to the refrigerator and pulled out a gallon jug of milk. At home, he drank right out of the container, but seeing his sister-in-law's narrow-eyed warning, he reached into the overhead cabinet and snagged a glass. After pouring about six ounces, he drank deeply and topped off the glass before replacing the container in the refrigerator.

"Wait till you see her," he enthused after another mouthful of cold milk. "She's beautiful. She has bright red hair and blue eyes and a button nose. She's always smiling and she never cries.''

"Mazel tov," said Clare, whose paternal grandfather had been Jewish, then she winked at her husband, and they both laughed. "We should be so lucky."

"I was wondering if you could help me," Gideon said, not getting the joke.

"What kind of help?" Clare turned to the dishes she was putting away.

"I'll need to buy furniture for Janna and things like that. Would you come with me?"

"Why don't you ask Lupe? I'm sure she'd be glad to help."

Gideon took another gulp of milk. "I stopped by her house, but she wasn't home." His confidence that she would be as thrilled as he was about his daughter had eroded. She'd told him he wasn't the man she thought he was. Bringing his baby to Coyote Springs wasn't likely to change that perception. If anything, Janna's presence would be a constant reminder of his failings.

"Besides," he added, "I'm not sure she would want to do this. I mean…under the circumstances—"

"Coward," Michael muttered with a sneer. He went to the refrigerator and removed a couple of cooked pork chops, which he began to bone and cube.

Gideon ignored the gibe. "Will you?" he asked Clare.

She curled her lips and narrowed her eyes in a *don't ask stupid questions* expression. "Of course."

"Thanks," Gideon replied with a relieved sigh.

"You say you're bringing her home a week from

Sunday," Clare noted. "That only gives us about a week to get everything done."

"That's when Spooner thinks I can get her. He's working with the other lawyer to finalize all the paperwork."

She nodded and held out a large glass bowl and a carton of eggs. "Get crackin', bro."

He placed the bowl on the counter and began breaking eggs into it.

"Who are you taking with you when you pick her up?" Clare asked.

Baffled, he asked, "Taking with me?"

"Five hours in a car may be easy for you, but it isn't for a baby," Clare informed him.

"I...I figured she'd nap." He used the whisk she handed him to beat the eggs into a froth. "Don't cars usually make babies sleepy? I've heard of parents with cranky kids driving around all night to get them to sleep."

"Some of them do." She set a large copper-clad stainless-steel skillet on the largest of the gas range's burners. "Others get sick."

Oh, God. He hadn't even considered what he would do if Janna got sick on the way.

Clare adjusted the flame and added oil to the pan. "It's a weekend. Ask Lupe to go with you."

Lord, how he missed her. On the drive back from Dallas, he'd visualized her sitting on the seat beside him. He'd talked to her and conjured up the sound of her voice as she responded. It had been an emotional roller coaster. At one moment, he was happy, fantasizing about her being by his side. The next, he'd glance over, see the empty seat and his mood would plummet to the depths of loneliness. The thought that she might never be there brought him to the edge of despair.

"She won't have the time," he insisted. "Final exams are coming up. She needs to study. Besides, she has her own family commitments."

This time, Clare tossed him one of her *can't believe this jerk* looks. "You better take someone."

"How about you?" Yeah, that'd work. "Come with me. You know all about kids."

The expression on her face shifted to *I should have kept my big mouth shut.* "I also have a family who needs me."

"Michael's a big boy who can get along without you for one day."

"Can't do," she said without any hope of compromise. She removed a plastic bag of leftover peas from the refrigerator and added them to the beaten eggs. Michael had already contributed the chopped onion and diced pork. "I have a meeting Sunday with the Citizens for Better Schools, which I positively can't miss," Clare explained. "And Sally has a piano recital in the afternoon."

Gideon gazed at his brother.

"Don't look at me," Michael objected. "Sally is my daughter, too, and I wouldn't miss one of her recitals for the world."

"We can drive up Saturday night, pick up Janna in the morning and be back in time for the recital. I'd like to hear her play, also."

Clare snickered but didn't say anything as she

added the omelette mixture to the skillet. It hissed when it hit the hot oil.

"Can't, brother. Sorry," Michael said. "I have work to catch up on around here, especially since I'm flying to Houston Monday to talk to Nedra Cummings at the bank. Apparently, she's planning to put more Number One land up for sale."

"That witch." Nedra Cummings, the Homestead Bank and Trust vice president in charge of investment management, had been Adam First's nemesis during the bank's takeover of the Number One. Seeing the breakup of the family ranch had been gut-wrenching. On the other hand, the huge sums the sales were garnering was greatly enhancing his personal wealth.

"I'll check with Julie. Maybe she can go." Gideon spoke without much enthusiasm.

LUPE CLIMBED out of her car Saturday morning, opened the Chevy's back door and reached for one of the bags of groceries. Behind her, she heard the kitchen screen bang and the scamper of sneakered feet.

"Did you get caffe mocha ice cream?" Miguelito asked eagerly as his mother thrust the paper sack into his arms.

"I went to Athon's," she explained. "They don't carry that brand. I got vanilla. You can put chocolate syrup on it."

"It's not the same." He peeked inside. "You got the store brand. Gideon always gets Bells."

Lupe could feel her temper beginning to rise. Gideon routinely bought the best of everything, which would have been fine if she could have afforded it, too. But she wasn't independently wealthy. Even with the extra money Elena brought in from her sewing, they lived on a carefully balanced budget. Gideon didn't seem to understand that, and neither did her nine-year-old son.

"Gideon doesn't do the shopping. I do. If this brand isn't good enough, you can go without."

"Jeez," he groused, and stomped toward the house.

"Miguelito—" But he was already through the back door. He'd become surly to the point of disrespectful since she'd told him the wedding was off.

Teresita was less demonstrative, but Lupe recognized she was very disappointed. Disappointed. Now that was an understatement. The kids had made Gideon a part of their lives—thanks to her encouraging them. She'd hoped they'd become a part of his, too, but he'd stopped coming by. Not that she could blame him. It was easier this way. How did you pretend you were nothing but friends with a man who'd put a ring on your finger and asked you to marry him? She had no idea how she was supposed to act around a man whose mere presence sent her heart rate skipping and her pulse humming. She certainly didn't know how she would handle the situation if he did show up, so she told herself she was glad he didn't.

Her concern at the moment, however, was her son, who was plainly feeling abandoned and rejected. He was hungry for a male role model in his life, and Gideon had seemed to fit the bill perfectly—upbeat, a wonderful coach and tutor and a good friend to a boy who missed having a dad.

Lupe huffed. Miguelito needed a man in his life. What about her? She hadn't realized how true that was until Gideon came along.

How could things have gone so wrong so fast? A call from a lawyer and so many lives had changed. No, she reminded herself, it wasn't the phone call that had altered everything. It was Gideon's lying about it. Only a fool would trust a man who lied.

She'd lain awake for several nights after giving him back the ring, wondering if she'd overreacted. Regardless of his flaws, she still loved him. And she was convinced he loved her.

She grabbed the other two bags of groceries, shifted her hip to close the car door and went inside. Elena was unpacking the bags the boy had brought in. "You remembered cilantro, good."

Lupe grunted and deposited her burden on the kitchen table. Her mother-in-law cast her a worried glance.

"I'm fixing *pollo diablo* tomorrow for dinner," Elena commented. The spicy chicken dish was one of Lupe's favorites.

"Sounds good," she responded without enthusiasm.

The two women moved around each other in silence for a minute, stowing canned goods in the pantry and produce in the refrigerator. Lupe was about to excuse herself so she could study for a test coming up on Monday when they heard a vehicle pull into the driveway. Elena parted the ruffled curtain over the sink and peeked outside.

"A truck," she said, "but I don't recognize it. Did Gideon buy a new one?"

Lupe shrugged. "Not that I'm aware of, but you never know." She went to the back door, opened it and stepped onto the small stoop. The wind chime Gideon had given her several months ago tinkled in the gentle breeze.

"Clare," she said in total surprise. "I didn't expect—" Gideon's sister-in-law had never stopped by before. It could only mean bad news. Had he been in an accident? Was he injured, dying, dead? She banished the thought and the pain it would bring. "Is something wrong? Has someone been hurt?"

Clare slammed the cab door and tucked the keys into her jeans pocket. "Everything's fine. May I come in?"

"Of course." Flustered and relieved, Lupe stepped aside to let her guest enter.

Several inches taller than Lupe, Clare mounted the steps and placed a hand on Lupe's shoulder. "Actually, I have some news you're going to like."

Lupe raised an eyebrow and followed her visitor inside.

"Hello, Elena," Clare greeted the older woman, who was standing inside the doorway. "Sorry to barge in on you like this. I hope I'm not interrupting anything."

Elena seemed as flustered by the newcomer's appearance as her daughter-in-law. "You are always welcome. Let me get you something to drink." Without waiting for a response, she went to the refrigerator and removed a pitcher of iced tea. "Lupe, take Clare into the living room. She will be more comfortable there."

"If you don't mind," Clare said, "I'd just as soon stay right here in the kitchen."

Elena quirked a small smile as she poured three glasses of tea. Wasn't the kitchen the heart of a home, especially for women? She joined the other two at the table. "Did you say you had good news?"

Clare grinned and nodded. "Gideon's keeping his baby."

A quiver of excitement ran through Lupe. He'd made the right decision, after all. The joy was immediately followed by concern. Raising a child was difficult for two people. For one man by himself, it was even more of a challenge. Was he up to it? "What made him change his mind?"

Clare's hand shot out and she covered Lupe's. "He—"

"I was sure he'd do the right thing!" Elena exclaimed, and beamed at Lupe. "Didn't I tell you?"

Smiling at Lupe, Clare spoke. "He didn't really change his mind. He just made it up. He stopped by last evening after he got back from Dallas. You should have seen him. He was downright bubbly." Clare laughed. "He said all it took was one look at Janna and he knew he couldn't let her go."

"I'm so glad," Lupe said, and tried to put on a happy face. She was indeed relieved that he'd finally come to his senses, but it would have been nice if he'd dropped by himself to tell her, instead of sending his sister. Why hadn't he? Had it gotten to the point that he was embarrassed to see her? Or was he mad at her because she'd had so little faith in him?

As if reading her mind, Clare said, "He drove by here before coming out to the ranch. Apparently, you weren't home."

"Oh." Lupe felt a ridiculous wave of relief wash over her. "The kids had practice last evening. We were home by nine o'clock, though."

Clare sipped her tea, squinting in amusement over the glass's rim. "He didn't leave our place until after ten."

"Ah."

"He's making arrangements through his lawyer with the Runyons to bring the baby home next Sunday. He asked me to help him get his apartment ready. I thought you might like to give me a hand."

The question sprang to Lupe's mind: *Why didn't he ask me?*

"What can I do?" Lupe laughed. "I don't own a bulldozer."

Clare chortled. "He is a bit of a slob, isn't he?"

"We gave away all Teresita's baby clothes a long time ago," Elena added.

"I don't have any of my girls' things, either," Clare agreed. "She probably won't need clothes for a while, anyway. The Runyons have apparently bought her truckloads, and I'm sure they'll be sending them along. No reason not to."

"Are they very unhappy about losing their granddaughter?" Lupe asked.

"They put up some resistance, but they really don't have much choice under the circumstances."

"It is very sad," Elena contributed.

"We'll have to get a crib and a playpen," Clare announced. "Toys won't be a problem. The Runyons are supplying them, too, and of course we'll have to make his apartment childproof. I don't have to tell you how fast a fourteen-month-old can get into things. I'm also sure my dear brother-in-law doesn't have the foggiest idea what to do. A crash course will be in order."

Gideon was lucky to have a sister-in-law like Clare, but this should be Lupe's job, something she and Gideon should be planning and doing together. To resent Clare was irrational. Instead, Lupe ought to thank her for what she was doing—including her. The important person in all this was the baby. Gideon's baby.

"What about during the day?" Elena asked. "Who will take care of the little girl while he's working? Will he put her in a nursery?"

Clare shook her head. "He doesn't want to do that. He asked me to help him find a baby-sitter for during the day. I was hoping you might know someone."

Elena pursed her lips and raised her brows. "And he'll take care of her by himself at night?"

Clare grinned. "Yep."

Elena smiled. "He does not realize what it is like."

This time Clare chuckled. "I'm not sure how much he remembers about his younger sister and brother as infants. Probably not much, since he was only a couple of years older. He's seen Michael and me contend with our kids, of course, but as a visitor, and there are two of us. Frankly, I'm not sure he has any idea what he's letting himself in for. But he'll soon find out.''

Lupe listened to the exchange and saw the temptation in her mother-in-law's eyes. Elena wanted to volunteer to baby-sit for Janna. Lupe realized she was getting angry with Gideon all over again. If they hadn't broken up—if he hadn't lied to her—it would be a simple matter to ask Elena to mind the child during the day until they got married. She would love doing it. Afterward, they'd all be a family. Now he was going to invite a stranger into his home to take care of his daughter.

''I know someone who might be able to sit for him,'' Lupe commented to forestall her mother-in-law from getting involved and complicating an already difficult situation. ''Margarita Johnson.''

Marge was in her early sixties, a grandmother who had been widowed in the past year. She had children and grandchildren in Coyote Springs, but she still lived alone.

''Maybe,'' Elena agreed, her disappointment and awareness of what Lupe was doing manifest. ''We can ask her.''

GIDEON SPENT Saturday mornings at one of four different nursing homes in town, where he worked with the staff to help residents, some of them quite elderly, stay as limber as possible. He didn't prescribe treatment, but he could recommend various exercises that might help them improve their mobility. Most of his seniors were grateful for his efforts, looked forward to his visits and greeted him with smiling faces. New residents were often skeptical. He spent as much time as he could with them, listening to their complaints and trying to find the best approach for alleviating their problems. In fact, he spent a good deal of extra time just visiting, listening to repetitive stories and encouraging people to stay as active as possible.

It was almost three o'clock when he left the Golden Years Rest Home. He wondered what to do with Janna on Saturdays. It didn't take him more than a few minutes to realize the best thing was to bring her with him. She certainly wouldn't be in any danger in the safety-conscious environment, and it only took one child's coming into a common room for him to see how the residents' rheumy old eyes lit up.

Clare's pickup was parked outside his town house when he arrived home. He bounded up the walk to see what she'd bought, pushed open the front door, which was standing ajar—and was confronted with the sight of Lupe bending over the couch.

The effect on his libido was instant and over-whelming. He lusted after this woman more than he'd ever wanted a woman in his life. It took the power of every calorie of heat his body was generating to resist the urge to sweep her into his arms.

"Hi," he said tentatively, not sure what kind of reception he was about to receive from the woman who'd sent him back his ring. They hadn't seen each other since the night he'd confessed his guilty secret. There hadn't been any scenes, no shouting about his misdeeds, his deceit. He wished there had been.

His father was right. He should be confronting her,

challenging her to talk, to listen, to argue. At least then he would know exactly where he stood and if there was any chance for him to redeem himself. It would have been easier to live with than the silence that was so strained between them. Let her yell and carry on, and when her eyes were fiery hot, he'd pull her into his arms and smother her with kisses until neither of them could stand it any longer. Then they'd make love—mad, passionate, unbearably consuming love, and he'd ask her to marry him, and she'd say yes. And this time, they'd do it.

Her movements stopped at the sound of his voice, then she resumed gathering the newspapers he'd left scattered about.

"You're back," she said over her shoulder, as if there had never been anything between them. As if his heart wasn't pounding. As if he couldn't see hers was, too.

"From Golden Years."

She occasionally accompanied him on his Saturday morning missions if family responsibilities didn't intervene. "How's Mrs. Klepensnoor?"

"Feeling better." The centenarian's body was fragile, but her mind was still clear and sharp. "I had her up and walking today."

Lupe folded the papers into a more or less compact pile. "Good."

"She asked for you."

They stood half a room away from each other, trying to pretend there wasn't an electrical charge pulsing between them, that their eyes didn't meet and bounce off each other like two positive poles of a magnet.

"I'll try to stop in and say hello during the week."

"There you are," Clare said from the top of the stairs. "Come see what was just delivered."

"Been shopping, huh?" He was responding to his sister-in-law, but his attention was on Lupe, searching her eyes for answers. If any were hidden there, they were locked securely away. Gesturing with his hand, he invited her to precede him up the narrow staircase. The two bedrooms were on the second floor, his own and the spare he used as a catch-all.

He watched the back of her hips sway gently from side to side as she rose gracefully, erotically, ahead of him. Common sense and an instinct for emotional survival told him he should divert his attention, concentrate on other things—the furniture they had bought, his daughter coming home. But hormones were raging and other primal urges were winning the battle for another kind of survival.

"We didn't know where to put the junk you had stored in the second bedroom," Clare said, "so we moved most of it into the living room. You'll be a little crowded until you decide what to do with it."

He followed them into the guest bedroom. The previous owner had had unconventional tastes. The carpet was a somber olive green. The walls were painted in semigloss swirls of maroon and peach. The color of the woodwork was probably best described as brown. The room was dark and ugly. But since no one lived in it, he'd continually put off doing anything about it.

Clare and Lupe had cleared the room of every stick of furniture. Not that there had been much. A double bed. A couple of end tables with lamps. A chest of drawers. In their place, he found a new crib, a changing table, two matching chests of drawers, a playpen and a toy box.

He ran his hands over the polished surfaces. "Neat."

"This room needs brightening," Lupe informed him. "You have a week. I'd suggest painting it as soon as possible. Pink, maybe, with white woodwork. Not original, but nice and clean and light. At least she won't get nightmares. Be sure to leave the windows open after the paint dries, so the smell can dissipate by the time you bring her home."

"Good idea. Speaking of bringing her home," he said, tossing Clare an imploring glance for support, "I was wondering if you could come with me when I pick her up."

"Me?" Lupe drew back. "I thought you were going to ask your sister."

He was tempted to cast his sister-in-law a disgruntled expression. He would have preferred it if Lupe had believed she was his first choice. But this was his own fault. Clare had suggested he ask her, and he'd been the one who'd resisted. Michael was right; he was a coward.

"I'm asking you. I'd really appreciate your help. You're experienced with babies. I'm not. Neither is Julie," he added quickly. In fact, he'd asked his sister, and she'd turned him down flat. She, too, had exams to study for. But he didn't have to tell Lupe that.

Lupe stared at the stained carpet. "I'm not sure this is a good idea, Gideon."

"Please," he said. "For Janna's sake."

There was hurt in her eyes when she lifted them to his. Because he was using his daughter to manipulate her? Or simply because she didn't want to be with him? At the moment, he didn't care which, as long as she'd say yes.

"Next Sunday?" she inquired.

He felt the first heartbeats of hope. "Yes." Maybe he should offer to go up there on Saturday evening so they wouldn't have to make the entire trip in one day. But she might refuse if it meant spending a night with him, even though they'd be in separate motel rooms. Hell, he'd even offer to put her up in a separate motel, if that was what it took.

"I usually go to mass on Sunday morning with the children, but I could go on Saturday night, I suppose."

He didn't even realize he'd been holding his breath. "Then you'll come with me?"

"We'll have to leave very early. I can study in the car—on the way up, at least."

"Thank you," he said humbly.

He had to tamp down the urge to grab her in his arms and dance around the room. Giving in to the strange feeling of lightness he felt, as if a great weight had been lifted from his shoulders, he said, "I don't suppose I could talk you into helping me paint, too..."

She stared at him, then burst out laughing. "Don't push it, buster. Bribe one of your students."

He was smiling from ear to ear; he couldn't help it. She was still mad at him, but she'd go with him to Dallas. She'd sit next to him in the car, and even if they didn't talk, she'd be there with him. "Now, why didn't I think of that?"

CHAPTER SEVEN

GIDEON picked Lupe up at her house at six o'clock Sunday morning. She carried a stack of books with her. She was still cramming for finals. He'd never seen her so early in the day, with sleep still in her eyes and a lethargy in her movements. He imagined seeing more of her this way, hair tousled, but with her head beside him on a pillow.

"I brought a pillow and blanket," he told her. "Why don't you curl up in the back seat? It's going to be a long trip."

"I have to study," she reminded him, her voice husky and sexy as hell. *I want to wake up every morning with that sound in my ear,* he told himself. *With this sight to feast my eyes on.*

"Catch some Zs," he advised her. "You'll be more alert when you do crack the books."

The debate with herself lasted almost three seconds, then she climbed in the back seat of the Explorer. He watched her turn on her side, tuck the pillow under her head, fold her hands prayerfully beside her face and draw up her knees. He caught a glimpse of white bra strap against smooth olive skin as he covered her with the soft wool blanket. His respiration shuddered as he took a slow deep breath. He shut the back door and got in the driver's seat. His jeans were definitely too tight.

Nearly two hours went by before she began to stretch. Then she sat up, alert and curious. "Where are we?"

"Close to Comanche. Ready for something to eat?"

"I'll let you know after my first whiff of coffee." She folded the blanket into a neat square and placed it on the far end of the seat.

"Breakfast coming up."

He pulled into a crowded truck stop on the near side of the small North Texas town. While she went to the ladies' room, he got a booth and ordered them juice and coffee.

"We're making good time," he told her when she slipped into the seat across from him. She'd combed her hair and put on lipstick. Nothing loud, just a subtle pinking of her lips. Damn, but he wanted to kiss that mouth. "We should be there by eleven."

She nodded nonchalantly, added cream and sugar to her coffee, took a grateful sip and picked up a plastic-coated menu. "If we eat now," she muttered as she browsed the selections, "we won't have to stop for lunch."

A harried waitress came over to take their orders. Lupe requested a bowl of cornflakes, a sweet roll and a container of yogurt. Gideon selected pancakes and sausage. They needed to talk, but the place was too noisy, too distracting and public to carry on a serious conversation.

Service was prompt.

"Barely six weeks to graduation." He slathered whipped margarine between oversize flapjacks and drowned them with imitation maple syrup. "Excited?"

Pride glowed in her smile. "It doesn't seem possible. I'm not sure what I'll do when I don't have tests to study for and papers to write."

He could think of several ways to keep her occupied. "There'll be work, which always expands to fill the time available," he assured her.

"So I've noticed." She spooned up a mouthful of cereal. Somebody dropped a coin in the jukebox, contributing a rock number to the collage of discordant sounds. It effectively cut off any further conversation.

They'd shared plenty of meals together, mostly lunches and suppers, but occasionally breakfasts. This one was different, though. It wasn't the noise or the frenetic atmosphere. An invisible shield loomed between them. He could imagine her delicate flowery fragrance, even though the scent was buried under the strong smells of breakfast foods and burned coffee. If he reached across the table, he could even touch her. Yet, they were out of contact, as far apart as two people on different continents.

They finished their meal, ordered coffee to go and returned to the car. Lupe moved to the front seat. *That's better,* he thought. *Now we'll have a chance to talk.* But she strapped herself in, opened one of her textbooks and totally ignored him. That didn't keep him from periodically glancing at her legs, the soft smoothness of her bare arms and the fullness of her breasts. Inevitably, he had to tighten his hold on the steering wheel to keep from reaching over and insinuating his fingers in the long strands of her jet-black hair.

Between erotic fantasies, Gideon's mind strayed to questions of whether what he was doing was right for his child, whether he was up to raising her by himself, what it would be like if he could share this experience with the woman sitting next to him. What could he do to convince her to take him back—with his daughter?

Life had been so pleasant, so idyllic until a few weeks ago, when everything seemed to come crashing down around him. He didn't resent the baby. After all, it wasn't Janna's fault she was born. The fault was in her parents.

After half an hour, Lupe gave up trying to study. She'd gone over the same page repeatedly and absorbed none of it. She closed the book and laid it aside. They were drawing closer to the Metroplex; traffic was getting heavier.

She crossed her arms below her breasts. "Tell me about Becky."

The invitation to talk about the mother of his child startled him, even though he'd sensed her curiosity. She hadn't missed his surreptitious glances her way, either, or how his hands had tightened around the steering wheel after each one.

"She was my age," he said on a deep breath. "We shared a couple of classes in high school. She was active in the drama club."

"Becky was an actress?"

He shook his head. "She took a few bit parts, but

her real interest was in constructing sets. She was a graphic artist with talent.''

''Was she athletic?''

He checked the rearview mirror, clicked his blinker and pulled into the left lane to pass an eighteen-wheeler. ''She liked to play tennis once in a while, and she was a good swimmer, but she wasn't on any team.''

''What did she look like?'' Lupe pictured a girl who was tall, with flowing blond hair and blue eyes, the perfect match to Gideon's Scandinavian handsomeness.

He switched blinkers, reverted to the right lane and hit the resume button on the cruise control. ''Well, let's see,'' he temporized. ''I guess the best way to describe her would be short and dumpy with straggly mouse-colored hair and buck teeth. I tried to talk her into getting the wart removed from the side of her nose, but she was afraid of needles.''

Lupe snorted. ''I'm not sure if you're telling me what you think I want to hear,'' she speculated, ''or if you have a weakness for ugly women.''

He stuck his tongue in his cheek. ''Oops. Stepped in it, didn't I?''

She pursed her lips. ''Of course, you might try telling me the truth.''

''Ouch!'' He breathed deeply. ''She was fairly tall, about five-nine. Long blond hair, very green eyes, and she had a dimple in her chin.''

Lupe wondered what he'd ever seen in her if his taste ran to Nordic blondes. She was petite, and had black hair and brown eyes. Her complexion was nowhere near fair, and she definitely didn't have a dimple in her chin. "She sounds beautiful."

His countenance grew serious. "Not nearly as beautiful as you."

She gave him a sidelong glance. "I'm not digging for compliments, Gideon." Although secretly she liked that he'd given her one. She decided not to remind herself that he didn't always tell the truth, that he said what was expeditious.

He gazed at her for a moment before focusing on the road ahead. "I know that." He shot her a quick grin. Not fawning, but enough to let her see he was sincere. "It also doesn't change what I said. You are beautiful, Lupe. Beautiful in a way Becky couldn't possibly match."

And how was that? she was tempted to ask. But this wasn't about her.

"Did you date in high school?"

"Occasionally, nothing steady." He veered around an ancient pickup driven by a little old man who might have bought it new. "A bunch of us used to go to a pizza parlor following football and basketball games. After a while, we tended to pair up into couples. She and I were comfortable in each other's company."

Comfortable enough to go from pizza parlor to bedroom. When Lupe was in school, she used to envy some of the Anglo girls who seemed to do whatever they chose with very few restrictions. They wore the kinds of clothes her parents would never tolerate, put on makeup a year or two before she was permitted to use lipstick, and they went wherever they wanted and stayed out till late—even on weeknights.

Her parents were very traditional. She had plenty of friends, but she was never allowed to be alone with boys. If they went places, it was always in groups. Dances and parties were either at someone's home or at the church hall, and they were always closely chaperoned. Some girls balked, but there weren't any unplanned pregnancies.

"Even in college, we didn't actually go steady," Gideon explained. "We dated more often, but we had no claims on each other."

"You were just good friends." She hadn't meant it to sound judgmental, but from the way he regarded her out of the corner of his eye, she could see he took it that way. For a moment, she expected him to object, but he didn't.

"Yes, we were just good friends." He let a minute go by. "I didn't love her, Lupe, and she didn't love me."

Silence lingered between them for several minutes. Lupe gazed out her window at the flat Texas land going by. Fences and open prairie, small stands of stunted live oak. A few cattle. An occasional oil jack. Rarely was one pumping. A dream of wealth on hold, or abandoned.

Why had he told her that? Was she supposed to be pleased that there hadn't been any commitment, any promises?

And what kind of warped values did she have that she was actually pleased? He'd told her he'd never said *I love you* to another woman, and she yearned desperately to believe him. But how could she be sure? He said he didn't engage in casual sex, which meant he had to feel some sort of emotional bond with his bed partner. He also said he and Becky were good friends. Lupe couldn't imagine having sex with a friend without feeling it was more than just companionship.

"She never told me she was pregnant, Lupe."

"You don't have to explain, Gideon," she assured him.

"Don't I?" The set of his jaw told her he had to spell this out. She owed him that much.

"Let's get something straight. I didn't abandon her—or my child," he elaborated. "The last time we met—I hadn't seen her in a couple of months—she invited me to lunch. She wanted to say goodbye because she was moving to Dallas. She must have known she was pregnant, but she didn't utter a word to me about it. I suppose I should have realized there was something different about her, but I didn't."

"At two months, she wouldn't have been showing, Gideon."

He shook his head. "Not that way. I've always said there's a special glow about a woman when she's pregnant."

The comment surprised her and had her glancing over at him. Miguel used to say the same thing—that she was most beautiful when she was pregnant. He teased her that he wanted to keep her that way because he loved to see her soul reflected in her eyes.

"Maybe she had that glow and I didn't notice it," Gideon accused himself. "Or maybe she just didn't have it. If what her aunt Vanessa says is true, Becky didn't have very strong maternal instincts.''

"What do you mean?''

''She apparently moved in with her folks because they would give her the freedom to come and go as she pleased. She returned to her job as soon as she could after Janna was born.''

"A lot of women go back to work after giving birth,'' Lupe said.

"She didn't have to. She could have spent more time with her daughter. Instead, she left her to her aunt and a nanny to take care of.''

And you were considering putting her up for adoption so you wouldn't have to bother with her. But Lupe didn't say it.

"Why do you suppose she never told you about the baby?''

He let the question hang in the air for a long minute before attempting an answer. ''My bet is she was afraid if she told me I'd ask her to marry me, and she wasn't interested in marriage—to me or anyone else.''

"Would you really have proposed to her?'' Lupe had to know. It was important.

"Yes.'' There was no hesitation.

"Because you loved her?''

He stretched his arms out as he held the steering wheel. ''I didn't love her, Lupe.'' Anger and frustration gave an edge to his words. ''And she didn't love me. We never discussed marriage. Not once. For a very good reason. Neither of us was interested in spending our lives with the other person. Beyond the surface of our friendship, we really weren't compatible.''

Were she and Gideon compatible? Lupe wondered. For a long while, she'd thought they were, but now she was seeing all the little cracks she'd never noticed before—or didn't want to see. The way he used money. The way he lived in constant chaos. His attitude toward premarital sex. Did it extend to extramarital affairs?

''You said Becky wasn't the maternal type—that she left the care of Janna to her aunt and a nanny. Yet she chose to have her baby rather than abort it the way some women do with unplanned pregnancies.''

Gideon blanched. ''She wouldn't kill our baby. And she didn't neglect her. Janna was well taken care of. She seems like a happy child. But damn it, Becky should have told me,'' he asserted between clenched teeth. ''I would have proposed, and she would have turned me down, but at least I would have known I had a daughter, and I could have been a part of her life.''

This time Lupe did say it. ''Yet a few weeks ago, you were thinking of putting her up for adoption.''

''It was a stupid idea. All right?'' The muscles in his neck were taut until he took a deep breath. ''Pike said Becky's parents offered to keep her. It seemed like a logical solution.''

''What changed your mind?''

''I saw her, Lupe.'' He turned his head to meet her eyes. It was for only a second, but it was enough to convey the force of what he felt. ''I held her in my arms. She called me her daddy." His voice had gone soft, vulnerable. He clenched and unclenched his jaw muscles and stared straight ahead at the busy highway in front of him.

They were between Fort Worth and Dallas, and traffic had intensified. Gideon sat straighter in his seat, craning his neck for a better view as he wove between cars and trucks on his way to their exit. While his posture stiffened, Lupe let hers relax. There was nothing she could do about road conditions. She waited until they had turned off the interstate and were driving at a more leisurely pace along secondary roads before asking, "Were Becky and her folks close? Is that why she moved back in with them?"

Gideon snorted. "Becky was a very independent person. Self-absorbed and opinionated. Until last week, I'd met her parents briefly only twice, but I'd say she inherited those qualities from them. I imagine she moved back in with them because it was convenient."

"You make her sound awfully cold, Gideon."

He sighed. "A part of her was. She could be selfish, but she wasn't a bad person. Actually, I suspect you would have liked her. You just wouldn't have been close friends."

He turned into an upper-class development. A few of the houses were single story, but most of them were two or even three stories tall and would easily qualify as mansions. Gideon pulled into the circular driveway of one of the larger homes.

There was no reason for Lupe's heart to be hammering, but it was. She caught the masked expression on Gideon's face and realized he was as uncomfortable as she was. He smiled at her. "Ready?"

She nodded. He came around to her side of the car, helped her out and escorted her to the front door. He rang the bell and was about to reach for her hand when the door opened.

"Hello, Gideon," Vanessa greeted him. She offered Lupe a pleasant smile and extended her hand. "I'm Vanessa Cramer, Becky's aunt."

Gideon had said she was in her late forties or early fifties, but she had bags under her eyes that made her appear older. Lupe clutched her hand, which felt clammy. "I'm Lupe Amorado."

"They're waiting for you in the living room." Vanessa ushered them in and closed the door behind them, then led them into a very large, open room.

Albert Runyon was standing by his wife, who was seated in a high-backed chair. Their posture reminded Lupe of royalty receiving visitors. Gideon walked to the older man and offered his hand. "Mr. and Mrs. Runyon, this is Mrs. Lupe Amorado. She's come to help me with Janna on the trip home."

Sylvia nodded acknowledgment of her presence. "Very wise of you, Mr. First, to bring a nanny with you." She turned to her younger sister. "Vanessa, why don't you take Lupe upstairs. She can help Kim pack the rest of Janna's belongings."

The humiliation on Lupe's face cut into Gideon like a knife tearing his chest open. He barely managed to suppress the urge to lash out at the narrow-minded prejudice of the old woman. What he wanted desperately to announce was that Lupe was his fiancée.

"You seem to have jumped to an unwarranted conclusion, Mrs. Runyon. I didn't say Mrs. Amorado was a nanny. She happens to be a close personal friend." He was tempted to demand an apology, but one requested was worthless. Instead, he simply stared at her hard enough to make her squirm.

"Sorry." Sylvia said it to him rather than to the person she'd offended. If anything, her tone betrayed more annoyance than contrition.

Gideon shot Lupe a glance. Her expression was stoic, but he could feel the humiliation twisting behind the calm facade.

With a thin smile in appreciation of his effort, she turned to Vanessa. "I would like to see the baby, though."

"Of course." The younger sister led the way to the hall. "She's a real angel."

When they had left the room, Mr. Runyon said to Gideon, "I can't stop you from doing this, Mr. First, or I would."

"I told you we shouldn't sign those papers," Mrs. Runyon declared with a scowl. "Janna belongs here. With us. Not a stranger."

Albert rested a hand on her shoulders. From the continued rigidity of her posture, it didn't seem to bring any consolation.

"I realize this is terribly difficult for you both," Gideon said sympathetically, addressing Mrs. Runyon, whose lips bunched in disapproval. "I'm sure you love her. But this was Becky's wish."

"Rebecca was a fool," she snarled, her voice quivery. Albert tightened his embrace, and this time she yielded to it.

"We want to continue to see her," the old man announced.

"Of course," Gideon assured them both. "Coyote Springs is a five-hour drive away. You're welcome to visit us whenever you like."

The unhappy old man closed his eyes and nodded gratefully.

"Now," Gideon began, "if you'll excuse—" He turned toward the doorway just as Vanessa, Kim and Lupe appeared. Lupe held the little girl in her arms, and for a moment, Gideon's heart stopped. She looked so perfect with a baby cradled against her breasts. His baby. The expression on her face was one of pure delight. Janna gazed at him with recognition and curiosity.

"Come to Daddy," he coaxed, and held out his arms.

Janna peered at him skeptically. Her eyes passed over her grandparents and she gazed at Vanessa, as if asking her permission. The great-aunt smiled and nodded reassuringly as Gideon approached slowly. But at the last minute, Janna recoiled from him and burrowed deeper against Lupe's breasts.

"Okay," he said softly, and stroked her small back with a gentle hand.

"She's a little overwhelmed right now," Lupe remarked to him.

"I reckon so," he replied, stunned by how much it hurt to have his little girl pull away from him. His baby. His daughter. He wished at that moment he'd been in her life sooner. "We'll give her time to adjust. Do you mind holding her?"

Lupe smiled at the baby. "Why don't you start loading her things?"

"Kim and I'll help." Vanessa's voice was tight with emotion.

The four adults and one child proceeded to the front door, where two large pieces of soft-sided luggage stood beside two even larger cardboard boxes. "Enough clothes to last until the ones I already shipped arrive," Vanessa explained, indicating the suitcases. "And her toys." She nodded to the boxes, then pointed to a shopping bag. "I left out a few of her favorites for the trip back."

Vanessa and Gideon stowed the items in the back of the Explorer while Kim retrieved the car seat from the Mercedes parked in front of the garage. She installed it behind the driver's seat, showing Gideon how to properly secure it. With reassuring sounds, Lupe buckled the child in and slid onto the seat beside her.

Mrs. Runyon had separated herself from her husband and was moving toward her granddaughter.

"You be a good little girl now," she crooned, and kissed the child's cheek—the only genuine affection Gideon had seen her show toward her grandchild. "And we'll see you real soon."

"Bye-bye, sweetheart," Mr. Runyon said, his voice less firm than his wife's as he bent to kiss the child's brow. "If you need anything…" he started to say to Gideon, then grasped his hand with surprising strength. "Take good care of her." His eyes were glassy.

"I promise you, I'll do everything in my power to make her happy. You have my word on it. You also have my address and telephone number. Call or visit us whenever you like."

Vanessa, her face swollen and tearstained, was the last to kiss the child goodbye. She tried her best to be upbeat, but her distress conveyed itself to the little girl, and Janna began to cry. Lupe combed the unhappy child's curly head with gentle fingers and quietly sang a sweet melody. It seemed to do the trick. Janna calmed down.

Gideon took Sylvia Runyon's cold hand in farewell, but when he turned to Vanessa, they embraced. "I'm so sorry," he said quietly in her ear.

"Don't be," she assured him as she wiped her cheek with the back of her hand. "It's the best thing for Janna."

Gideon held both her moist hands in his. "Come see us."

"I will," she murmured in reply. "God bless you."

Gideon climbed behind the wheel and started the engine. With a nod to the bystanders, he slowly pulled out of the driveway. Lupe held Janna's hand up to wave at her grandparents and great-aunt.

The first hour, Lupe entertained the baby, who seemed perfectly happy to play with the toys that had been brought along. Gideon felt strangely contented as he drove the open highway, his daughter jabbering away in her car seat behind him, the woman he had expected to marry delighting in the little girl's vitality, soft music playing on the radio. The sun was shining, the air clear. A sense of peace and everything being right with the world seeped into his psyche.

In the second hour, Janna became a little more restless. Lupe had learned from Kim that the child knew some songs, so she coaxed her into a sing-along. On an impulse, Lupe sang to her in Spanish. Janna seemed bewildered at first by the unfamiliar sounds. She kept watching Lupe's mouth and even put her fingers on her lips as if she could touch the strange syllables.

"Do you think you can sing that?" Lupe asked her.

Janna paused and nodded.

Lupe sang a short phrase. "Now you."

Janna mimicked it.

"Very good," Lupe praised her. She sang another line in Spanish.

This time Janna's imitation was even better. More remarkable still was that she carried the tune correctly, as well.

Gideon was all ears as he watched his daughter in the rearview mirror. "Is she as good as I think she is?"

"Better," Lupe confirmed joyfully. "Kim said she liked to sing, but I had no idea…. At her age, most kids are just beginning to express themselves in more than one word. She's using whole sentences—"

"Does she understand Spanish?" he asked in Spanish. But it quickly became obvious she didn't. Gideon wasn't surprised. "She will. I'll ask Mrs. Johnson to talk to her in Spanish as well as English."

Lupe continued to sing to the child in Spanish, Gideon sometimes joining in, and the fourteen-month-old parroted their words. After a while, the novelty wore off, however, and Janna became cranky.

"What's the matter?" Gideon asked from the front seat.

"She might be hungry."

"Can't you distract her?" he asked over the baby's wails. "Give her something to play with," he suggested.

"Babies have three basic drives," Lupe explained patiently. "To eat, sleep and be comfortable. There are no substitutes. You can't distract them from one with another."

"We'll be in Abilene in about thirty-five minutes. We can stop there for a bite. I'm getting hungry, and I bet you are, too."

"We can't wait that long," Lupe insisted. "If my nose isn't mistaken, she also needs changing. Now."

"Can't you do that back there?"

"In a moving car? Get real. Not only could it be messy, but it's unsafe. You'll have to stop."

Gideon grunted. "There's a picnic area up ahead."

The next half-mile seemed interminable as Janna screamed at the top of her very healthy lungs. Finally, Gideon pulled into a turnout, where a concrete picnic table and benches hovered under a sprawling live oak tree.

"Okay, baby," Gideon said as he jumped out of the car and opened the back door. It took him what seemed an eternity before he was able to unsnap the baby-seat harness. She practically jumped into his

arms. "Pee-hew." He twisted his mouth and blinked.
"You really do need changing."

Lupe had exited the other side of the car and
walked around to join him.

"Here, take her." He offered the still-crying baby
to her. "I'll grab the bag."

With a fiendish smile, she said, "Uh-uh. I'll get the
bag. You attend to your daughter."

"But—"

Her eyes twinkled as she spun around and retrieved
the diaper bag from the floor of the back seat.

Gideon had changed a diaper or two, but that had
been a while back, and mostly wet diapers on his kid
brother or his nephews. This was considerably different. He clamped his jaw and swallowed hard when
he uncovered her, then held his breath the entire time
he worked at wiping away the mess.

"Better get used to it," Lupe advised him. He definitely wasn't seeing the humor in the situation when
he glanced up and saw her grinning at him from a
considerable distance upwind. "You probably have
another year of diapers."

He rewarded her with a disdainful glance. "She'll
be potty trained within three months."

A wider grin creased Lupe's face. "Uh-huh."

"You'll see. Any kid who can sing in English *and*
Spanish is smart enough to learn to use a toilet."

She snickered with undisguised humor. "Good
luck."

A clean diaper did the trick. Janna resisted getting
back into her car seat, but she settled down when
Lupe gave her a pacifier.

"Those aren't good for kids," Gideon commented from the front seat as he pulled out of the picnic area.

"Since when?"

"I read it in a book."

Lupe chuckled. "She's quiet, so let her have it. When you get home, you can take it away from her if you want, but right now, I value my eardrums."

Gideon said nothing, but the frown he sent her in the rearview mirror clearly indicated he wasn't pleased. After a few minutes, Janna grew restless again.

"What are you doing?" he asked when Lupe went rummaging in one of the carryalls.

"Getting out some baby food. I'm sure she's hungry."

He checked his dashboard clock. A few minutes after three. "But it's not her dinnertime yet."

Lupe screwed up her mouth and shook her head. "I don't think she can tell time, Gideon. She's hungry. I'm going to feed her."

"You'll spoil her appetite."

"For what?" She was getting a little annoyed. "Janna's hungry. She eats. What else is she supposed to do with an appetite?"

"Lupe—"

"Shut up and drive. You can read her all the parenting books you want when you get her home."

Checking the rearview mirror a few minutes later, he could see his daughter gobbling down the jarred fruit Lupe was feeding her.

"She likes applesauce," Lupe commented happily. "But then, I guess most kids do."

"I'm not sure she should have apples," Gideon opined. "They can be a problem with hyperactive children."

"She's not hyperactive, Gideon. She's hungry. And I doubt Vanessa would have included applesauce if Janna had bad reactions to it."

He grunted.

At last, they reached the outskirts of Coyote Springs. Gideon glanced over his shoulder at his sleeping daughter and wondered, not for the first time, how Becky could have been so cavalier about having a baby. What could be more important than the life and welfare of a child?

Five minutes later he pulled into his driveway.

Lupe looked around the living room as she entered behind Gideon, who held Janna in his arms. The usual newspapers weren't strewn around—they were stacked on the coffee table. And there were no used paper plates left on end tables and chairs, though there were a few soda cans. Several of the things she and Clare had removed from the extra bedroom upstairs— books, magazines, racks of CDs and a shopping bag filled with audio and VCR tapes—were still tucked into corners.

"Poor tyke's exhausted from all the traveling," he murmured as he carried Janna up the stairs.

Lupe followed.

The spare bedroom, now the nursery, was a complete surprise. The walls had been painted a rose pink. The woodwork was a brilliant white. A plush dusty-rose carpet had replaced the olive-green shag rug. The room was spotlessly clean and bright and smelled, not of paint, but of a delicate floral scent.

Gideon carefully laid Janna in the crib, where yellow ducks and pale-green frogs dotted a peach-colored flannel sheet.

"Should I take her clothes off?" he asked.

She nodded. "And cover her."

Before stepping out of the room, Gideon engaged a switch on a small plastic box on a shelf over the toy box.

"An intercom," he explained. "I've got it hooked up to my room, the living room, kitchen and bathroom downstairs.

Lupe was impressed, and let it show in her smile.

"I'll help you bring the rest of the stuff in," she offered when they returned downstairs.

She toted the suitcases into the house while he wrestled with the big cardboard boxes.

"Let's leave them here," he suggested. "I'll put this stuff away after she wakes up."

"I suggest you do it now. When she wakes up, you'll be busy doing other things."

He smiled at her. "Okay."

They moved around quietly in the nursery, so as not to disturb the sleeping child, and had everything put away in a matter of minutes.

"I didn't even think about the suitcases this morning," he admitted, after carrying them empty downstairs. "I'll ship them back to the Runyons tomorrow. How about something to drink?" He walked toward the kitchen.

She automatically trailed behind him. "I really

have to be leaving.'' Using the wall phone, she called for a cab to take her home.

''Can't you spare a few more minutes?'' he implored. ''We need to talk.''

About what? She wanted to ask. But the answer was obvious. *About us.* ''There really isn't much to say.''

He met her eyes. ''What about us?'' His voice was low, intimate. It should be the prelude to a kiss.

She turned away. When she didn't respond, he went to the refrigerator and removed two cans of Sprite. He handed her one.

''I still love you, Lupe.''

Don't do this, she nearly cried. *Don't torment me with protestations of love.* Her fingers shook as she popped the top on the sweaty can. But she didn't lift it to her lips.

He cupped his hand around her elbow. Gentle persuasion. A reminder of what it felt like for them to touch. ''Whatever your opinion of me,'' he said, ''my love for you hasn't changed.''

She bit her lip and refused to meet his eyes.

''I care for you, too, Gideon,'' she finally said, simultaneously slipping out of his reach. She wasn't willing to use the L-word now, not after all that had happened. ''But things have changed.''

''I haven't,'' he told her.

And maybe that's the problem, she almost countered. All she did was shuffle her feet. His piercing gaze was making her nervous.

''You haven't,'' he added.

She wondered if that was true. She'd lost something in the past few weeks. Not innocence so much as naïveté. She wasn't as trusting as she had been. Didn't take people at face value as she once had.

"We can still be friends, Gideon. Let's leave it at that."

The taxi arrived out front and blew its horn. She moved quickly to the living room.

"You have a beautiful daughter, Gideon," she said over her shoulder as she put her hand on the doorknob. "If you need anything, let me or Elena know."

And she was gone.

CHAPTER EIGHT

LUPE STOPPED BY Gideon's office the following Friday afternoon. Her days had been hectic, filled with last-minute lab reports and more cramming for final exams. She'd wondered how Gideon and Janna were getting on all week, but she'd told him to call her if there were any problems. Since he hadn't, everything must be going all right.

As she approached his closed office door, she decided he must not be in. No music. He always had music playing. Not a sound emanated from behind his door, though the light was on. She was familiar with his teaching schedule, so she knew he wasn't in the classroom. Probably in a conference with one of the coaches or working with an athlete to improve performance.

She should simply walk away, but something compelled her to turn the knob. It wasn't locked. She opened the door.

There he was at his desk, his head resting on the usual messy pile of papers. Alarm froze her in her tracks. What was wrong? A half-eaten sandwich was beside the desk lamp. Had he gotten food poisoning? Was he having an allergic reaction to something he ate?

Then she heard it. A soft wheezing. He was snoring. Gideon First was sound asleep.

She put her hand to her mouth to stifle a laugh. Poor guy. She remembered what it was like when her two children were infants. She'd had Miguel to help her then, to give her a little respite in the evenings and on weekends, and still she'd been exhausted most of the time. Only the joy of being a mother had kept her going. Gideon had no one. He was a single parent. It couldn't be easy.

She started to back toward the door. He roused and slanted a bleary eye at her. It took several seconds before the situation registered. Then he jumped.

"Oh, Lupe, I…" He rubbed the bridge of his nose.

"Rough night, I gather."

His smile was twisted in irony. "You might say that. I'm glad you stopped by. I've missed you."

"Actually, I just wanted to remind you that you promised to come to Miguelito's soccer game this evening and help out with coaching."

He blinked slowly. "Tonight? Oh…but I—"

"Miguelito's been telling all his friends you'd be there. According to him, you're the best coach in the whole wide world."

She wondered about the vicious streak that had her twisting the knife. He'd opted out of her son's life. No, that wasn't completely fair. She'd pushed him out of her children's lives.

Gideon ran his hand down his face. "Tonight."

He was obviously exhausted. It would have been charitable to let him off the hook. But Miguelito was counting on him.

"At seven o'clock," she confirmed.

"I'll have to get a baby-sitter," he mumbled, to himself as much as to her. "I don't know who. Maybe Mrs. Johnson can suggest someone."

Lupe regarded him with sympathy. "If you can't find anybody, why not bring Janna along? I'd love to see her, and I'll be happy to watch her while you're coaching."

"Would you?" His face lit up. "That'd be great."

ONE OF THE subconscious images floating around in Gideon's head ever since he found out he was a father was of his arriving home in the evening and having his little girl run into his arms and give him a big kiss. That picture was now a conscious wish that made the fatigue vanish. It also put a bounce in his step as he walked up the narrow path to the front door of his town house. In a quiet little corner of his brain, he acknowledged that the prospect of seeing Lupe tonight added to his stimulation.

He inserted the key in the lock, opened the door and was about to call out "I'm ho-o-me," but the TV was blaring an afternoon game show. Mrs. Johnson was ensconced in a corner of the couch, her knitting needles clicking in her fingers. Janna was sitting on the carpet a few yards away, playing in a field of bright plastic blocks. Her cupid's bow mouth forming an *O*, she was absorbed in her tiny world. She glanced up, saw him and returned to her playthings.

He was devastated. Suppressing the disappoint-ment, he went over and picked her up. "Hi, sweetheart.'' He planted a kiss on her soft cheek. ''Did you have a good day?''

''*Mira,* Daddy,'' she said, pointing to the floor. ''*Tengo un* jack-n-box.''

Gideon couldn't help but laugh. In less than a week, his daughter was speaking Tex-Mex, that colloquial combination of English and Spanish.

''You have a jack-in-the-box, huh?'' He looked to Mrs. Johnson for an explanation.

''It was my grandson's,'' she said. ''He's too old for it now.''

Janna struggled to be put down. With amazing dexterity, she forced the puppet into the box and slammed the lid shut, then twisted the crank. It played ''Pop Goes the Weasel'' and the jack sprang out. Janna laughed and did it again.

Gideon laughed with her. ''Did you thank Mrs. Johnson?'' he asked.

''*Gracias, Señora* Johnson,'' Janna said, pronouncing the last name in English.

''*De nada, chiquita.*'' The woman grinned from ear to ear. ''She's a good baby,'' she said to the proud father. ''And she likes to get into everything.''

Taking consolation in the knowledge that his daughter was bright and curious, he tickled her under the chin.

''Did she have her nap?'' he asked.

''Yes, but it was late. She just woke up a little while ago.''

Which meant she wouldn't be ready for bed until even later. Great, Gideon told himself. He'd been hoping to arrive home and find her ready to go to sleep right after he fed her. In spite of the snooze he'd taken at his desk in the office—he reckoned he'd slept for nearly an hour—he was dragging physically, even if his mind was all keyed up.

"I'm supposed to help coach a soccer team this evening. Do you know anyone who might be available to sit with her for a few hours?" he asked.

She shook her head. "Not on such short notice and on a Friday night." Then she added, "Shouldn't you be spending some time with her yourself?"

He didn't miss the note of censure. He couldn't deny Mrs. Johnson was right. Too many kids got bounced from one sitter to another and never really developed a close attachment with their parents. According to the books he'd read, it was one of the reasons for children to rebel in their teenage years and cultivate all sorts of bad habits. But he wasn't intentionally avoiding a chance to be with his daughter, he reminded himself. He'd made this commitment before he'd even found out he was a father, and it wasn't right to disappoint Miguelito and his team when they were counting on him. He'd certainly be more careful about making promises to other people in the future, but for this evening, he had to keep his word.

"You're right," he conceded, "but I promised a bunch of kids to help them, and I don't like letting them down. I'll just take her with me."

Mrs. Johnson nodded. "She'll be ready to eat in about an hour. Her food is on the kitchen counter. All you have to do is heat it up. By the way, you need to go shopping tonight. I wrote out a list. You're almost out of diapers, too. I noticed she's getting a little bit of a diaper rash, so you better change her often. Medicated powder is on the shopping list, and don't forget to use it every time.''

She gathered her purse and knitting bag, then, raising a brow, strode over to the piece of paper she'd left on the sofa table. ''Almost forgot baby shampoo.'' She wrote it down. ''Be sure you don't use the regular kind, because it'll burn her eyes. She has real nice, expensive clothes, but I noticed some of them are getting a little tight, so you'll have to replace them pretty quick.''

Holding Janna in his arms, he examined her and found a small abrasion an inch or so below her left shoulder.

''What's this?'' he asked sharply. ''She's been hurt.''

Mrs. Johnson compressed her lips for a moment in exasperation. ''Nothing mysterious or sinister, Mr. First. She fell against the corner of one of the boxes you have crammed in the corner.''

Scanning the room as she straightened, Mrs. Johnson added, ''It would be a good idea if you cleared this place out some. There's an awful lot of stuff around for her to get into. Toddlers like to roam, and this clutter is dangerous.''

Gideon tried to absorb it all. It seemed overwhelming. He hadn't slept more than three or four hours a night since he'd brought Janna home. Between the schoolwork he did here because he didn't have the luxury of staying late at the office anymore, doing laundry—how could one little kid go through so many clothes—cleaning up after her, entertaining her,

fixing her meals, changing her diapers, reading her
bedtime stories... How did mothers do it?

He thanked the sitter, saw her out and turned to
objectively assess the living room. It truly was a mess.
Neatness had never been one of his virtues, but apparently now the mess had become a hazard. Silently,
he vowed to correct that.

LUPE WONDERED first if Gideon, given his exhaustion,
would even show up at the soccer game this evening,
and second if he would bring the baby with him.
Janna was a beautiful child, bright and cheerful and,
Lupe realized, very intelligent. Miguelito had been a
little slow to start speaking. Everyone agreed it was
because he was in a bilingual environment. When he
did begin to talk, though, he'd spoken both languages
without difficulty. Teresita had been the same way.
Lupe was curious to see what Janna would do, having
started with English alone.

She put on a pair of jeans and a red T-shirt with
You Can't Fool Mom printed on the front. Only after
she looked at herself in the mirror did she remember
that Gideon had given it to her after Miguelito had
tried to put one over on her. She should probably
change the shirt, but she was in a hurry.

One of the neighbors was picking up Teresita after
school to take her to her gymnastics class and would
bring her home when it was over. Terry, as she preferred to be called these days, was doing very well
and her coach was advising her to enter the competition in Dallas in a few weeks. Lupe had been active
in sports when she was young, too, but her family

hadn't encouraged her, partly because they didn't have the money for private lessons and expensive uniforms or the other accessories athletics involved, and partly because athletics wasn't considered an appropriate pastime for a girl.

Several people greeted her as she made her way to the bleachers on the long side of the dusty field. It would be a few more minutes before things got started. She scanned the crowd for Gideon. He was notoriously late for nearly everything, so she was surprised when she saw him pull into the parking lot behind her car. He got out and opened the back door of the vehicle, reached in, removed a diaper bag, placed it at his feet, then reached in again. A minute later, he stepped back with Janna in his arms. Lupe wasn't sure why the sight made her vision mist over.

He hadn't been able to find a baby-sitter. She watched him bend and grab the bag, stand tall and straight, then move toward the stands. Abandoning her seat and soft-drink cooler, Lupe rushed to meet him.

"Hi, Gideon."

There were bags under his eyes, but his face brightened at the sight of her. "Hi."

She walked closer and placed her hand on Janna's bare arm. "Hello, sweetie. Aren't you the pretty one."

"It's a good thing you reminded me about the game tonight," Gideon confessed, "or I would have forgotten it."

She grinned. "That's why I reminded you."

"It was too late for me to get a sitter."

"That's all right." Lupe put out her arms to the little girl. "Come on, honey. Let's let Daddy do his thing and we'll sit on the side and watch." Janna didn't hesitate to climb into Lupe's arms.

"You're sure you don't mind?" Gideon asked.

Lupe nodded, still smiling. "We're fine." He gazed at her for what seemed like an eternity. "Is that her diaper bag?"

He almost jumped. "Ah, yeah. Um, I'll carry it back to the stands for you."

Lupe shook her head. "That's not necessary. Just give it to me." He handed her the bag. "Now, get out there with the kids. Miguelito's been a pill lately. Maybe this game will work off some of his temper."

"What's he mad about?" His voice trailed off.

She could see and hear in his embarrassment that he knew the answer even before he finished asking the question. Since a reply wasn't necessary, she turned away before he had a chance to comment further and strolled with the baby in one arm and the bag in the other hand to the stands.

A whistle blew, and the teams lined up.

A toddler is a magnet for mothers, and Janna First was no exception.

"Whose baby is that?" Lupe was asked.

"I didn't know he had a kid," another commented with a sly glint in her eye.

"How old is she?"

"Where has she been all this time?"

"Who's the mother?"

And then, in sotto-voce one-on-one conversations, some of them would commiserate.

"It must have been devastating learning he had a kid by another woman."

"No wonder she broke up with him. I don't blame her."

"Well, with looks like his, I guess you can't expect him not to play around."

Lupe bit her tongue at the comments, and her lip when no one was watching. They were right on all counts. It was devastating. She was correct to call off their engagement. And as she gazed across the field at the tall, blond athlete running up and down the sidelines, gesticulating encouragement to the small boys, she saw one of the most attractive men she'd ever met. How could any woman resist, and how naive of her to think he would?

Janna was growing restless, so Lupe got up and started strolling with her alongside the grandstand. His little girl. She could see him in her features, in the subtle dimple in her chin, the curve of her mouth, the pure blue of her eyes. Gideon's baby. His daughter.

After a long walk, Janna raised her arms to be picked up. Lupe hugged her tightly and pressed her cheek against the child's as she moved slowly to the bleachers.

"Are you hungry, baby?" she asked when they reached her place on the end of the bottom row of benches. Gideon better have remembered to bring something for Janna to eat. As she opened the carry-all, she heard two women snickering behind her.

"I noticed she's not wearing that big diamond ring he gave her."

The other tittered. "Wanna bet it isn't at the jeweler's being sized?"

"Well, I guess he's come to his senses, or his family gave him an ultimatum. Asking one of them to baby-sit is one thing, but marrying her is another."

Lupe's fingers trembled as she opened a plastic bag containing orange wedges. Burning humiliation made her want to hunch her shoulders. Inviting Gideon here had been foolish. Being with him was an even bigger mistake. Fighting back tears, she offered the baby a piece of fruit.

THE GAME was a close match. Miguelito's team was playing good defense, but their offense, which he usually commanded, was the pits. He'd missed several goals that should have been shoo-ins, and he lost the ball three times on aggression. Only one other kid on his team, Jarvis Hume, came close to him in speed and dexterity, and he was getting increasingly vocal and insulting in calling Miguelito on his screwups.

By halftime, the score was tied two-all. Standing on the sideline and periodically conferring with the team's coach, although officially he was a spectator, Gideon cheered till his voice was raw. When the whistle blew and the boys were coming in off the field, he jogged forward to meet them.

"Hey, Mikey, what's the problem out there?" He dropped an arm across the boy's shoulders. Miguelito shrugged, dejected.

"This isn't like you," he insisted. "What's the scoop?"

Jarvis was passing. "He's turned chicken," he said

savagely, then sneered at his teammate. "Afraid the ball might hurt you? Maybe you should try out for the girls' team, Mikey." He drew out his name in a girlish taunt. "You sure don't know how to play with the boys."

Miguelito whipped out from under Gideon's hold. "Stuff it, pea brain."

"Who you calling pea brain, turkey?" Jarvis was a good two inches taller than Miguelito and twenty pounds heavier.

"Maybe no brain would be better," Miguelito hurled back.

"Gobble, gobble, gobble."

In a fraction of a second, Miguelito bunched his right hand into a tight fist and planted it squarely on Jarvis's mouth. The bigger boy staggered, from both the impact of the punch and the shock of it. The crowd went instantly silent and was staring, appalled.

Miguelito, equally shocked by his own action, had already retreated a step, but seeing the fight stance his adversary had assumed, braced himself for a counterpunch. Bleeding from a cut lip, Jarvis spat out a curse and was about to charge full body into his opponent when Coach Dayton grabbed him around the waist from behind and lifted him off the ground. Gideon simultaneously put a vise grip on Miguelito's torso, pinning his arms to his sides.

"Chill out, both of you," Dayton blared. He and Gideon made eye contact from behind the two combatants.

"Go get that cut taken care of," Gideon suggested. "And I'll deal with this one."

Dayton nodded agreement, slowly released his hold on Jarvis and escorted him to the bench.

Jarvis's mother, a hefty woman in a shapeless green-and-orange dress, stormed out of the stands and cradled her son's face between pudgy hands. The kid wasn't pleased with his mother's fussing and made sounds to indicate it. She spun and charged toward Miguelito, and for a minute, Gideon was afraid she might accost him. Instead, she planted herself squarely in front of him, hands on her hips.

"You're all alike, aren't you? Hitting people is all your kind knows."

Lupe, carrying Janna, had moved closer to her son but hadn't yet had a chance to say anything. Gideon caught the expression, the kind of humiliation he'd seen on her face when Mrs. Runyon had assumed she was a servant.

"You're nothing but a little thug," the woman ranted. "Now everybody can see your true color." Still steaming, she wheeled and returned to embarrassing her own son.

"Miguelito," Lupe started to reprimand him, then stopped. She stared at him, too hurt to go on.

Her son hung his head, lower lip quivering.

Gideon touched Lupe's arm. "Will you let me talk to him?" he asked softly in her ear.

She paused for a moment, unsure. Their eyes met, and a message of concern and devotion passed between them. She nodded.

Miguelito tried to move away.

"Hold it right there," Gideon called in a voice that

wasn't loud but was firm enough to brook no argument.

The boy halted, his head still downcast.

"Stand up straight, turn around and look at me," Gideon commanded.

Miguelito's posture didn't significantly improve, but he did turn and raise his head enough to face Gideon under tightly knit black brows. Tears of anger and humiliation were close, but he managed to hold them in check.

"The first thing you do," Gideon informed him in no uncertain terms, "is run five laps around the field. Don't jog. Run. I'll be watching and counting. While you're at it, think hard about what you just did and why—and the consequences. Then we'll talk." Seeing hesitation, he ordered in a controlled bellow, "Go. Now."

The boy trotted off.

"I said run, Mikey. Move your sorry butt."

The boy took a few more steps, then shot into a full sprint.

Lupe walked beside Gideon, his baby in her arms. "It's my fault," she said. "He's so angry at me. I've tried to explain, but he won't listen."

Gideon scowled.

Janna was squirming. Lupe concentrated on rubbing her back, in an attempt to contain her boundless energy. "Ever since I told him we weren't getting married, he's been sulky and surly and neglecting his chores. He flew into a rage at his grandmother the other day, and I had to send him to his room. I wasn't sure he would stay there. He's got me worried, Gideon.''

He knew that when parents broke up, kids often felt abandoned and blamed themselves for the adults' failures. He and Lupe weren't married, and Gideon wasn't Miguelito's father. But he would have to be totally blind not to see the boy hero-worshiped him.

"He's a good kid," Gideon assured her.

The ripples from a pebble dropped in a pond apparently had no limits, he ruminated. His lie, his deceit, his terrible lapse in judgment were hurting the very people he wanted to protect. He'd betrayed the fatherless boy who looked up to him. If only time could be reversed. If only he could remove the sadness he saw on the face of the woman he loved.

"Do you trust me enough to handle this?" he asked.

He didn't miss the doubt that shadowed her features. The questions lurking in the depths of her eyes burned like acid, eating away at his confidence. With her support, he felt he could do anything. Without it, he felt helpless, aimless, useless.

"I trust you," she said after a moment's hesitation that lasted too long.

She didn't trust him, but she wanted to. Maybe that could be the start of a new relationship. Or was it merely the echo of one that was ended? She wasn't sure of him, but she was willing to give him this second chance. *Don't blow it,* he told himself. *This time, give her reason to respect you.*

"He'll be all right." Gideon wanted to make it a promise, but it would have been a promise he didn't have the power to keep. He'd made promises in the past. No matter what words he used now, he couldn't be sure they would help her son. The damage was done, and he'd done it. He could only pray the trust she was giving him wasn't misplaced—again.

"I hope so."

The phrase could have been an indictment of him, or it could have been a vote of confidence. She was blaming herself for her son's problems. Blaming herself for poor judgment in putting so much faith in the man she loved.

"Daddy play ball," Janna said, and reached out to him.

"Hey, sweet pea." He took her into his arms and kissed her soft cheek. "Are you having a good time watching the soccer game?"

"Me play ball."

He grinned at her. "When we get home, sweetheart, we'll play with your ball. Can you say soccer ball?"

"Sock ball."

He laughed. "That's close enough for now." He put her on the ground. "You go with Lupe and watch, and I'll be with you later, okay?"

Janna nodded solemnly. Lupe took her by the hand and started leading her to the stands. Janna turned, looked at him and stretched out her free hand. The pressure around Gideon's heart contracted painfully.

He smiled through the ache. "Bye-bye, sweetheart," he said, and waved. "See you later."

How in God's name could Becky have resisted that smile, that tug? All week long, through sleepless exhaustion and constant activity, his mind had bounced between contemplation of the woman who'd borne his child and the woman he wanted to bear his future children. For a while, he'd hated Becky for her selfishness, for keeping knowledge of Janna from him, for being such an indifferent mother. Eventually, though, he realized it wasn't hate he felt, but pity. Pity that she'd never experienced the joy of being a parent, of being responsible for the life of another human being.

He saw, too, a terrible irony. Becky would have understood his lie, his equivocation, his dissembling about the paternity test. After all, hadn't she lied to him? Maybe they'd had more in common than he realized.

The whistle blew, ending the break. Miguelito came running back and skidded to a breathless stop in front of Gideon. "Where's Mom?"

"Watching the game with Janna."

"I want to go home," he announced between heavy pants. "Now."

The pugnacious demand hardened Gideon's tone. "You're staying here."

"Why?" the boy objected. "I ain't playing soccer ever again."

"Come with me." Gideon led him across the unpaved parking lot to his Explorer. He put down the tailgate and sat on it, inviting the young athlete to hop up beside him.

"Okay, Mikey, what's really going on?" he asked in a less challenging tone. "What was that all about back there?"

"Jarvis called me a turkey."

Gideon snorted. "Seems to me you started the name-calling when you called him a pea brain. Punching him was wrong. Do you know why?"

"Mrs. Glades, the principal, says we're never supposed to hit anyone. Fighting is always wrong."

"That's partly right. You're not supposed to start fights," Gideon corrected him. "If someone hits you first, you better hit him back—hard enough so he'll think twice about taking another swing at you. That's called self-defense. If you don't defend yourself, you're a victim. But when you throw the first punch, Mikey, you're a bully. Do you understand the difference?"

"He started it by calling me a turkey," the boy protested.

Gideon asked, "Did you ever hear the rhyme 'Sticks and stones will break my bones, but names will never hurt me'?"

He received a begrudging nod.

"You don't have a choice about sticks and stones hurting you. You do have a choice about whether you let words hurt. You can call names back, but that just makes you as much of a jerk as the guy who called you names. It's much better not to respond to name-calling at all."

The boy hung his head like a whipped puppy, not convinced.

"What are you going to do now?"

In the smallest whisper, he said, "Say I'm sorry to Jarvis, the team and the coach."

"You left someone out."

Miguelito's brow furled.

"How about your mother? What you did reflected on her and embarrassed her."

Miguelito bunched his mouth, his eyes glistening. Saying you were sorry to the people you love was never easy. "Then can we go home?" he pleaded. "I don't want to play soccer, anyway."

"In that case, there's no point in apologizing to the team, because you don't really mean it," Gideon said coldly.

The boy raised his head and gaped at him, completely thrown off by the declaration.

"You joined a team, Mikey. They need you. If you quit now, you're letting them down. All the apologies in the world won't help them win."

Miguelito twisted his hands together. Gideon could feel the urge to bolt welling up in the kid.

"Nobody'll want to play with me anymore."

"Then you'll have to earn their trust. You won't do that by hitting other people or by quitting. Quitters are losers, Mikey, and you're not a loser—not unless you let yourself be."

A stiffening of his back was Miguelito's sole response. He'd play. And if Gideon was any judge of pride, he'd play harder than ever.

He dropped off the tailgate, waited for Miguelito to jump down, then closed the back of the SUV.

"Why'd you and Mom split up?" he asked as they walked to the playing field. "Why aren't you and Mom getting married, like you said you would?"

It was Gideon's turn to fess up. "That's my fault,

Mikey, not your mother's. I told her I loved her, but I wasn't completely honest with her.''

"You mean you don't love her?"

Oops. He'd have to be more careful about how he said things. "I love your mother very much, Mikey. But I told her a lie and now she doesn't trust me."

"About Janna?"

The simple answer was yes, but if he said that, the boy might resent the baby and blame her for the breakup.

"No," he said. "This happened before she found out about Janna."

Miguelito wrinkled his forehead, not understanding what Gideon was talking about.

"Not because of her, son, but because of what I did. I screwed up."

"Can't you just say you're sorry? She'll forgive you."

"I have, son, but saying the words isn't enough. Sometimes it's necessary to prove you mean them. Apologizing is only the first step. Like telling Jarvis and the team you're sorry. You still have to prove to them they can trust you and depend on you."

"So why don't you prove to Mom that she can trust you?"

"I would, son, if I knew how."

CHAPTER NINE

MIGUELITO did his duty. He begged the forgiveness of Jarvis and the team. The coach had every right to bench him for the rest of the game. Perhaps it was Mikey's sincerity that kept him from doing so. More likely, though, it was the score that persuaded him to put his star player back in. They were losing eight to three.

"Show them what you're made of," Gideon whispered in his ear just before the boy ran onto the field. "Give it all you've got."

Gideon was proud of the performance Miguelito turned in, undoubtedly his best to date. The opposition gained one more point; Mikey scored four—still not enough to win the game, but a respectable loss.

"You handled the ball real good out there," Dayton told him when the team came off the field. "If you'd played that way the first half, we would have won."

The boy's face transformed from a pleased-with-himself smile to a dark pout of humiliation. Gideon felt sorry for the kid, but he agreed that the put-down was deserved. He also knew the experienced coach and grandfather would capitalize on Mikey's strengths and his need to excel at the next practice.

Lupe waited at the foot of the stands after everyone had abandoned them for the parking lot. Janna was fidgety, insisted on being held but squirming when she was.

"I'm sorry, Mom," her son said, when he joined her. He followed Gideon's advice and succeeded in keeping his head up as he offered his apology. "Face her like a man," Gideon had counseled the boy.

"I'm sorry, too, Miguelito," she responded in Spanish. "You disgraced yourself and you disgraced me today."

The boy stiffened, not happy at being reminded of his offense. "I said I'm sorry."

"There's no excuse for what you did. You're grounded for the next two weeks. No soccer. No sports—"

Miguelito's eyes went wide with shock. He cast a seething look at Gideon. This wasn't supposed to happen. He pleaded with his mother, "But, Mom, there's a softball game next Friday."

"Not for you there isn't."

"But the team needs me," he shouted.

"That's it, Miguelito. Not another word. Now, go to the car and wait for me there."

Gideon watched the boy stomp off, tight jawed and on the verge of tears, then turned his attention to Lupe. She appeared even more miserable than her son.

"You're making a mistake," he said quietly.

She'd been toying with Janna's hands, but her head shot up. She hadn't expected him to challenge her authority.

"I understand that you're upset by what Mrs. Hume said. I am, too. But don't take it out on Mikey."

Perhaps because she had Janna in her arms, she didn't raise her voice. "Thanks for trying to help, Gideon, but this is for me to handle."

"He's a good kid, Lupe," Gideon persisted. "He's also still a boy who's made a mistake. One he's learned from. Don't blow this incident out of proportion."

"Gideon, please stay out of this."

"I'm sorry, sweetheart, but I can't. One of the things I explained to Mikey was that by acting irresponsibly he was letting his soccer team down. Now you're forcing him to do the same thing to his softball team. If enough kids don't show up next Friday, the game will be forfeited, and they'll blame him. Is that what you want?"

"Of course not, but—"

He saw the doubt in her eyes and the dilemma it produced. "But you've made your decision and you're afraid to back off because it'll make you appear weak."

He could tell from her pained expression that he was right. She'd boxed herself into a corner and wasn't sure how to get out of it without losing face.

"It took a lot of courage for Mikey to stand in front of Jarvis, the team and the coach and say he'd screwed up and was sorry. I am fully aware that mothers know everything," he said with a grin and a wink, "but occasionally they do make mistakes. Not very often, mind you. Just once in a while." He held out

his hands to Janna and was flooded with pleasure
when she leaned eagerly toward him.

"And this is one of them," Lupe posited.

"Mikey won't love you less for changing your
mind, Lupe. He'll love you more."

He could see by the contrite expression on her face
that she'd relent. They started walking toward the
parking lot.

"You feel I'm too controlling, don't you?" she
observed.

"I think you're trying to do the job of both parents.
That's no mean trick." *I'd be perfectly willing to relieve you of half the burden,* he had the urge to tell
her, but decided this wasn't an auspicious moment.

They arrived at the point where they had to separate to go to their individual vehicles.

"Thanks for taking care of Janna," he said. She
was restless in his arms, and he wondered if it was
because his little girl missed the soft warmth of
Lupe's caress. He certainly did.

"She's tired," she said, noting the child's squirming in his arms. "Probably overtired. It's been a busy
day for her." She held out the carryall she'd been
toting. "Don't forget your bag."

"Thanks," he repeated, and watched her retreat toward her car and her son.

IT WAS DARK and long after Janna's bedtime when
Gideon arrived home. He'd stopped at the supermar-
ket for the things Mrs. Johnson had put on the list,
and he picked up a few things for himself, as well,

mostly frozen dinners that he could pop in the microwave.

Janna had grown increasingly cranky. He changed her diaper, but that didn't help. He fixed her something to eat, but she didn't want it. He gave her a bath, which he'd learned usually had a soothing effect, but she continued to bawl.

He was at his wit's end after two hours of her increasing crying. Holding her in his arms, he went to the phone and started to dial Lupe's number. She'd said to call if he needed anything. But that had been last weekend after they'd picked Janna up at the Runyons'. She hadn't renewed the invitation tonight at the soccer game. Besides, it was after eleven o'clock. Janna had been fine when they'd left the ball field. Lupe would dub him a complete incompetent if he called her at this hour simply because the baby was crying. She might even consider it a ruse to lure her over here. Not that he was above using that kind of trick to get her back, but this wasn't a game. He was genuinely concerned something was seriously wrong. Janna got irritable when she was tired, but this was beyond irritability. He dialed his sister-in-law.

Clare was sleepy voiced when she answered the phone but became immediately alert when he explained his concern. She asked several questions. He'd done all those things, he assured her—fed Janna, changed her diaper, bathed her.

"Is she running a fever?"

He placed the palm of his hand on his daughter's forehead the way he'd seen mothers do. Her skin was warm, but he realized he had no way of determining whether what he was feeling was normal or hot. All he knew was that she was screaming.

"I can't tell," he replied in exasperation.

Patiently, Clare mentioned she'd left a thermometer in his medicine cabinet. Still carrying the crying child, he retrieved it. "How can I put it under her tongue when she's crying so hard?"

There was a quick snort of aggravation, or maybe amusement. "Gideon, it's a rectal thermometer."

"A rec…oh." He paused. "I've never used one of these. I mean, isn't it dangerous—"

"They've been in use for quite a while now." Definitely annoyance now. "Insert it about an inch and hold her butt so she can't dislodge it. Keep it there for at least a minute. Two would be better. Do you know how to read it?"

It was his turn to be irritated. "Of course I can read a thermometer."

He laid Janna in her crib, opened her diaper and, holding his breath, gently inserted the instrument.

"I'll hang on," Clare encouraged him. "What did you and she do today?"

While his daughter continued to cry, he held her tiny cheeks and did his best to keep her still. "We went to a soccer game," he said absentmindedly. "Lupe was there. She held Janna while I helped Mikey. Janna was no trouble for Lupe at all. I had to do some grocery shopping after that. She cried a lot, but I figured she was overtired, even though she didn't get to have her nap until late today."

"It's been long enough," Clare stated.

Gideon removed the thermometer and held it up to read it. "My God. It says one-oh-two."

"Okay."

"Okay?" he repeated in outrage. "She's burning up, Clare. I better call nine-one-one."

"Gideon," she snapped. "Calm down. Babies often run higher fevers than adults."

He was scared. No denying it. His baby was sick and he didn't know how to help her. "What should I do?"

Unruffled, Clare said, "Take her to the emergency room. It could be tonsils or an earache, or she could be teething."

"Maybe I should call an ambulance."

"Gideon, you don't need an ambulance. You don't need paramedics. All you have to do is get in your car and drive to the hospital. Welcome to parenthood, Daddy."

"Will they let me stay in the room with her? I'll call the dean tomorrow and tell him I can't come in next week."

"Gideon," Clare said patiently, "you need to stay calm. This probably isn't serious. Babies get sick. It's hard to watch, but you won't do her any good by overreacting. Take her to the emergency room. They'll want you to stay with her while they examine her. Depending on what the problem is, they may give her a shot and you'll both be on your way."

"But shouldn't they keep her for observation or something?"

"They'll decide that," she said sympathetically.

"Call me when you get back, and let me know how things go."

"But—"

"No matter the hour. Promise?"

"So you are worried?" he persisted.

"Instead of jabbering with me on the phone, why don't you get in your car and take your daughter to the emergency room?"

His hands were shaking while he re-dressed the baby. She continued to cry, even though he held her tight and tried desperately to reassure her everything was going to be all right.

She screamed when he buckled her into her car seat. He felt as if he were abandoning her when he closed the back door and climbed behind the wheel. He should be holding her, making sure she knew he loved her. But he couldn't drive and hold her at the same time. Maybe he should have asked his neighbor to drive him to the hospital. Or called a taxi.

Coyote General was less than half a mile away, but as he maneuvered there through side streets, it seemed like a trek across a continent.

The receptionist seemed unmoved by his plight, even though Janna was wailing at the top of her lungs. "If you'll have a seat over there, someone will be with you in a minute."

He was inclined to argue, to shout, to demand immediate attention. Couldn't this woman see his daughter was in agony? A single sympathetic glance from the lady behind the desk, however, stopped him. On reconsideration, Janna's bellowing was statement enough. Less than two minutes later, a nurse appeared and invited him behind the wide swinging doors to the treatment area.

"Poor thing," the middle-aged woman crooned.

She asked the predictable questions. Gideon answered as best he could, kicking himself for not quizzing Vanessa more closely about the baby's medical history. Guilt riddled him whenever he had to answer with "I don't know" or "I don't think so." Needing to justify himself, he explained he'd only recently received permanent custody of his daughter. The nurse nodded understanding but made no further comment. She checked the baby's heart and blood pressure, then put a digital thermometer under her arm and held it there for mere seconds.

"One-oh-two-point-three," she confirmed.

"It's getting higher," Gideon blurted.

The woman gave what he supposed was intended as a comforting smile. "The doctor will be here in a minute."

Janna was still crying, but it was more the whimper of exhaustion. Her face was red. Great tears were running down her blotched cheeks. Gideon had never felt more helpless in his life. He held her, stroked her back, trying to soothe her, but nothing worked. She continued to cry.

ROSALITA SOTO stopped by Lupe's house on Monday evening. "Your former fiancé was in the emergency room Friday night."

Lupe's heart jumped. "Gideon? Why? What happened? What's wrong?" She put her hand over her mouth. "Janna. Something happened to Janna."

She'd been fidgety toward the end of the game. Had she been coming down with something? If she was and Lupe hadn't recognized it, he'd be right to blame her. After all, she'd raised two babies.

Elena, who was sitting at the kitchen table beside her, reached out and covered Lupe's hand. "Was it the little girl?" she asked Rosalita.

"*Sí*. She is such an adorable tyke. But she had an earache."

Lupe remembered the ear problems Miguelito had had when he was small. Nothing was harder than seeing her child in pain and not being able to make it stop, at least not right away. The constant crying was heartrending and nerve-racking.

"Serious?" Lupe pressed her.

"Difficult, but he got good treatment and took the sweet darling home. Poor man. He looked exhausted." Rosalita sighed. "He's finding out it's not so easy being a single parent, especially without a mother's instinct. He asked a million questions, worrying about everything."

Lupe remembered finding Gideon asleep at his desk at school. She'd been tempted to stop by his house over the weekend to thank him for coming to the game Friday night and dealing with Miguelito. Whatever he'd said to the nine-year-old, it had worked. Her son was still angry, but his manners had improved, and he didn't argue with her when she told him to do something around the house. She'd considered Gideon's advice and commuted his grounding to three days. She didn't want to convey the wrong message. Saying he was sorry didn't exempt him from the consequences completely.

Janna had been cranky when Lupe had finally turned her over to Gideon at the ball field. She figured it was because the child was tired. She hadn't bothered to check to see if she had a fever. She should have.

"Will Janna be all right?" she asked.

"She'll be fine. Dr. Taylor give him antibiotics for her. But you know how ear infections are. They take time."

Anywhere from one to three days, in her experience. Days that were very difficult. Lupe wondered if he was getting any respite. When her babies had been sick she'd never been able to sleep soundly, even when Miguel was home. Maybe Gideon wasn't a very competent parent yet, but she was certain from the look she'd seen in his eyes when he talked about Janna or held her in his arms that he was a very loving and caring dad.

"Didn't he tell you about this?" Elena asked.

"I haven't seen him."

She'd spent all her free time today in the library. Normally she would have made at least one pass by his office to see him or to leave a note to tell him she'd stopped by. That had been before they broke up, of course. Since then, she'd only gone by his office once—and found him sound asleep.

"Oh," Elena remarked.

Lupe had no problem reading the subtext in her mother-in-law's commentary. She wasn't happy with her.

TUESDAY MORNING, Gideon finished a session with a runner on the varsity track team who was having trouble regaining his speed after recovering from a pulled hamstring. He'd spent the better part of an hour with the nineteen-year-old, watching him run, evaluating his technique, putting him through a series of exercises and coaching him on his style. The sophomore's problem wasn't unique. He was afraid of harming himself again and was holding back. Ironically, it only made him more vulnerable to further injury.

Sort of paralleled Lupe's relationship with Gideon. She was holding back out of fear of being hurt again, too. He couldn't blame her. Giving him her heart had brought her pain. She wasn't likely to do it again. But the comparison ended there. Or did it?

Gideon recommended some exercises for the young athlete to rebuild the strength he'd lost in the hamstring while it was recovering and to restore the guy's confidence in his body's ability to perform at max output. Mental attitude was vitally important to success in competitive sports. Mind-set often made the crucial difference between a winner and an also-ran.

Too bad he couldn't do the same for Lupe.

He returned to his office and called home to find out how Janna was doing. Mrs. Johnson assured him she was fine, that she'd eaten well, had her nap and was playing contentedly with her favorite blocks. He considered it more suitable for a girl to play with dolls, but the books he'd read assured him that at the toddler stage boys and girls were the same as far the need for physical and mental stimulation, agility training and play. When the moment arrived, though, he looked forward to presenting her with her first doll.

"The living room is much better now," Mrs. Johnson added.

He'd been too worried to go to sleep the past couple of nights, so he'd used the time to clear out the place.

He'd neatly bundled piles of old magazines, catalogs and newspapers, then loaded them into the back of the Explorer. On his way to the office that morning, he'd dropped them off at the recycling center. He'd also filled the Dumpster at the end of the covered parking area with the kinds of accumulated junk that either couldn't or wouldn't be repaired.

"I'll get the rest of it cleaned out within a couple of days." He had several pieces of furniture the Salvation Army had promised to pick up. "Did you give Janna the medicine?" The doctor had been very emphatic about completing the full series of antibiotics even if symptoms were no longer present. He understood that. It was like continuing a particular exercise to strengthen a muscle even after it had recovered from an injury.

"Right on the dot, Mr. First. Don't worry. I'll take good care of her."

"I know you will, Mrs. Johnson. Thank you."

Don't worry, she'd said. He'd never worried more in his entire life. In the past, the biggest of his personal concerns had been tests, swimming competitions and writing his master's thesis. He'd been vexed about the ranch when his sister had sold controlling interest to the Homestead Bank and Trust, and concerned about his father when he'd realized the old man was losing control of the family's extensive holdings. But those troubles had been different. They'd been on the outside, something he could separate himself from. A child wasn't like that. Janna was part of him, and so terribly dependent on his doing the right thing that he sometimes broke into a cold sweat out of fear he'd fail her.

He hung up the phone a minute later and rested back in his chair. He could feel the adrenaline draining from his limbs, from his will. He'd never been so tired in his life. He doubted that he'd had more than six hours' sleep in the past three days.

A tap on the door had his eyes springing open. "Dr. Williams." He rose in place.

The dean waved him back into his seat and took the one on the other side of desk. He was a medium-sized man in his late forties with a small potbelly, which he disguised with well-tailored suits. "How are things going, Gideon? I understand you have your daughter home with you now."

Gideon nodded. He hadn't made any secret of his newfound fatherhood. Word had already spread that Lupe had broken off their engagement because of it.

"It must be exciting having a little one around. I remember when my first kid was born. It was one of the most exhilarating experiences of my life."

"She's a—"

"Handful," the dean finished with a chuckle.

Gideon grinned. "That, too."

Williams crossed his soft hands across his middle. "The timing on this may not be very good, but there's a special conference on physical rehabilitation for challenged children in Austin this coming weekend, and they've requested a kinesiologist attend, specifically you.''

"Me?"

"By name."

"I'm flattered, but why me?"

"Apparently you were recommended by Craig Robeson, who is a major contributor to the rehab center that's sponsoring the conference. I understand he's also your brother-in-law."

Kerry had married the billionaire last fall. They lived in Dallas most of the year and made frequent trips to West Texas to visit the family. At the moment, they were on a safari in Africa.

Gideon nodded. "When did you say this conference is being held?"

"This Saturday and Sunday at the Hyatt Regency."

Lupe should come with me, was Gideon's first reaction. Physical therapy for young children with chronic or congenital disabilities was what she was writing her thesis on. It was also the thesis on, and the area in which, she intended to specialize in their PT center. Gideon wanted to work chiefly with a slightly older group, concentrating on injury recovery and occupational therapy. He planned, as well, to remain as a consultant with the university and work with athletes who sustained sports-related injuries.

He could ask Lupe. Except with finals upcoming, a seminar like this might be an unwelcome distraction if the techniques under discussion challenged the prevailing professional wisdom.

Of course there was Janna to contend with. Lupe would probably insist they take her along, which was fine with him. But then one of them would have to stay with her while the other attended sessions, or he'd have to hire a total stranger to stay with Janna— and he didn't want to do that.

Maybe it would be better if he didn't invite Lupe, after all. It still left the problem of who would stay with Janna while he was away. Perhaps Mrs. Johnson would be available, but he doubted it. She'd made it pretty clear she reserved her weekends for her family.

"I'll have to check on the availability of a baby-sitter," he told the dean.

"Certainly. But you'll have to decide by tomorrow, so I can let them know in time to get someone else if you can't attend."

The easiest thing would have been to say no, but Gideon was interested in getting into rehabilitation work. It was what he and Lupe had dreamed of— having their own rehab center.

The dean left a minute later, and Gideon picked up the phone. Mrs. Johnson couldn't do it. She recommended another woman, but she wasn't available, either.

He called the Number One. Clare and Michael were taking their kids to Six Flags this weekend.

He called his father and Sheila, but they were flying to Houston on Friday to spend a couple of days with one of Sheila's daughters, her husband and their kids. They'd just returned from an overseas military tour of duty and were on their way to a new stateside assignment.

He called his sister Julie. She laughed and told him no way. She had exams to study for, too.

Maybe Elena would be willing to keep Janna for the two days. That would work perfectly. He could extend an invitation to Lupe, let her decide if she wanted to go.

Then he reconsidered. Asking Elena to baby-sit would only complicate matters. If Lupe decided to go with him, she'd lose valuable study time and maybe her objectivity. If she didn't go, Janna would probably be a serious distraction. He'd seen how much she enjoyed being with his little girl. He exhaled in frustration. Nothing was simple anymore.

He was about to pick up the phone to call the dean and turn down the conference offer, when he saw Karida standing in the doorway.

"Hi," she said softly. "Dr. Williams told me you needed someone to look after your little girl this weekend so you could attend a conference in Austin."

As if for the first time, he noticed she was the kind of woman he used to go out with before he met Lupe. Tall and willowy. With blond hair and hazel eyes that were almost golden. She ran every day and had the healthy glow of an athlete. A couple of years back he wouldn't have hesitated about asking her out. Even now, he couldn't help but admire her feminine allure, but he felt no compulsion to get caught up in it.

"Yeah," he admitted, "but I'm not having much luck."

Karida smiled. She really was a very beautiful woman, and unless he'd forgotten how to read signals, she wouldn't be averse to their spending time together.

"I can take her," she said.

Gideon's head shot up. "You?"

She laughed. "I do have some experience caring for people," she reminded him.

"I know you do," he said, remembering how devoted she'd been to her terminally ill mother. "It's just that…well, I didn't imagine you'd want to tie yourself down on a weekend with someone else's kid."

She fixed him with a serious expression. "I don't have any problem with your child, Gideon. If I can help, I'll be glad to."

"You're sure?" Maybe this was the solution to his problem.

"I'm sure," Karida said.

He got up from behind his desk, crossed to her and gave her a peck on the cheek. "You're a lifesaver. You really are." He leaned against the desk. "She won't be any problem. She had an earache over the weekend, but that's all cleared up now, and giving her the rest of her antibiotics will guarantee it stays that way. Come over to the house tonight and I'll introduce you to her, and you can make sure you want to do this. If you still do, I'll let the dean know tomorrow that I can go to the conference."

"Glad to help. I'll see you this evening. What time?"

"If you get there around five, you can help me feed her, and we can have dinner together."

"Five o'clock? Okay. I'll be there."

CHAPTER TEN

BECAUSE the conference started at eight o'clock on Saturday morning, he'd driven to Austin on Friday night after helping Karida feed Janna and put her to bed. The weather had been clear, the road open, so the three-hour drive to the capital city had been uneventful. His biggest concern had been staying awake, which he ensured by drinking plenty of coffee. The painfully long stretches between rest stops also prevented him from dosing off.

He arrived at the Hyatt Regency after ten, registered at the front desk and called Coyote Springs from his room to check on Janna. Karida assured him his daughter was tucked peacefully in for the night.

"Has she been any trouble?"

"Not a peep from her," Karida told him. She would be sleeping in his bed, of course, since the second bedroom was now the nursery. It had been a long time since he'd had a woman in his bed. The one he wanted there was Lupe, but it seemed that was not to be.

He unpacked his hanging bag, left a request for a wake-up call with the front desk and crawled into the sack. The next thing he knew, the telephone's harsh jangle was wrenching him from a deep sleep. Groggily, he reached over to answer it—and sat bolt up-right. The only one who knew his specific location was Karida. She wouldn't be calling so soon unless something was wrong. Something must have happened to Janna. He shouldn't have left her.

"Good morning," a mechanical voice said. "This is your wake-up call. Have a nice day."

There must be a mistake. He'd just gone to bed. He reached over and turned the digital clock to face him. Seven a.m. He twisted to look at the drapes pulled across the window. Sunlight was peeking through the crack. He'd slept eight hours straight. If the condition of the bedclothes was any indication, he hadn't moved a muscle during the entire night.

Resisting the temptation to curl up and go for another eight hours, he bounced out of bed, took a shower, shaved, dressed and went downstairs to the continental breakfast the hotel was providing for conference participants. The coffee was hot and strong. He devoured two cups of it and had a piece of melon and a sweet roll.

Dr. Williams had furnished him with the literature the Metroplex Rehab Center had sent him about the conference, but Gideon had been so busy with other things he'd barely skimmed it. There was a big board set up in the dining room, showing the agenda for the next two days. Most of the subjects were predictable. Occupational rehabilitation for job-related injuries. Physical therapy for hip and knee replacement. He'd have to check that one out to see if there were any new developments that might help Nick.

There were also several topics that would especially have interested Lupe.

Closed head injuries in preschool-age children. He
didn't dwell on the fact that some of them would be
the result of accidents, others the result of abuse.

Prosthetic therapy for amputees. The science of
prosthetics had made incredible advances in the past
twenty years.

Early electroneurological intervention for spinal
cord injuries. This was one of the most promising
fields in medical and therapeutic science. Microcom-
puterization held out tremendous hope for electroni-
cally bypassing spinal cord damage and restoring
function to paralyzed limbs. The bionic man. Gideon
had no doubt that someday the most common forms
of paralysis would be alleviated, if not completely
cured.

He regretted not bringing Lupe now—for several
reasons. He'd have to be sure to pick up whatever
literature they distributed and take it to her.

The attendees all identified themselves at the beginning of the first session. He recognized several of
them and exchanged nods, but most of the people
were strangers. He was surprised, therefore, when a
woman came up to him as they were getting ready to
break for the noon meal and introduced herself.

"Mr. First, I'm Marla Hastings." She extended her
hand. "I believe you're acquainted with my boss,"
she commented as they shook. "Craig Robeson."

He smiled. "He's my brother-in-law."

She was around thirty, with high cheekbones, wide-
spaced dark sloe eyes, mahogany-brown hair, a pert

nose and a sensuous mouth. Gideon wondered if all his brother-in-law's female employees resembled *Playboy* centerfolds with their clothes on. Recalling the adoration on Craig's face when he and Kerry toasted each other with nonalcoholic champagne at their wedding, he suspected it wouldn't make any difference if they did.

"Yes, I know," she said in a voice that sounded more southern than Texan. "He sends regards from Nairobi."

They entered the dining room. The maître d' greeted Marla Hastings by name and led them to a table for two in a quiet corner.

"I didn't find out he was sponsoring this conference until I received the invitation." Gideon accepted a menu from the waiter.

"A friend of his, Hank Dawson, and his wife have adopted several handicapped children," she explained. "As a result, he's become interested in physical therapy and rehabilitation, especially for children."

Gideon shouldn't be surprised. On one of his early visits to the ranch, Craig had asked for a tour of the university campus and the facilities in the department of physical therapy. Gideon had been flattered, but Craig had said nothing about his having a personal interest in the subject.

His sister Kerry had once remarked that Craig liked to play his cards close to the vest. Gideon understood now what she meant.

"He would like to expand the Metroplex Rehabilitation Center he established a few years ago in Dallas and asked me to approach you to see if you might be interested in heading the effort.''

Gideon was stunned. He'd dreamed of opening his own rehabilitation center with Lupe and Nick. Taking over a fully established center was a completely different matter. On the one hand, it meant bypassing the difficult period of uncertainty and growth. On the other, they'd also be giving up the satisfaction of starting from scratch and the heady pleasure of succeeding on his—on their—own.

Was Lupe still willing to work with him? She'd broken their engagement, but she hadn't said anything about pulling out of the business partnership. Or was that understood? The truth was, he hadn't asked because he was afraid of the answer.

And what about Nick? Okay, so his best friend was unhappy with him right now about what he considered Gideon's high-handed approach to building them a rehab center. He still didn't understand what the big deal was, but he respected his friend, and if Nick didn't want Gideon using his money to build them a facility, Gideon would go along with it. In this case, if they took over the Metroplex Center, Gideon wouldn't be the one footing the bill. The place would already exist; Nick couldn't argue with that.

The big question was whether they'd be willing to relocate to Dallas. Both of them were born-and-bred Coyote Springs natives. Leaving their hometown permanently would be a big step for them. Especially for Lupe and her kids. Would Elena come along?

''Are you interested?'' Marla asked.

Living in the Dallas area would also mean Janna

would be close to her grandparents and Aunt Vanessa—assuming the retired stockbroker stayed in the vicinity. Gideon suspected she would, especially if her great-niece was nearby.

"Tell me more," he invited Marla.

She gave him a broad grin. "If you have the time this evening, we can get together and talk in more detail."

Gideon found it difficult to keep his mind on the subjects being discussed that afternoon. After the last session was over, he went to his room to freshen up and call home for the second time that day. He could hear "Old Macdonald" in the background. Must be the tape of the kiddy songs he'd bought a couple of days ago.

"How's my girl?"

"She's beautiful, Gideon."

Without realizing he was doing it, he expanded his chest.

A few minutes later, he met Marla in the bar downstairs. She had a glass of wine. He was inclined to order a beer for himself, but chose instead a soft drink. He was still feeling tired, and the subject of their discussion was too important to let alcohol and fatigue gang up on him.

An hour later, they went into the hotel's main dining room and continued their discussion.

"You'll have a virtually unlimited budget," Marla told him. "Mr. Robeson expects the place to be run efficiently for efficiency's sake, not for profit. If you need new equipment, more facilities, more staff, you'll get it."

"Sounds ideal," he commented.

She smiled. "It is. I'm not sure he would make the same offer to someone else, but he trusts you. You're family. That means a lot to him."

Indeed. Craig had been the only child of an alcoholic father and a weak, battered mother. The remarkable thing was that when he finally decided to get married, it was to Gideon's sister Kerry who was an alcoholic and had been a battered wife. Their courtship had been tempestuous, yet anyone seeing them together now recognized instantly that they were deeply in love. They found strength in each other. It was the way he'd hoped his marriage with Lupe would be. Kerry's weakness was alcohol. What exactly was his?

"I must say, though, that he didn't choose you because of family ties. He's a very particular man when it comes to his investments."

"That's a comfort," Gideon responded lightly. "Tell me about the center you have now. When can I visit it?"

KARIDA WAS about ready to pull her hair out. Ten minutes after Gideon's phone call late Saturday night, Janna had woken up and started crying. At first, Karida thought the cause was a dirty diaper, but that didn't prove to be the case. Maybe she was thirsty. Karida gave her juice, but that didn't satisfy her. She opened a jar of fruit, but the toddler wouldn't eat. In fact, she managed to knock it out of Karida's hand, splattering apricot mush all over the living room carpet.

Gideon had told her about the baby's earache and the sign of her grabbing her ears. But there were no such gestures now. Since a fever was a symptom of infection, she used the high-tech electronic thermometer Gideon had bought to check her temperature. Ninety-eight point six. Janna could have been teething, Karida supposed, but there were no indications of tender gums.

Eventually the kid had quieted down, but when she was put into her crib, she started bellowing all over again. Karida had spent several hours holding the child in her arms. Which was how she'd fallen asleep, only to wake with the worst crick in her neck she'd ever experienced.

Before dawn on Sunday morning, the baby began crying again. Once more, Karida checked her temperature. Normal. Checked her mouth. No evidence of painful teething. Checked her diaper for the hundredth time. The kid didn't even have a rash to complain about. So what was the problem?

Janna did quiet down enough to eat her breakfast, which was when Gideon had called.

"Everything's fine," Karida had assured him.

"I should warn you," he told her. "She likes to play with her cereal."

Karida laughed—it seemed to her own ear a little hysterically. "I'll keep that in mind."

In fact, gooey oatmeal already covered the high chair and most of the table nearby. Fortunately, the drinking cup had a no-spill top; otherwise juice would have been broadcast all over the floor, as well.

"I won't be here at the hotel today. There's something I have to check out in Dallas, so I probably won't be getting back to Coyote Springs until very late this evening. Will that be a problem?''

Karida's heart sank. She was hoping he might say he was coming home early. Still, she'd signed on to mind his baby....

"I'll be here," she said brightly.

"Give Janna a big messy kiss from her dad, will you?"

"You got it." She'd calculated the way to Gideon's heart might be through his daughter. But if he had any interest in Karida at all, he was hiding it very well. She'd hoped spending a little time with him would get his testosterone levels stimulated now that he had split with Lupe, but she hadn't seen any signs of it, and she'd looked.

When Janna seemed more interested in playing with her food than eating it, Karida put her on the floor while she cleaned up the mess. A minute later there was a thump and a pop, followed by Janna's terrified scream. Karida bolted into the living room.

The child was sitting on the floor by the end table, the heavy brass lamp beside her. Karida could see the tiny shards of glass from the broken light bulb on the carpet inches away.

Her hands shaking, Karida picked up the baby and examined her. No cuts or marks. She let out a suppressed breath, shut her eyes and said a silent prayer of thanksgiving. Apparently, the baby had just scared herself. Karida hugged the little girl and made ineffective cooing sounds.

An hour later, though Karida could find no reason

for it, Janna was still crying. Nothing distracted her. Not food. Not music. Not holding her. It was all too much, too overwhelming. Karida was afraid to leave her alone, yet the place was becoming a shambles. Caring for her mother had been difficult enough, but her mother had been a grown woman, able to communicate her needs and explain any discomfort. Karida had no idea what was wrong with the baby, and the crying was becoming a real problem—for Karida. Her patience was wearing thin. Gideon wouldn't be home for another ten or twelve hours. She wasn't sure she could last that long.

"I'm ashamed to say I'm at my wit's end," she told Clare on the telephone a few minutes later. Gideon had given her his sister-in-law's number in case there was a problem and she couldn't get through to him.

Clare sympathized. "It's hard when you're not used to kids. Hell, it's hard when you are. Tell me what's been happening."

Karida did, even as she held the crying baby in her arms. "I hate to ask you this, but is there any way you can take her? I volunteered for this, but I had no idea—"

"No need to apologize. At least you recognize your limits. I respect that. And so will Gideon." Karida doubted that. Any notion she might have entertained of impressing him had fled before a screaming child.

"Can you hang on a little while longer?" Clare asked.

"Of course. I feel so bad about this."

"Don't. Relief will be on the way in a few minutes."

"Thank you."

Less than fifteen minutes later, the doorbell rang. Still holding the crying baby, Karida went to answer it. "Lupe!" A feeling of shame and of being betrayed shivered through her.

"Clare called me. I live only a few blocks away." Lupe extended her arms to the baby. Janna went to her as if she were being rescued from an ogre and instantly went from crying to sobbing.

"How do you do that?" Karida asked almost angrily, though the quiet was a tremendous relief.

Lupe smiled. "I wish I knew. I had the same problem with my Teresita. She'd cry her head off when I held her and then Miguel would get home, take her into his arms and she'd snuggle against him and go to sleep. It used to really tick me off."

They moved into the living room.

"You all right?" Lupe glanced at the fallen lamp and the other debris on the floor.

"I am now. Well, better, at least. I feel like such a failure."

Lupe stroked the baby's back. "Being an only child, you wouldn't have had any experience with this. Did you ever do any baby-sitting?"

"A few times, but the kids were older. I could talk to them and explain things." She grinned sheepishly. "And yell at them, if I had to."

Lupe stuck a finger tentatively inside the diaper to check it. "It's different with infants and toddlers."

"So I've learned." Without her usual makeup and

with her eyes puffy from lack of sleep, Karida lacked her usual cool glamour.

"Did you get any sleep last night?"

Karida smiled wanly. "A couple of hours."

"Why don't you go on home," Lupe said kindly. "I'll watch her until Gideon gets back."

"You don't mind? It won't be until late."

Lupe shook her head. "We'll be fine. Go on. Get some rest." She petted the child in her arms. "Janna and I are old friends."

They discussed what the baby had eaten and when, and confirmed where things were.

"This place was neat as a pin when he left Friday night, and look at it now."

Only then did Lupe inspect the room. There was the obvious mess, which she'd noticed when she'd first arrived—the overturned lamp, a cookie or cracker crushed into the carpet and a soda can on its side, apparently empty when it was knocked over since there were no wet marks. But the room itself was different. The clutter was gone from the top of the coffee table. There were no boxes stacked in the corners. A stereo that Gideon said needed a little work was missing, along with an extra set of speakers.

Amazing. He'd cleared the place out.

"It resembles L.A. after a quake," Karida complained. "Since Janna seems content with you, let me at least clean up some of this before I go."

Eager to assuage her sense of guilt, Karida set about removing the debris, including running the vacuum repeatedly over the area where the light bulb from the fallen lamp had shattered.

Lupe wandered to the kitchen. It, too, was neater. A miracle she had never expected to see. ''When did Gideon say he'd be home?''

''He didn't give me a specific time. Said only that he was driving to Dallas, so he probably wouldn't be in until late tonight. Do you want me to come back later and relieve you?''

''I'm fine,'' Lupe assured her. ''If I need anything, I can call Elena. Between the two of us we should be able to handle just about any crisis.''

After a moment's pause, Karida said, ''I envy you.''

She went to gather her things from the upstairs bedroom. Ten minutes later she planted a kiss on the thumb-sucking child's cheek, thanked Lupe for being a lifesaver and was gone.

GIDEON AND MARLA had to take separate vehicles to Dallas, since he'd be driving from there back to Coyote Springs. He would have preferred to have company on the three-hour trip, specifically Lupe, or, lacking that, to spend the hours discussing more details about his brother-in-law's offer with Marla, but the drive, even alone, wasn't unpleasant. He played three Beethoven symphonies on the way.

Marla was no slouch behind the wheel and, after a few minutes of testing Gideon's willingness to keep up, stepped on the accelerator. The highway speed limit was seventy. She pushed close to eighty on the open stretches where they had clear visibility. Gideon maintained a safe distance but never lost sight of her. The Metroplex Rehabilitation Center was located on the southwest edge of the sprawling city. The ten-thousand-square-foot facility was not more than five years old, well designed and expensively equipped. Gideon was fascinated by its octagonal floor plan. He'd never envisioned a therapeutic center laid out in this fashion, but he instantly realized that it was economical and efficient. Nick would love it. And so would Lupe. The entire building was light and cheerful, clean and modern, but far from cold.

Marla had called ahead, and even though it was Sunday, senior members of the staff were there to meet them. The current director gave him the grand tour. He was a small man of fifty who had recently been diagnosed with cancer and was unable to maintain the heavy schedule his position demanded. His assistant, a much younger woman, made it very clear she wasn't interested in the chief's job. Her forte was in public relations and awareness, and according to Marla, she was exceptionally good at it. The center's chief accountant reminded Gideon of a slightly younger version of Albert Runyon in appearance. Lanky and in his sixties, he made no secret of the fact that he loved what he was doing and had no intention of retiring until he was forced to. At Marla's behest, he explained the center's funding and went over their latest cash flow and income and expense reports. Many of the details were over Gideon's head, but as far as he could determine, nothing was held back.

The last member of the reception committee was the man who was temporarily filling in as chief therapist, Mailer Shanks. He was afflicted with a clubfoot, and he was the orthotist, the person who designed and fit prosthetic devices. Gideon was no expert on architectural design or accounting procedures, but he did know physical therapy, and he was impressed by Shanks's expertise in an area that wasn't his primary specialty.

Over the next several hours, the group discussed the planned expansion of their services. Gideon's enthusiasm grew exponentially as details were revealed. This was exactly the kind of operation he, Lupe and Nick had dreamed about, one that incorporated a broad spectrum of rehabilitative services, as well as a public education program.

It was past five o'clock when they finished discussing the center's plans and projected timetables. Marla offered to buy him an early dinner before his journey back to Coyote Springs, but he declined. He didn't like to drive on a full stomach, but more than that, he was eager to see his daughter.

Marla gave Gideon one of her cards at the entrance to the center. "Let me know when you'll be bringing your associates to Dallas to see this place. I'll send copies of the plans to you by courier tomorrow. You should receive them Tuesday. If you don't, call me."

Gideon held out his hand. "Thank you, Marla. And thank Craig for me, since you're likely to talk to him before I do."

"Will do. And give that little girl of yours a big kiss for me."

He almost blushed. The evening before, he'd played the typical proud papa, waxing poetic about his beautiful daughter, her instant ability to speak two languages and carry a tune.

He unlocked his Explorer and stepped inside. "I'll call you one way or another," he told Marla just before he put the vehicle in gear.

"Drive safely."

He pulled out of the sweeping driveway. The sun was in his eyes as he headed west. He'd had another full night's sleep and felt elated by this new professional opportunity.

For the moment, though, he was eager to see his little girl. She seemed to have settled in with Karida all right. The house had been quiet when he'd called that morning, and Karida had sounded chipper. Too bad he wasn't interested in her. He pondered. She was a very attractive woman and apparently had a way with kids. A winning combination.

But she wasn't Lupe.

He spent the nearly five-hour trip to Coyote Springs sorting through the details he'd learned in Dallas. Lupe would love the facility, and Nick would be pleased with its organization. Gideon liked Craig's approach to expansion. He didn't intend to add on to the existing facility; it was efficient and self-contained. Enlarging it wouldn't improve it; in fact, it would probably make it less responsive to client needs. Craig's plan was to build more of them, not only in the Dallas-Fort Worth area, but in outlying towns, as well.

As he approached the outskirts of Coyote Springs, however, Gideon put considerations of rehabilitation centers aside and visualized his redheaded daughter sitting in the middle of the living room, playing with the dolls he hadn't yet bought her. The woman he pictured sitting on the floor beside her, helping her dress and groom the little mannequins, wasn't Karida Sommers, but Lupe Amorado. The image put a smile on his face and an ache in his heart.

Of course he wouldn't find either of them waiting for him. It was nearly ten o'clock. Janna would be sleeping contentedly, and it wouldn't be Lupe sitting on the couch watching the news or reading a magazine, but Karida.

He pulled into his reserved space under the covered parking area near his town house. After grabbing his single piece of luggage from the back seat and the attaché case full of the brochures he'd collected at the seminar in Austin, he marched to his front door with a bounce in his step.

He put his key into the lock and flung the door wide.

"Karida, I'm home."

He stopped dead in his tracks. "Lupe... what... what are you doing here?"

CHAPTER ELEVEN

"HELLO, GIDEON," she said with apparent calmness, though her blood was close to the boiling point. She continued to spin a top for the baby on the floor.

"Wha-what are you doing here?" he repeated.

"Karida couldn't stay. Clare asked me to come over and fill in."

He closed the door and moved inside the room. "Couldn't stay? I don't understand. Has something happened? Is Karida all right?" He seemed awfully worried about her. Maybe their relationship wasn't so casual, after all.

"Karida's fine." She made it sound as matter-of-fact as possible, but from the expression on his face, he must have detected the bite in her voice. "She was just a little overwhelmed by Janna. She'd never taken care of a baby before. The child's crying all the time was getting on her nerves, so she asked for relief."

He went over and picked his daughter up and cradled her in his arms. "Hi, sweetheart. Did you miss your daddy?"

"Oma Donel."

"Have you been singing 'Old Macdonald Had a Farm'?"

Janna nodded happily. "Ee aye ee aye oh."

With a mirthful chuckle, he started singing the song with her. She mimicked the words remarkably well, considering she had little or no idea what they meant, and maintained the melody perfectly.

Lupe watched and listened. No matter what his other flaws, there was no doubt he loved his little girl.

"Why isn't she in bed at this hour?" he inquired when they finished the song.

The challenge in his question sparked anger, but she managed to keep it under control and her voice sweet. "Because her schedule is all messed up. You'll have to ask Karida why."

"You said she was crying," he reminded her. "When I called this morning everything was quiet, and Karida said Janna was fine."

She didn't like the implication that she was making this up. "You must have called during one of her few quiet moments." Lupe kept her face bland, her words temperate. "And she probably wasn't eager to tell you she was having such a hard time handling a fourteen-month-old."

"But she—"

"She what, Gideon?" Lupe pressed him. "If she told you she was an experienced baby-sitter, she lied."

"But..." He was beginning to sound like a motor-boat. "Why was Janna crying?"

Lupe shrugged. "Kids get in cranky moods. You can't always explain them. In this case, Karida's own tension probably set Janna off. Babies are very sensitive to it. Whatever the reason, Karida had no idea how to handle the situation."

"Why didn't she tell me? Why didn't she call me?"

"As I said, I don't suppose she wanted to bother you. After all, there wasn't much you could do from Austin. Or from Dallas."

He coaxed Janna's head onto his shoulder and stroked her back. "You think I'm neglecting her, don't you?"

Did she? Perhaps he'd made mistakes, a few wrong judgments. But it would be unfair to accuse him of neglecting his daughter. One had only to watch his eyes as he held her or hear him brag about her accomplishments to be convinced he loved her deeply.

"No, Gideon," she said softly. "I don't think you're neglecting her. But I am disappointed that you'd leave her with a stranger. Janna's life has been disturbed enough, and she's only now recovering from a painful earache. What was so important about this trip that you had to leave her?"

He had the decency to avert his eyes. "That's what I need to talk to you about."

Lupe ignored him. "Janna needs consistency, stability in her life, Gideon, and she's not getting it— not from you—if you're never here."

His impulse was to argue with her, that was clear, but he suppressed it. "I'm doing the best I can, Lupe."

She almost said *It isn't good enough* but managed at the last moment to hold her tongue.

He swiveled his head to gaze at his daughter. She'd dropped off to sleep. "Let me put her down for the night and then we can talk. It's been an interesting two days. I have a lot to show you.''

Her brain told her it was time to pack up her books and leave. He didn't need her.

A couple of hours after Karida left, Janna had gotten sleepy, and Lupe took her upstairs for her nap. Having seen how organized the downstairs was, Lupe couldn't resist the temptation to check out the rest of the house.

The nursery was every bit as neat and clean as it had been when she'd helped him bring the baby home. She could attribute some of that to Mrs. Johnson, who prided herself on keeping things orderly, but obviously Gideon was doing his part, as well. Lupe had considered him incorrigible, and he'd proved her mistaken.

When she'd been here last time, she'd caught a glimpse of his bedroom, enough to see that it was crammed with all the things he'd moved from other areas. Karida had left the door ajar, so Lupe didn't feel too guilty pushing it the rest of the way open to see what changes there might have been. Her eyes grew big at what she'd found. Not only had all the clutter been removed, but the room looked positively habitable.

Except the bed wasn't made. So that was where Karida had slept last night. It was the logical place, of course. There was no other bedroom, but the realization that her friend had slept in Gideon's bed was unsettling. Nonetheless, she started arranging the bedclothes. The drawer of the nightstand wasn't completely closed. She reached over to shut it, and something caught her eye. Instead of pushing the drawer in, she pulled it farther out—enough to see several shiny foil-wrapped packets of condoms.

Lupe had stopped breathing. Condoms in Gideon's nightstand. No telling how long they'd been there, but the drawer had obviously been recently accessed. The only other things in it were a pair of fur-lined leather gloves and an electric razor, still in its box. Neither would be a reason to go into that drawer. Except the condoms.

Karida had slept in Gideon's bed last night, when he wasn't here. Had she slept in it when he was? Is that why he'd called on her to stay with Janna, because she was a regular visitor and Janna would be familiar with her?

Biting back the tears she refused to let fall, she'd closed the drawer, left the bed unmade and walked out of the room.

Downstairs, sitting on the couch, she'd contemplated going upstairs to see if there were any empty foil wrappers in the bathroom wastebasket. But she wouldn't sink that low. If Gideon was sleeping with Karida, it was his business. At least he was using protection. But then, he claimed he'd used protection with Becky, too. And he claimed his affair with Becky had only been casual sex. Is that what it was with Karida? Casual sex? A diversion? An amusement?

She'd given him back his ring, she reminded herself. She had no claims to him.

And obviously, he didn't owe her anything.

Watching him climb the stairs with the sleeping

baby in his arms, Lupe continued to debate whether she should go or stay. Go...but she was curious about what had lured him out of town and away from his daughter.

"Have you eaten?" she called.

He shook his head and disappeared at the top of the stairs.

She went to the kitchen and found some cheese ravioli in the freezer and a container of sour cream with a current date in the fridge. There was even a bag of salad makings in the crisper that appeared to be fresh. Amazing. After setting a pot of water on to boil, she spooned the sour cream into a glass dish, got out two small wooden bowls and filled them with the medley of salad greens.

Gideon walked into the room. His face had a fresh-scrubbed look; his blond hair was damp and combed. He didn't seem nearly as tired as he had at the game more than a week earlier. Apparently, he'd gotten a chance to catch up on his sleep while he was away. She'd assumed his nap at the office had been as a result of Janna keeping him up at night. Now she wondered if it hadn't been Karida.

"I guess I'm hungry," he commented. "That looks good."

"I'll fix them Russian style." It was one of their favorite quick dishes.

"Sounds great."

He removed two plates from an overhead cabinet, set them on the table and stepped to the drawer where the silverware was kept. It wasn't the first time they'd worked together in the kitchen, side by side, in a sort of spontaneous choreography. They fell easily into the pattern again, despite the tension smoldering inside her.

"Let me tell you about this conference I went to. Its main focus yesterday was on physical therapy for children with chronic disorders, exactly the type of PT you plan to do."

He must have known what would be presented at the conference before he went, she ruminated. He could have invited her. But he hadn't. He hadn't even told her he was going.

"I didn't attend the sessions today, but I brought back all the handouts I could get hold of for you."

"Gee, thanks." Disappointed that he didn't seem to notice the sarcasm in her reply, she got out a skillet, set it on the range and added a pat of butter.

"But the best part was the woman I met. We spent today together," he continued. "Her name is Marla Hastings."

Lupe turned and stared blankly at him, though her heart was hammering. He'd met another woman and he was bragging about it.

"She works for Craig," he explained.

One of his brother-in-law's employees. Maybe this Marla was an old married woman or some cold business executive, but Lupe's imagination conjured up a sexy personal assistant with the skills to charm a man.

"He and Kerry are on safari in Africa, their belated honeymoon. He built a PT center in Dallas a few years ago and wants to expand it. He had Marla ask me if I would be interested in taking over as director."

He'd decided to leave Coyote Springs and move to Dallas. That would probably be good for Janna; she'd be close to her other grandparents.

"Congratulations," Lupe said tightly as she removed the cooked ravioli and placed them on paper towel to drain.

"It's a great opportunity for us," Gideon said.

Lupe slanted him an inquiring glance. "Us?" She slipped the pasta into the bubbling skillet.

"For the three of us. You, me and Nick." At her surprise, he added, "I realize we'll have to convince Nick, but between the two of us, I'm sure we can."

Lupe shook her head. Gideon didn't seem to understand his friend's reason for opting out. Or hers.

"Craig wants to build three more in the next five years. We'll have a full staff and virtually an unlimited budget."

"In Dallas." She thought for a minute he might be talking about building one of them in Coyote Springs.

"In the Metroplex. For now. Later we can develop in other directions. Where will be up to us."

She turned the sautéing pasta. "I'm not interested," she said flatly. "You can talk to Nick and see if he wants to go, but I'm staying here."

His voice turned harsh with anger. "Is it Dallas or is it me you're not interested in?"

She whipped around to face him. "Coyote Springs is my home. It's where I intend to stay. Besides, I'm not sure we can work together anymore."

"Is something burning?" he asked with a grin.

Lupe jumped and turned to the smoking pasta.

"Damn." Two of them were black on the bottom, the others more brown than they should be.

"At least consider it," he proposed. "Right now isn't the best time to make a decision." His gaze threatened to melt the resistance she was determined to maintain. "You're tired," he said sympathetically as he got a couple of cans of Sprite from the refrigerator. "How long have you been here?"

"Since around noon," she mumbled.

Using a hot pad, she carried the skillet to the table and scooped the cheese-stuffed ravioli onto their plates. Four instead of six for herself, and an even dozen for him. She deposited the skillet in the sink and spread her hands on the edge of the counter.

"If you needed someone to stay with Janna, why didn't you phone me, Gideon?" she asked over her shoulder, then turned to face him. She had to return her hands to the counter behind her so he wouldn't see them shake. "I told you I would help if you needed me." *But you don't need me, do you?* "You didn't even tell me you were going out of town." Hurt slipped into her tone, and she hated herself for it. This wasn't supposed to be about her, about them. It was about a child. His child. The child he didn't know he had and didn't want when he found out about her. "Why did you leave Janna with Karida?"

Several beats went by before he answered. "She offered to mind her, and—"

"And what?" She hardened her voice to keep it from quivering. "Karida doesn't know a thing about taking care of a small child."

His hands were braced on the back of the chair in

front of her plate. He was probably getting ready to pull it out for her. Ever the gentleman.

"I didn't realize that," he explained, still looking bewildered. "She reminded me she was experienced as a caregiver. Her mother—"

He was telling her Karida was the instigator. It might explain the woman's shock when she saw Lupe standing on the threshold instead of Clare. Karida's remarks about Gideon reverberated in Lupe's mind— that he was a gorgeous hunk, a perfect catch.

Twice betrayed, Lupe realized. Not just by the man she'd given her heart to, but by a close friend.

"Her mother was a chronically ill and dying adult, not a healthy, growing, energetic child. There's a difference."

"I'm aware of that," he growled, anger creeping into his response.

"Why didn't you call me?"

He took a deep breath. "I didn't call you, Lupe, because I knew you were studying for exams and I felt I'd already imposed on you enough."

"Imposed on me," she repeated, as if she couldn't quite comprehend the words. "Is that what you think it was when I agreed to go with you to Dallas to pick up Janna? Is that how it appeared to you when I took her in my arms at the soccer game while you coached my son and took a hand in teaching him responsible behavior? Does it seem like an imposition when I hold your daughter in my arms and kiss her?"

She thought she was fuming until she realized tears were running down her cheeks. The humiliation of being so vulnerable thickened her voice.

He made a move toward her, his arms outstretched. Awareness that she wanted him to hold her more than anything in the world brought heat to her face. She skirted the end of the table, keeping it between them.

"You still haven't answered my question, Gideon," she challenged him. "Why didn't you call me when you needed someone to take care of your baby while you were out of town?"

"I wanted to. I almost did. But you said it was over between us, remember?" he retorted, his baritone voice raised. "You told Karida you weren't interested in raising my illegitimate kid."

She was stunned, numbed by his declaration. Then the full meaning began to cut deeper than she could ever have imagined.

"Karida told you that?" Her voice sounded thin, strangled, even to her. Her mind raced. She remembered her friend commiserating with her, telling her it was just as well she found out about him now, that she didn't know how many other illegitimate children might be out there. That it would be tough on any woman to bring up someone else's love child. Lupe hadn't argued with her. Had Karida construed that as rejection of Gideon's baby?

"When you told her about Janna, you told her you didn't want to have anything to do with raising my bastard daughter."

"I never said that," she shouted, then lowered her voice, mindful of the sleeping innocent upstairs. "I never said that, Gideon," she enunciated in hushed outrage.

"That's what she told me."

Lupe stared at him through tear-filled eyes. "And you believed her?"

"What was I supposed to think?" he countered, his chest rising and falling with barely suppressed resentment. "What is it you expect from me, Lupe? I made a mistake in not telling you the whole truth when that lawyer called, and I apologized for it." When he received no perceptible reaction beyond the chill in her stare, he released his grip on the chair, took a pace away and turned again to face her.

"I disappointed you," he acknowledged, "when I suggested that it might be best for Janna to stay with her grandparents. Was I being selfish?" He shrugged. "Yeah, probably. But I was also trying to think of my little girl."

Lupe's eyes flashed with doubt.

"All I knew about her was that she'd lost her mother," he tried to explain, "and she was living with grandparents who presumably loved her. You decided," he emphasized, "that I should bring her home without a moment's hesitation." He filled his lungs with air and slowly expelled it. "Well, I did bring her home," he reminded her. "And you're still not satisfied. So I ask the question again, Lupe. What do you want from me?"

She moved shakily from the table and entered the living room. He followed. Lupe picked up her books on the couch and the purse that lay beside them and strode to the front door.

"Lupe," he called contritely.

She turned toward him, her hand on the doorknob. Her cheeks were wet, but she refused to brush them dry. Through blurring tears, she studied the man she thought she loved, the man she'd anticipated spending the rest of her life with. At this instant, she wanted to feel nothing toward him except perhaps the coldness of indifference. All she could hope for was distance.

"Goodbye, Gideon."

Quietly she closed the door and slipped away.

GIDEON WAITED until Tuesday afternoon before stopping by to see Nick. He'd received the courier package from Marla describing the rehab center in Dallas and detailing the plans for expansion. She'd been considerate enough to send the fact sheets in triplicate, so he didn't have to run off copies. He held on to the set for Lupe, for the time being. Maybe after she calmed down she'd be able to examine this proposal objectively. At the moment, she was too distracted by her anger at him.

Life at the town house had begun to settle into a routine the past week. Mrs. Johnson kept the place neat and orderly, but she let him know she wasn't a housekeeper. So Gideon had arranged for a maid service to come in twice a week to do the major cleaning. The household chores he'd never paid much attention to in the past—like doing laundry at regular intervals and putting things away—were becoming part of his daily existence. Instead of such mundane activities irritating him, as they had previously, he found himself taking pride in getting them done. He wouldn't win any good housekeeping awards, but he'd improved enough that the place looked and felt habitable. No, more than that. Like a home.

"Let me tell you about this conference I attended last weekend," he began enthusiastically. Nick had missed their swimming sessions the day before because he had an appointment in town. Probably, Gideon surmised, to inspect more prospective sites for their PT center.

Gideon had noticed, however, that his friend was limping more than usual. Maybe Craig's proposal would take his mind off some of the pain. Gideon told Nick about his visit to the Metroplex Rehab Center in Dallas, and the offer he'd received to become its director.

"Congratulations," Nick said.

"You should see the setup of the place. The floor plan is octagonal, and probably the best design I've run across. Take a look at that stuff when you get a chance," he said, pointing to the thick folder he'd laid on Nick's desk. "This is a fantastic opportunity for us."

"I'm not interested," Nick declared unequivocally. He didn't even glance at the blue folder mere inches from his hands.

"I realize this is a big change from what we originally had in mind," Gideon acknowledged, "but please give it some consideration before you decide."

Lupe had turned down the opportunity. Gideon had hoped he could convince his friend and between the two of them they'd be able to bring Lupe around.

"There's really nothing to talk about."

"I expected you to jump at this chance." Gideon

felt his whole world crashing down around him. "You'll make a lot more money than you would if we started from scratch. Check out the salaries Craig is paying. I've highlighted your position as head of administration. It's at least twice what we could possibly pay you here."

Nick shook his head unhappily. "This has never been about money, Gid. I thought you of all people would understand that. I'm not interested in heading some well-run bureaucracy. I'm doing that now. I want the challenge of starting something new and making it prosper."

Gideon told himself he should be offended by his friend's facile rejection, but the truth was that he did understand what Nick was talking about.

"I'll turn it down then, since neither of you is interested."

"Don't do it on my account," Nick objected. "If you want this job, go for it."

The message took a moment to sink in. "We're partners," he reminded him.

Nick's brows were raised, his hazel eyes steady and challenging. "Are we?"

"What do you mean? Of course we are."

Nick rubbed the back of his neck. "I've never felt your equal, Gid. At first, I admired your take-charge attitude. Even within partnerships, there has to be a dominant personality, someone who's willing to finalize decisions. So I was flexible and accommodating. But I don't see that we're really getting anywhere. I identified properties that I judged would suit our needs, but you rejected all of them. Even when I got owners to make concessions, you found problems. Then, unexpectedly, you decide you'll build to suit. Never mind that we—Lupe and I—don't have the money to invest in new construction.''

"But I've got the funds," Gideon remarked with heat. "What's the point of having money if I can't put it to good use?"

"No argument about what money is for. But when you talk about spending *your* money, the PT center isn't *ours* anymore. Sorry, my friend, but I don't want to work *for* you. I'd rather keep your friendship."

Gideon sat across from him, speechless. "I had no idea you felt this way, Nick. Why didn't you say something sooner?"

"I tried to, Gid. More than once. But whenever I raised an objection, you brushed it aside. I felt like I was whispering in a hurricane."

"I'm sorry."

"Yeah," Nick said. "Me, too."

CHAPTER TWELVE

LUPE PHONED the dean's office Tuesday morning, expecting Karida to answer. Instead, a strange female voice informed her Ms. Sommers was off that day.

"Is she sick?" Lupe asked, genuinely concerned. Deciding she needed more time to cool off, she hadn't tried to contact Karida on Monday.

"I believe she took a personal day," the woman replied. "She'll be back tomorrow. May I help you?"

"Thanks, but I'll get in touch with her then."

Karida's absence might have been planned, or a genuine emergency could have developed. If it was an attempt to avoid Lupe, knowing that by now Lupe had probably figured out what was going on between her and Gideon, the ploy wouldn't work.

Lupe considered calling her at home but nixed the idea. Another day for emotions to settle down wasn't a bad thing. She might be able to see things a little more calmly by then.

More calmly, perhaps, but her overall attitude hadn't changed. She was furious at her *friend* for what she considered the worst kind of deceit.

A few years earlier, Lupe would have passively withdrawn to lick her wounds. She certainly wouldn't have considered confronting the person who'd offended her. But the years since her husband's death had taught her to be aggressive in making sure her children were treated equitably in school and advancing her own education. In the past two years, spending time with Gideon had equipped her to hold her head up high in the company of the rich, powerful and prestigious.

Another thing she'd learned was that in social situations, other people had only as much power as Lupe gave them, and Lupe wasn't about to give Karida any. Karida had betrayed a trust and she'd have to answer for it.

Immediately after Lupe's seminar on special physical education let out at 12:50 on Wednesday, Lupe walked directly to the student union cafeteria. Karida usually took her lunch break between 12:30 and 1:30. There was a chance she had opted to eat at her desk, in which case Lupe would seek her out there. But the stately blonde was sitting alone, eating a salad and browsing a magazine, at a table that was half-hidden behind a large square pillar.

Lupe walked directly to her. "We need to talk," she said quietly.

For a moment, Karida's casual movements froze, then her features dissolved in a sort of resignation. She closed her eyes and nodded. "Okay," she said submissively, putting down her fork. She gathered her periodical and handbag and rose from her chair. "Where do you want to go?"

"The gazebo will be fine, if it's available."

Lupe led the way, and Karida followed her to the quiet place out of earshot of passersby, where a few weeks before they'd shared coffee and Lupe had spilled her guts.

They climbed the three steps to the ornate pavilion and sat far enough apart to make it obvious they weren't enjoying each other's company, but not so far that they had to raise their voices to be heard.

Lupe placed her leather book bag on the wooden seat beside her, straightened her back, folded her hands in her lap and faced her erstwhile confidante. "What the hell do you think you're doing?"

Karida stiffened, then sat very still while she regarded Lupe from under arched brows. "What do you mean?"

Lupe had promised herself she would remain cool and steady during this discussion. Pacing herself, she filled her lungs with air and let it out. "Oh, I'm sure you know." In spite of her resolve, her voice hitched. "Karida, I can't believe you'd do this to me."

Karida peered at her, her expression blank as she waited.

"Not too long ago we sat in this very spot," Lupe reminded her, "and I told you about Gideon. About his baby."

"You said it was all over between you," Karida replied. "You broke your engagement to him."

Where Karida was heading was obvious. She'd argue that Lupe had abdicated all claim to Gideon, that when she returned the big diamond Karida had so envied, she was declaring him available to any woman who chose to use her charms and skills to attract him. And Karida certainly had both.

"I told you things in confidence. I thought you

were my friend,'' Lupe said, her voice hardening with the pain of having been stabbed in the back. "I didn't expect any of what I said—or what you imagined I said,'' she emphasized tightly, "to be repeated.''

"I didn't—'' Karida started to object.

"Least of all to him. How could you?'' Lupe's voice was rising in anger, in spite of her resolve not to let it. "I certainly didn't expect you to tell him things I never said.''

Karida's eyes narrowed with exasperation. "What the hell are you talking about?''

Lupe could see the other woman's mind working even as color was staining her smooth, fair complexion. She was calculating how to defend herself—or to escape.

"You told Gideon,'' Lupe reminded her, "that I didn't want to have anything to do with raising his daughter.''

The sun caught the stray wisps of Karida's hair, giving her the golden glow of a halo, a sharp contrast to the pinched expression on her face. "You said how hard it would be—''

"You said that, Karida.'' Lupe cut her off. "I didn't.''

Karida huffed disdain. "Well, you sure as hell didn't contradict me,'' she snarled. "I knew what you were thinking. It was only natural.''

Lupe's chest was getting tight. Her respiration was labored. She fought back her own temper, determined to maintain the upper hand with the force of logic.

"As I recall,'' she said reasonably, "you were the one who speculated about how hard it would be for a woman to bring up someone else's kid. And you're right. So I didn't contradict you. What I also didn't point out was that raising other people's children is a two-way street, that it can be equally difficult for a man to bring up another man's kids.''

Karida's face went slack as her jaw fell. Under other circumstances, Lupe would have laughed at the stunned gape. Apparently, the parallel between Lupe mothering Gideon's daughter and his assuming the role of father for her two children had never dawned on Karida.

Lupe let the moment linger, using the interval to buck up her courage for the next question. Mere anticipation of asking it had her pulse accelerating and a slightly queasy feeling souring her stomach.

''Are you sleeping with him?'' There, the words were spoken. Now all she had to endure was the answer.

She watched Karida's eyes grow big, her expression transform into one of shock, or perhaps it was outrage at her boldness. ''Did he tell you that?''

Lupe's belly did a sickening somersault. ''He didn't have to.''

''You must be out of your mind,'' Karida said with a disgusted wave of her perfectly manicured fingers.

''Am I?'' Lupe realized her hands were shaking. ''You slept in his bed the other night.''

Karida's face broadened into a smirk. She folded her arms across her chest. ''Actually, I slept in his bed two nights.''

Lupe's heart tumbled. A flat denial was what she'd anticipated. She wasn't sure if she would have believed it, but it would have given her hope. She'd been counting on her instincts to tell her if the woman was telling the truth.

"Two nights?" she repeated in a shaky voice that was just above a whisper. "You slept with him two nights?"

Karida barked a mocking, bitter laugh. "Now who's jumping to conclusions, Lupe? I said I slept in his bed two nights. Friday night and Saturday night. He left for Austin Friday afternoon. That's when I went over to take care of Janna."

Lupe felt hope bubble once more. Still, she had an uncomfortable feeling that the table had turned, that she was no longer in command of the situation.

Nervously, Karida asked, "Is that how you do it? Get him all hot and bothered and then hold out for a wedding ring? That seems so manipulative to me. I want an honest give-and-take relationship when I find the one I can trust the rest of my life with. By the way, what makes you think we're doing it, anyway?"

Lupe pressed the tips of her fingers to her temples. Maybe she'd misinterpreted.

"There were the condoms. That's what alerted me," she explained scornfully. "And someone had been in the drawer recently."

Karida laughed again, this time with a twist of humor. "It would serve you right if we had. You've been holding back on loving just to see how much you could push him before he turned on you. But you've got it all wrong."

The catharsis of confession seemed to lighten Karida's tone. "Janna woke me up Sunday morning before the crack of dawn. She was crying again. I had no idea what was wrong with the kid. Still don't.'' She shook her head, then dragged a hand through her loose, shoulder-length hair. "Thank God I don't have any children. I'd make a terrible mother. I simply don't have the patience to give them the attention they demand.''

She lowered her head reflectively for a moment, then looked up and continued. "Anyway, I was roused after hardly an hour's sleep and woke with my nose all stuffed up, so I went looking for a tissue. In the dark. I felt the foil packages.'' She grinned. "And figured out what they were. But I didn't get a chance to even muse about them. Janna was screaming her head off. I rolled to the other side of the bed and went to her.'' She added miserably, "For all the good it did.''

The explanation sounded plausible enough, and Lupe wanted desperately to believe it. But there was still that niggling doubt. Karida had acknowledged having the hots for Gideon.

"If you weren't interested in…sleeping with him,'' Lupe ventured, surprising herself at her unwillingness to say *having sex,* "why did you offer to baby-sit for Janna when you admit you don't like small children?''

Karida stood up stiffly, self-consciously, and blew the hair from her face. "I—'' she began, then waved her hand as if to erase what she had been about to say. With a dissatisfied shake of the head, she started pacing in front of Lupe, her dressy heels clicking on the painted wooden floor of the gazebo.

"It was an impulse," she admitted. "A stupid one, as it turns out. Did I want to have sex with him?" She shrugged elegantly and gave Lupe a weak smile. "I won't deny it. I've been alone for a long time, Lupe, and I would have jumped between the sheets with Gideon without a second's hesitation if he'd asked me."

"Why did you lie about me?" Lupe asked, hurt rather than anger sharpening her words.

Karida turned away and hung her head. "I saw what was happening between you and Gideon, the way you seemed to be avoiding each other, and I thought…"

She spun to face her old friend, remorse in her eyes. "I'm not proud of myself, Lupe. What I did was wrong, and I'm sorry." She bit her lip, then seemed to brighten. "Of course, it was also a waste of effort."

Lupe's whole body seemed to vibrate as she let the words sink in. Gideon hadn't had sex with Karida.

"He sees me as a woman." The statuesque blonde moved to the rail and peered across the well-maintained lawn toward the bell tower that was a landmark of the campus. She spun around and fixed her gaze on her friend. "But he's not interested in me, Lupe. There's only one woman he cares about, and that's you. I don't understand everything that's going on between the two of you, but for some reason he still wants you, even though you don't deserve him."

GIDEON DISMISSED his kinesiology class and packed up his notes. The semester was nearly over. A few more classes to teach, mostly review and emphasis on key points, then he'd proctor the final exams. After that...

He'd expected to be working with Nick and Lupe on their PT center this summer, so they could be ready for the fall. But that plan was dead. And they all seemed to conclude he was the one who'd killed it.

He walked to his office, half-aware of the clouds beginning to form an overcast in the west. They probably wouldn't bring rain, certainly not in sufficient quantity to break the drought now in its fifth year. And as much as people prayed for much-needed precipitation, they tended to become moody when the sun wasn't shining.

The real sunshine in his life these past few weeks had been Janna. He'd never realized how much a child could fill a man's world. But he'd had a difficult time trying to concentrate on anything else since his confrontation with Lupe after he'd returned from Dallas. They'd had disagreements before, like the one over disciplining Miguelito at the soccer match, but their other disputes had taken on more the aspect of a reasoned discussion than an argument.

She'd said she didn't believe they could work together anymore. Reluctantly, he was beginning to agree. He'd always admired strong personalities. The First family was full of them, from his occasionally domineering father to his elder brother who inevitably accomplished whatever he set out to do. His sister Kerry was positively pigheaded. She'd carried a grudge for nearly twenty years and then found the courage to overcome alcoholism. His younger sister Julie was as tenacious as everyone else in the clan, even if she was inclined to be less dramatic about it. Sheila, his father's new wife, certainly fit the pattern. She'd stood up to Adam First and the Homestead Bank and Trust, defeated one and taken the other prisoner. Of course, he'd never put it that way to his father. Gideon was beginning to wonder now, though, about himself.

He'd never doubted that strength was one of the qualities that attracted him to Lupe. But if opposites attract, and she was the strong one, did that mean he was weak?

She seemed to think so. Nick, on the other hand, had called off their partnership for exactly the opposite reason—because Gideon overpowered their relationship and tried to force his agenda without consultation.

Gideon shook his head and smirked, not at the humor but the irony. Sometimes a guy just couldn't win.

He let himself into his office, pleased with the order he'd managed to establish out of the previous chaos, and was about to set his folder down on the middle of the desk blotter when he saw the note: "Call Hazel in the registrar's office."

He knew the number by heart and dialed it immediately.

"Oh, Professor First. I figured I ought to let you know. Mr. Siler's had a little accident. He tripped on the front steps this afternoon and injured his right knee. I wanted to call nine-one-one, but he wouldn't let me. Lisha drove him to the emergency room at Coyote General.''

The clock above the door showed a few minutes after four. Mrs. Johnson had specifically asked him to be home by five today because she had some things she had to do with her grandchildren.

''When did this happen?''

''About an hour ago. He was coming back from a meeting at the dean's office. He'd been limping pretty bad all day—''

''I'll go see him. Thanks for calling.''

What should he do about Janna? He could go home, relieve Mrs. Johnson and take Janna with him to see Nick at General, but hospitals were by definition unhealthy places, and he didn't relish exposing his daughter to any more germs than he had to. Besides, it would soon be her dinnertime, and he was loath to disrupt the schedule he'd finally gotten her on.

There was an alternative. Maybe more than one kind of healing could come out of this misfortune. He picked up the phone and called Lupe's house. Miguelito answered the phone.

''Are you coming over?'' the boy asked eagerly. *I've missed you* was silently communicated over the line.

''Can't tonight, Mikey. But one day soon.''

''Yeah, sure. That's okay.'' But it was clear that it wasn't. ''You want to talk to my mom?''

''Please, or your grandmother if your mom isn't available.''

A moment later Lupe was on the line. ''Gideon?''

"Hi."

"What's the matter?"

Telephone calls didn't used to mean something was wrong. "Nick fell and bunged up his knee. He's in the emergency room."

"Oh, dear, I'm so sorry. How serious is it?"

"I don't know. Um, do you think you could do me a favor? Mrs. Johnson needs to go home at five today, and I was wondering if you could mind Janna while I check to see how Nick's doing."

Gideon could hear her hand covering the mouthpiece and her mumbling behind it. "I'll go over to your house right away," she said in a businesslike fashion. "Do you have any idea how long you'll be?"

"If he's lucky, not more than an hour or so. But I can't say for sure."

"Don't worry about it. Take however long you need. I just hope Nick's all right. Be sure to give him my best."

"I will." This conversation felt oddly impersonal. He didn't want it to end that way. "Look, Janna will have to be fed—"

"You don't have to worry about her, Gideon. I'll check with Mrs. Johnson to find out what needs to be done and take care of everything. Janna will be fine."

"I know she will...and thank you."

He passed on a couple of tidbits of information that Mrs. Johnson may not have, like Janna's favorite bedtime story and the music tape he played for her when he put her down for the night. Caught between concern for his friend and a desire to stay on the line longer with the sound of Lupe's voice in his ear, he finally hung up.

LUPE COULDN'T quite make up her mind what the call from Gideon meant. Did he merely need someone to baby-sit his daughter while he visited a sick friend? Or was there more to it? Whatever the reason behind it, she was glad for the opportunity to be invited to his house.

The harshness of his complaint the last time they'd been together had left her speechless and shaken. She'd returned to her house late. Elena had waited up for her—dozing in a chair in the living room. She had been grateful her mother-in-law was too sleepy to notice that Lupe was upset.

Lupe had slept very little that night. Gideon's ugly words kept ringing in her ears. She'd had no idea she'd been so judgmental and self-righteous, but on consideration, she began to see he was right. She'd demanded a kind of perfection from him that was both unreasonable and unrealistic. What exactly had Gideon done that was so bad? She couldn't remember. But she could recall the things she'd accused him of and the unkind value judgments she'd made. He hadn't abandoned his child. He'd loved her.

"Is something wrong?" Elena asked. She was preparing the teriyaki marinade for the pork chops she'd barbecue on the gas grill in the backyard. "Are you going somewhere?"

"Nick's in the hospital. Apparently, he's injured his leg."

"I'm very sorry to hear that. Is Gideon picking you up so you can visit your friend?"

"No," Lupe responded. "He asked me to watch Janna while he visits him." She looked around at the dinner preparations under way. "I have to leave right now. I'll grab something to eat over there."

She kissed her children goodbye, grabbed her books and a Sprite and dashed to her car. Ten minutes later, she pulled into the parking lot in front of Gideon's town house.

"My grandson, Curtis, has a track meet this afternoon and then a band concert tonight," Mrs. Johnson explained to Lupe. "I promised not to miss either of them."

The older woman ran down the list of things to be done, what she was planning to feed Janna if Gideon had not shown up when he promised and the baby's normal bedtime routine. Lupe absorbed it all without much effort. It was a pattern she was familiar with.

After Mrs. Johnson left, while Janna was contentedly watching a cartoon on TV, Lupe set about preparing the child's dinner. Out of curiosity, she spoke to her in Spanish and was utterly amazed to find the little girl understood every word. They settled down to a quiet evening of playing games and singing songs in both languages.

GIDEON FOUND his friend stretched out on a gurney, his badly swollen right knee supported by a pillow. Nick was trying to put up a brave front, but Gideon knew him well enough to realize he was in considerable pain.

"Dumb thing to do," Nick chided himself for Gideon's benefit. "You'd think at my age I'd be smart enough to pick up my feet when climbing steps."

"Have they given you anything for the pain?"

He closed his eyes and nodded. "Some Tylenol 3. They offered me something stronger, but I won't be able to get anything done if I'm zoned out."

"You won't be able to get anything done if you're in agony, either."

"It's not that bad."

"If you think that, I'll ask the nurse to bring a mirror so you can see what pain looks like."

"Stop preaching," Nick said irritably.

Gideon grinned. "Not a chance."

Nick smiled weakly.

"Has Kasselbaum been here?"

"They called him. He should be by in a little while."

On cue, the orthopedic surgeon entered the cubicle. He was a small man, with wavy steel-gray hair and wire-rimmed glasses. His smooth, unlined face belied his nearly fifty-plus years.

"Hello, Gideon," he said even before greeting his patient. They shook hands. "Well, let's see what we have here."

The examination of his patient didn't take long. The diagnosis was predictable. "I've examined the X rays. Nothing's broken, but there's a lot of fluid on the joint. We'll have to aspirate." He slipped the X rays he'd brought with him onto the wall-mounted viewer and indicated the affected areas of the joint.

"As you can see here—" he pointed at the black-

and-white fuzzy image "—the cartilage is virtually nonexistent. You have bone rubbing against bone, my friend. I don't need to remind you there's only one remedy."

"Replacement." Gideon cast a concerned glance at his friend.

"No." Nick was emphatic.

"One of the best indicators for joint replacement is running out of other options and having nothing left but pain." Kasselbaum faced his patient squarely. "I'm not prescribing any more cortisone shots or anti-inflammatory medication," he declared authoritatively. "They relieve the pain temporarily, but they also accelerate deterioration."

"I don't want surgery," Nick insisted.

Kasselbaum shook his head. "You're putting off the inevitable, Nick. The sooner you get this done, the better. The longer you wait, the greater the deformity we have to work with, the more complicated the procedure and the more difficult your recovery."

"No." Again Nick was adamant.

"Let me know when you change your mind," the surgeon said with obvious disapproval.

"Why?" Gideon asked, when the doctor had left the room.

"This is my decision, Gid, not yours."

Gideon smothered an urge to argue. Instead, he decided on persuasion. "I'm not challenging your right to make the choice, Nick. I'm simply asking why you're making one you know is wrong."

"Damn it. I'm in enough pain without you badgering me," Nick complained.

Gideon was undeterred. "This condition won't get any better, old buddy, and your chances of making a complete recovery don't improve with delay. Actually, it's the opposite. And there are some other things you need to consider. For example, as the pain increases you'll have no option but to take narcotic painkillers, because they'll be the only ones that work. Then you'll become dependent on them. Is that what you want—to turn into a drug addict?"

Nick fumed, than flared. "Butt out, Gid. You know as well as I do that when medication is given solely for pain, there's no danger of drug addiction."

"We also know it doesn't always work out that way." Gideon pulled up a stool and sat beside the gurney. "We've been friends too long for me to give up on you, Nick. I'll respect your decision when you tell me the reason for it. Level with me," he pleaded. "What's the hang-up?"

There was a long interval of tense silence. Finally, the man on the gurney spit out, "Because I'm scared. There. Does that satisfy you?"

The response shocked Gideon, but he did his best not to show it. He'd never even considered the possibility that his friend might be afraid. The guy had been a mountain climber, for crying out loud. The very notion of dangling off the side of a rock cliff hundreds, maybe thousands, of feet above the ground made Gideon's stomach feel hollow and his head swim.

"All right. I accept that." Phobias weren't reasonable, but he suspected his friend had a reason underlying his unreasonable fear. "Can you tell me why you're afraid?"

Nick rearranged himself uncomfortably on the paper-covered pallet, his averted glances testifying to his embarrassment at having to confess a secret weakness.

"I had an uncle who had a knee replaced. Everyone was pleased with the surgery. No problem, the doctors all agreed. Everything went smooth as silk. Gus was up and walking within two days, wincing and grinning at the same time. On the third day he suffered a pulmonary embolism and dropped dead. Just like that." Nick snapped his fingers. "Oh, but the surgery was successful," he added bitterly. "They buried him with a nice new plastic knee."

Blood clots were a danger in every invasive procedure. "When was this?" Gideon asked.

"About ten years ago."

"They've come a long way since then, Nick. I'm not trying to make light of this. It could still happen. But the chances of such a thing occurring were remote back then. Today it's even less likely."

Over the next three hours, Nick's knee was drained of the fluids that had accumulated in the painfully stiff joint. Gideon entertained his friend with tales of Janna's exploits, his newfound mania for neatness and the way the Homestead Bank and Trust was continuing to put large tracts of Number One land on the auction block. He also pointed out that his brother-in-law, Craig Robeson, was buying up a good deal of it for possible development.

Finally, Nick was seated in a wheelchair and rolled

out the front door. Gideon helped him into the front seat of the Explorer and drove him home. He'd arrange to have Nick's car, which was still at the university, brought to his house tomorrow.

At Nick's place, Gideon found a pizza in the freezer and threw it into the oven, grabbed a couple of beers from the fridge, popped the tops, and the two of them settled down to a bachelor meal. Gideon had called Lupe from the hospital before he left and told her where he was headed. He didn't tell her about Nick's fears.

"Take however long you need," she'd said. "Janna went to sleep at seven without any trouble, so I've been getting a lot of studying done." She chuckled. "Probably more than I would at home."

BY TEN O'CLOCK, Lupe's back and neck were stiff. She needed to stretch. Leaving her open books on the kitchen table, she climbed the stairs to the second floor and peeked into Janna's room. The fifteen-month old was flat on her back, her legs wide, arms spread, the stuffed animal she'd insisted had to be pressed at her side tossed onto the floor.

Lupe admired the curly red hair, the porcelain complexion and oval face. Janna had a hint of Gideon's dimples in her cheeks and the slightest of clefts in her chin. Someday she would be a beautiful woman. Lupe picked up the discarded toy and returned it to the side of the crib.

Her eyes were drooping. She ran a hand down her face and went into Gideon's bedroom to use his bathroom. Splashing water on her face didn't seem to wake her up, however. She dried herself, turned to the doorway and found herself facing Gideon's bed. It looked so inviting.

Karida had slept there when Gideon was away. Lupe stretched out on the forest-green coverlet, arms extended, and stared at the moon-shadowed ceiling. Was Karida right about her? Was she a tease, leading Gideon on, then pulling back? If she had been torturing him, she'd also been torturing herself. She wanted Gideon. She wanted him to make love to her. Almost from the first moment she'd seen him, she'd fantasized about spooning herself against him, their bodies tangling, shifting.

She curled up on her side and rested her head on the satin pillows. His scent, lingering there, prompted her to snuggle contentedly against the smooth fabric. It was time to stop the torture, she told herself as she drifted off.

CHAPTER THIRTEEN

IT WAS almost eleven o'clock when Gideon turned off the engine and climbed out of the Explorer. Daytime temperatures had diminished to a comfortable level, and the gentle breeze had a soporific effect.

He was tired. The hours spent with his friend had been exhausting but productive. Nick's next appointment with Kasselbaum was in a couple of days, and he'd agreed to let Gideon go with him to schedule the surgery he needed so desperately.

Living with pain and fear couldn't have been easy. Nick would go through with the surgery now, not because he'd lost his fear, but because he'd overcome it. Gideon had sensed his relief after having owned up to it. Strength and courage took many forms, he reminded himself.

He got out his key and opened the front door, expecting to see Lupe sitting on the couch, studying for finals. But she wasn't there. He strode to the kitchen, sniffing for the aroma of brewed coffee, but didn't detect any. Nor did he find her. Maybe she was upstairs with Janna. The baby had woken up the past few nights for no apparent reason, except for a need to be held. Fortunately, it hadn't taken long for her to fall back to sleep.

But Lupe wasn't in Janna's room, either. Finally, he saw her cuddled up on his bed, her arms tucked against her breasts, a contented smile on her lips. This was a fantasy he'd had for a long time—coming home to find his wife in bed, waiting for him. He did his best to ignore the fact that she wasn't his wife. She wasn't even in his bed, merely on it. Sound asleep. It was a pity he had to wake her.

He stood for several minutes watching her slow, gentle breathing. Desire nipped and bit. Heat, long banked, exploded into open flame. After moving quietly to the side of the bed, he sat on its edge, smiled at the woman sleeping there and brought his lips to her cheek. The scent of her hair in his nostrils, the smoothness of her skin against his mouth, the sweet warmth of her body close to his were as powerful as any aphrodisiac.

"Lupe," he murmured in her ear.

She stirred, a delicate flutter of lashes, a slow, sensuous uncurling of arms. She gazed at him with smiling eyes. "Welcome home."

He wasn't sure she was awake, wasn't sure he dared touch her again. He was a man on a tightrope, his balance precarious, his control slipping. The urge to touch, to kiss and caress, was as gloriously intoxicating as any liqueur and twice as powerful.

She raised her arms and wrapped them around his neck, capturing him, bringing him down to her. "I'm glad you finally got back."

"Mmm. Me, too." A firestorm rocketed through him. He risked brushing her lips with his, a fleeting touch like the wind outside the window, billowing and passing.

It wasn't enough. She tightened her hold. "Don't stop now."

This time he tasted, and was jolted by her response. She was the one who plunged, demanded, then accepted.

He repositioned himself so that his legs paralleled hers, his eyes at her level. The sensuous curve of her lips was all the invitation he needed. His mouth covered hers, his tongue arrogant, searching, pillaging. He bracketed her face and held her lips to his. Together they swam uncharted seas of taste and touch. His hands grew restless, toyed with her ears, trailed down the column of her neck to its base and kept moving. Her breasts were warm, soft and alluring. His reaction was hot, hard and ungovernable.

He unbuttoned her blouse and played his fingers across the swell of her silken bra.

Her breathing dragged with each butterfly stroke. She hitched the palms of her hands down the firm contours of his chest and closed her eyes to savor more deeply the quivering response of compact muscle. She released the buttons of his shirt, desperate for the feel of his flesh. An involuntary moan of pleasure escaped between her teeth as she made contact with his hair-dusted skin.

Sensations old and new, familiar and strange, had her head reeling, her respiration quaking, her core melting in liquid desperation. His mouth was wet against her bra as he teased her erect nipple. She lifted his face and smiled into his stormy blue eyes. ''Make love to me, Gideon.''

His breathing faltered as he squeezed out words. ''Lupe, are you sure?''

The plea in his voice, in his gaze, was like an ocean wave, irresistible, unrelenting and implacable. She was carried away on its crest, its height glorious. ''I'm sure,'' she murmured a split second before his mouth plunged to hers.

Gravity made them clumsy. Fingers trembled, uncoordinated, as they stripped each other naked. Her blouse. His shirt. Her bra. His T-shirt. He slipped his fingers under the waistband of her slacks. She was wet, waiting. She cupped the bulge of his jeans. He was hard, throbbing. She moaned with pleasure. He groaned with indulgence. Zippers parted. Breathing stopped.

They saw little of each other in the thin light of the moon streaming in from the warm summer night beyond the windows. But they felt. Pliant feminine flesh. Rigid masculine sinew. The sweep of desire. The urge of need.

Hot, pulsing, he reached across the bed to the drawer of the nightstand. Strange erotic sensations blazed through him as he removed a foil packet. His fingers blundered. It slipped from his grasp. On a stalled breath, he retrieved it from the coverlet beside her peaked breasts.

And stopped.

He fell against a pillow, tense, in agony. ''No.''

She wasn't sure she'd heard him. "Gideon..."

Squeezing his eyes shut, he took a racking breath. "Lupe—"

She lifted herself onto her side, facing him. "Gideon," she repeated, her voice soft, imploring.

"We can't do this, Lupe." His voice was a hoarse whisper. "It's wrong."

She must not have heard him right. "I don't understand—"

"This isn't right for us, Lupe." His voice was tormented, tense with erotic restraint. "Not until we're married."

She was naked on his bed, vulnerable to his every touch, and he was rejecting her. "You've made love with other women, but you won't make love with me."

"You'll regret this in the morning. You'll hate me."

The heat of desire transformed itself into tears of shame and humiliation. "I already regret it, Gideon." Her entire body shuddered on a thick sob. "I regret exposing my emotions for you to play with."

He reached over to brush away the tears coursing down her cheeks. Angrily, she slapped his hand away. "Actions may be more telling than words, Gideon, but yours are too often contradictory." She hiccuped. "And I can't trust either one."

"Lupe—"

She sprang from the bed, grabbed her discarded clothes from the floor and ran into the bathroom.

Miserable, he struggled into his jeans, covered his

bare chest with a now-wrinkled shirt and padded bare-foot to the living room.

Her eyes refused to meet his a few minutes later when she descended the stairs. Stiffly, she strode to the kitchen, packed her books and turned, only to find him in the doorway.

"Lupe," he pleaded with outstretched hands, "please listen to me."

She slammed her eyes shut and stood before him trembling. "I don't think I even know you, Gideon."

"I want to explain." Impatience hardened his words.

"Let me pass."

Her hair was in disarray. He ached to comb it with his fingers, pull her against him, but she was immovable. On a deep breath, he dropped his arms and stepped aside. She brushed past him, bolting like a frightened doe through the doorway.

He'd come so close to plunging into her, wrapping himself in the sweet warmth of her body—the fulfillment of his fantasies. The frustration of it unhinged him.

"You're absolutely right," he called, and followed her into the living room. "We aren't meant for each other. It's best we go our separate ways. Because no matter what I do, no matter what I say, you throw the wrong light on it." He was shaking with anger and heartbreak. He stared at her back as her hand clasped the doorknob. "Well, I quit."

A moment later, he heard the click of the front door as it closed behind her.

ELENA HUSTLED the family forward with a nervous sweep of her hands. "We don't want to be late. It'll be starting soon."

"We have plenty of time," her son Jesse assured her. More than a head taller than his mother, he affectionately draped an arm over her shoulders and gave her a gentle squeeze. "The ceremony doesn't start for another fifteen or twenty minutes. Relax, Mama."

"Besides," his wife, Tori, said, "they wouldn't dare start without you."

Elena broke into a broad grin and playfully slapped her daughter-in-law's arm. The Amorados, she decided, seemed to be attracted to blondes with blue eyes. Jesse's golden-haired wife was pregnant for the second time. Their firstborn, a son, promised to be every bit as handsome as his father. With medium-brown hair, hazel-green eyes and a tan complexion, the three-year-old was turning heads already.

Elena diverted her attention to Lupe's sister, who had driven up from San Antonio with her husband and children to attend this very special event. Felicia was three years older than Lupe, an inch or two shorter and fifty pounds heavier. Her husband, Danilo, matched her girth but was almost a foot taller.

"You must be very proud of your sister," Elena said, not for the first time. "She has worked so hard for this."

Felicia matched her enthusiasm and turned to her daughters. "Someday you will go to college, just like your Tía Lupe."

"Yes, Mama," the older of the two girls replied. Plainly, they'd heard the remarks before.

Graduation exercises at Texas University at Coyote Springs were held on Friday evening in the Coyotes' Lair, the school's athletic stadium. June temperatures had already hit the century mark. Fortunately, family and friends were seated in the relative coolness of the shady side of the stands, overlooking the playing field, where the graduating class of more than five hundred would sit on folding chairs.

Popular instrumental music blared from the big black speaker consoles set up at strategic points in front of the bleachers, an innocuous background noise that blended with the rumble and banter of human voices and was totally ignored. When it ceased, however, conversation waned as people settled onto the hard metal benches in anticipation of the coming event.

At last came the familiar strains of Elgar's "Pomp and Circumstance." From the arched entrance to the playing field on the east end of the stadium, the stately procession began. Learned academics and honored guests led the way in dignified, self-conscious splendor, their robes billowing in the gentle breeze. The graduates appeared, marching two by two in their plain gowns and plasterboard caps. As if on signal, the crowd smiled.

Since her last name began with *A,* Lupe was among the first to march down the red-carpeted path to the long rows of folding chairs.

"*¡Mira!*" Elena crowed, her bobbing finger outstretched. "There she is."

Others had joined the Amorados in the stands. Adam and Sheila First. Michael, Clare and their kids.

Since Gideon was part of the pageantry, Julie had won the honor of holding Janna, who smiled happily at all the attention she was getting from friends, family and strangers. Nick was there, too. Karida was not.

Gideon had taken his place on the dais with other members of the university's faculty and was in an excellent position to watch the procession as it approached. Like a compass needle swinging to magnetic north, Gideon immediately picked out Lupe, her hair forming a frizzy black wreath beneath her iridescent blue hat.

Gideon's heart ached with a melancholy gladness. This was her day, and he was unimaginably proud of her. But he'd hoped to share a greater role in it—as her fiancé. It could have been as her lover, he reminded himself, had he not gotten a sudden case of scruples. He'd dreamed for nearly two years of having her in his bed, their bodies heart to heart, hip to hip. After taking her to the edge of the cliff, he'd stepped back; he cursed himself, yet he knew he'd do it again.

He sat in his cowled robe, aware she wasn't coming to him ever again. He'd wanted to be a part of her life. Now he was a mere spectator.

When everyone was settled, the president of the university took his place at the podium, and the usual speeches followed, fine words that were forgotten five minutes after they were heard—if anyone had even listened. Gideon remembered someone once observing that people who were grinning from ear to ear rarely heard anything.

Half a dozen doctoral candidates received their Ph.Ds. At last, the names of the master's candidates were called. Abernathy, Adams, Amorado. Cheers went up from a section of the stands as Lupe, lips working nervously, fought to suppress the smile that lit her eyes. She accepted the rolled parchment that acknowledged her years of hard work, offered the customary word of thanks to accompany the perfunctory handshake and moved on. She met Gideon's eyes for a split second, and in that poignant moment time stood still, then rushed on.

The piece of paper in her hand was more than an academic degree. It symbolized a significant transition in her life and, in a sense, a separation from the world she'd grown up in. As she descended the stairs and returned to her seat, Gideon understood she was also passing out of his life.

The ceremony seemed to drag on interminably as name after name was called and cameras clicked. Finally, Clayton Zuniga accepted his diploma and left the platform. The president of the university spoke his concluding words, the audience broke into wild applause and tasseled caps flew high into the warm summer air. A moment later, pandemonium broke out as families and friends crowded onto the field to congratulate the graduates.

Gideon held back for several minutes while his family and Lupe's babbled around her. Then she caught his eye. Uncharacteristically reticent, he came forward. Extending his hands, he took hers, looked into her glistening eyes and did his best to smile.

''The big day,'' he said warmly, and gave her a collegial peck on the cheek. Her scent rammed hormonal signals racing through him, and he wondered if she could feel his pulse quickening. "Congratulations."

"Thank you," she said, "for helping me take control of my life."

He searched for subliminal meanings, for a hint of understanding, if not forgiveness. He found good manners and a self-possessed confidence that reared itself like an invisible wall. Still, he needed all the strength he could muster to keep from pulling her into his arms and smothering her with kisses.

"You did all the work," he reminded her pleasantly.

She smiled wryly. "And you gave me the inspiration."

He must be getting paranoid, but he was sure he detected irony in her praise.

Sporting a cane, Nick rescued him with a slap on the back. "Hey, did I hear somebody say something about food?"

Gideon broke contact with Lupe and joined the bustling crowd on its migration to the parking lot. To negotiate the exit bottlenecks as people maneuvered onto the city's streets took several minutes. The Amorado party reassembled at a restaurant several blocks away, where a private room had been reserved.

Gideon felt like an outsider. This wasn't at all how he'd envisioned Lupe's special day. Instead of simply holding her hands and mouthing platitudes, he'd expected to dance with her in his arms, give her an erotic kiss and watch her blush in front of everyone. Here was the woman he'd asked to marry him, the woman he dreamed of having in his bed for the rest of his life, the woman who had agreed to work at his side, to share his successes and failures, his joys and pains. To bear his children. And now they were treating each other like distant cousins.

"I checked on houses near us for you," he heard Felicia comment to Lupe a few minutes later as they inched through the long buffet that offered an assortment of cold salads and hot foods. They sidestepped, picking and choosing on their way to the baron of beef at the end of the line. "There are a couple that are definitely worth considering."

Gideon felt as if someone had run the razor-sharp blade of a knife across his belly. "In San Antonio?"

"In the new Suegra Heights development," Felicia elaborated.

"Who comes up with the names of these places?" Her husband, Danilo, chortled. "Can you imagine living in a place named for your mother-in-law?"

A sense of foreboding rattled Gideon. "Why would you be interested in houses in San Antone?" he asked Lupe.

She concentrated on spooning French-cut green beans with slivered almonds onto her plate. "A scout from the Santa Maria Rehabilitation Center in San Antonio came to see me last week," she mumbled.

That didn't surprise him. Graduate students were routinely sought after by big concerns. She'd been interviewed by a number of other institutions earlier in the year. But asking her sister to inquire about houses in the Alamo City was alarming.

His brow wrinkled. "Did they make you an offer?"

She nodded absently as she helped herself to a

small portion of country-fried potatoes. "As a staff physical therapist. Full-time, with all the benefits."

She might as well have poured vinegar on an open wound. For a moment, he stopped breathing.

"Congratulations," Nick said from behind Gideon. "The Santa Maria has an excellent reputation."

Gideon was afraid to ask the next question, but he had to. "Will you accept it?"

"Adam, are you really planning to eat all that?" she asked his father, who was moving up the other side of the long table. His plate was piled high with chicken strips, fried okra and mushrooms swimming in butter.

"Don't worry—" he winked at her "—I'm leaving enough room for the beef."

"I'm sure it's a consolation, dear," Sheila added from behind him, "that none of this food will go to waste."

"My waist," Danilo said with a chuckle. His plate was piled even higher.

"Are you taking the Santa Maria position?" Gideon asked again.

"I'm giving it serious consideration," she admitted, and walked to the round table where Elena and the children were already seated. Without thinking, Gideon followed, then stopped.

Elena extended her hand to the seat next to Miguelito. "Sit with us," she invited. "We do not get to see you much these days."

"Thanks, Doña Elena. The end of the school year is always busy, as Lupe can tell you. Final exams and all the administrative paperwork that goes with them.'' He speared a slice of yellow summer squash but didn't bring it up to his mouth.

"Why the Santa Maria?" he asked Lupe.

"It's one of the best in the country," she replied diffidently. "I'd get to work with a wide range of clients, including injured servicemen, and I'll be close to Felicia and her family."

From the expression on Elena's face, it was clear she didn't approve.

"How do you feel about this, Doña Elena?" Gideon asked her.

She bent her head to one side and shrugged eloquently. "It is her decision."

"Will you go with her?"

"She has asked me to."

"We're family," Lupe said pointedly.

"I don't want to live in San Antonio," Miguelito snapped. "I want to stay here."

"Me, too." His sister chimed in petulantly, and crossed her arms defiantly in front of her narrow chest.

Lupe spread a cloth napkin across her lap. "You'll like San Antonio," she said quietly, as if the subject were closed. "Besides, you'll be near your cousins."

"And you'll be in the same class with my Raymond," Felicia noted.

"I don't want to go to school in San Antonio," Miguelito whined, ignoring his aunt. "I want to stay here and be with my friends."

"We don't always get what we want in life," Lupe murmured.

"You'll make plenty of new friends," his grandmother told him in Spanish but without much enthusiasm.

"I don't need new friends," Miguelito complained more forcefully in English. "I like the ones I have here."

"We'll talk about this later," Lupe said on a note of finality.

The boy appealed to Gideon. "Tell her not to make us go."

"It's not my decision, Mikey." He put the piece of squash in his mouth, though it had grown cold and he had no appetite for it in any case.

"But she'll listen to you," the boy protested.

Gideon focused his attention on Lupe, who was too busy cutting off a bite-size piece of the roast beef on her plate to meet his gaze. "I'm not sure she will."

"Miguelito," Lupe snapped, "I said we'll talk about this later."

Gideon could see the steam rising against her son's aggravating persistence. "Have you formally accepted their offer?"

"Not yet." She peered across the table at him. "But I plan to."

"Maybe you ought to give it a little more thought," he suggested conversationally. "For the children's sake. After all, shouldn't their happiness be your first consideration?"

Zing. Bull's-eye. The lowered brows of a scowl lasted a mere second before she regained control.

"As you say—" she cut tenaciously into her roast beef "—it's none of your business."

Gideon closed his eyes and his mouth. She'd

balked at the idea of moving to Dallas, but she was
willing to take her children away from Coyote
Springs and go to San Antonio. Was it merely for the
opportunity to work for one of the foremost rehabilitation centers in the country—or to get away from
him?

No point in asking the question. He knew the answer.

GIDEON WAS at home the next morning, Saturday,
when the phone rang. He poured Janna her second
bowl of cereal before picking up the receiver. It was
Marla. They'd talked a few times since he'd returned
from Dallas, but he hadn't committed to his brother-
in-law's generous offer, and so far, Marla hadn't
pressed the issue.

"You realize the job of director is yours for the
asking, Gideon. But you'll have to make a decision
pretty soon, or I'll have to start looking elsewhere."

She quoted a salary. It wasn't exorbitant, but it
would allow a director to live in reasonable comfort.
Besides, as Nick had pointed out, this had never been
about money.

After leaving the dinner table in the restaurant the
previous evening, Gideon hadn't crowded Lupe.
When a small combo began playing dance music,
he'd left it to the other men in the room to sweep her
around the floor. The music was loud and Janna was
restless, so he'd used that as an excuse for leaving
early. No point in spoiling the rest of Lupe's evening.
She'd said she was going to accept the position in

San Antonio. Nick had made it clear he wasn't interested in being Gideon's partner.

"You've just hired yourself a new director," he
told Marla on the phone, and wished he could feel
good about it.

IT WAS Saturday evening, and most of the First family
were gathered on the patio behind the Home Place.
Sheila had served grilled breast of chicken and her
homemade potato salad for dinner. She hadn't told
anyone that she'd substituted no-fat, cholesterol-free
mayonnaise in the dressing. She wasn't worried about
Michael and his brood, or Julie, who was slender and
fit. But Adam's appetite seemed to have gone into
overdrive since he'd taken over the original sixty
thousand acres of the family ranch. Reverting to the
role of rancher rather than ranch manager, he was
more physically active than before, but so was his
appetite. He worked off the calories, all right, but the
high-fat diet bothered her, so she'd been quietly cutting back on the saturated variety.

"What was going on between Gideon and Lupe
last night?" Julie asked.

Gideon had announced the evening before that he
wouldn't be coming out to the ranch this weekend
because Nick was checking into the hospital to have
knee surgery on Tuesday, and he wanted to spend
some time with him.

Julie snickered. "They sure were dancing around
each other, weren't they?"

"They were supposed to be dancing with each
other," her father noted unhappily.

"I knew they were having problems—ever since Lupe found out about Janna," Michael added. "But instead of sparks flying last evening, I had the feeling I better be prepared to duck javelins. Do you know what the problem is?" he asked his wife.

Clare shook her head.

"A friend of mine told me she saw Lupe and Karida talking in the gazebo on campus a few days after Gideon got back from his trip," Julie reported. "She couldn't hear what they were saying, but the discussion appeared to be a heated one."

"Baby-sitting for Janna was a pretty transparent play for Gideon on Karida's part. I imagine Lupe was telling her friend to keep her hands off."

"Some friend," Julie said scornfully.

"Former friend," Clare admitted.

"Speaking of Gideon's trip," Craig said, "I received a call from one of my people in Dallas. She talked to Gid this morning. He's accepted the offer to head the Metroplex Rehab Center."

Sheila gasped. "He's moving to Dallas?"

"Looks that way," Craig confirmed. He and Kerry had planned to attend the graduation the day before, but their flight from South Africa had been delayed by weather. They'd arrived at the Number One only an hour ago.

"Idiot," Julie proclaimed.

Craig and Kerry both raised their brows.

"Not you," Julie said to Craig. "That stupid brother of mine."

"I agree," Clare added.

"He's a big boy now," Adam reminded them,

though it was obvious he wasn't any more pleased by the situation than they were. "Big enough to know his own mind."

"I'm not talking about his mind," Julie retorted. "His heart isn't in Dallas."

Adam worked his jaw. "Isn't that a bit presumptive of you?"

"Not presumptive, Dad," she said without taking offense. "Observant. This is his home, and Lupe is the woman for him."

"Uh-oh." Michael snorted and grinned at his father. "This might be a good opportunity for the men to retire to the smoking room while the ladies conspire."

"You don't smoke," Clare reminded him. "And you're part of this conspiracy whether you like it or not."

Michael slanted an amused grin at her. "Yes, dear."

Craig leaned forward, his elbows on his knees. "What are we conspiring?"

Kerry slapped his arm. "Jerk."

"So—" Julie rubbed her hands together "—how will we get them back together?"

An hour and another pitcher of iced tea later, Kerry said, "A family picnic, then. At the Home Place. Sounds good to me. Getting Gideon here won't be a problem, but how can we entice Lupe to join us?"

"Easy," Clare said. "We enlist Elena's help. From what she told me last night, she's no happier about this than we are. Miguelito and Teresita love coming out. If we say this is a farewell get-together for them,

Lupe won't have much choice but to show up. Even if Gideon's here," she added.

"When do you plan to have it?" Adam asked.

"Is next weekend too soon?" Julie asked. "I'm going hiking the following week, and I sure don't want to miss the fireworks."

Heads bobbed.

"Next weekend will be fine," Clare announced. "I'll drop by and visit with Elena tomorrow."

CHAPTER FOURTEEN

THE DAY of the farewell party for Gideon and Lupe turned out to be balmy with fairly low temperatures and only a gentle breeze blowing.

The festivities were scheduled to officially start around noon, but many of the Number One Ranch people had shown up the evening before to start mesquite fires to slow-roast slabs of beef brisket and *cabrito* overnight. Today, they'd barbecue pork ribs and grill catfish. The gala event, which resembled an old-time fair before commercialism had taken over, was spread over several acres below the Home Place. Large tents were set up for eating and dancing to the western band Clare had hired. Playing fields had been cleared for softball and soccer. Less strenuous games like horseshoes and darts were also available.

"Not too hard to tell the city slickers from the country cousins, is it?" Craig commented to Clare. They were standing on the front porch of the house, steaming coffee cups in hand, as they observed the scene below.

With Karida Sommers's help, Clare had quietly invited everyone from the university who worked with Gideon. Karida had declined the invitation to attend. Clare understood and didn't press. Perhaps sometime in the future Karida, Lupe and Gideon would be able to mend fences, but this wasn't the occasion for it.

Clare grinned. Dr. Williams was strolling around greeting people, wearing Bermuda shorts, a baggy T-shirt, white ankle socks and shiny penny loafers.

"When will the guests of honor make their appearances?" he asked.

"Elena said her brood would be here at noon. Gideon doesn't expect to arrive before twelve-thirty, which, on Gideon time, means not before and probably considerably after."

Craig chuckled. Gideon's tardiness was legendary.

Just then an Explorer pulled up in the parking lot not far away, and the doors opened.

"Our brother-in-law seems to have turned over a new leaf." Craig checked his watch. It was a quarter to twelve.

Gideon climbed out of his vehicle, opened the back door and a minute later approached with Janna in his arms.

Sheila stepped onto the porch. "He's early."

Janna insisted on being put down, so Gideon held her hand as they made slow progress toward the hundred-year-old ranch house. When they reached the foot of the steps, Sheila bent down and stretched out her arms. "Come on, sweetheart. Come to Grandma."

The baby scampered up the three stairs, Gideon hovering protectively behind her.

"You're early," Julie said from the doorway, making it sound like an accusation.

Gideon snorted. "Do you want me to go away and come back later?"

Ignoring the question, Julie asked, "Why are you early?"

On an indignant sigh, he said, "I got the laundry done last night, so I had more time this morning."

An amused smirk passed between Clare and her sister-in-law. Would wonders cease?

"I don't see Lupe's car," he commented with transparent casualness.

"She isn't here yet," Clare told him. "Should be any minute, though."

Dr. Williams approached the group. "You ordered up nice weather, Mrs. First."

Sheila and Clare both turned automatically, but it was Clare he was addressing.

"So this is Janna." He reached out slowly and offered his finger to the baby. "What a pretty little girl you are."

Adam joined them on the porch. "The prettiest little girl in the world," he crowed, "except for my other granddaughters, of course." He winked at Clare.

Gideon made the formal introductions. Dr. Williams had met Adam, who contributed generously to the university scholarship fund every year. Gideon introduced the other family members. They chatted amicably until Lupe's car pulled up a few minutes later.

Elena and the two children were the first to emerge from the vehicle.

"There she is!" Elena exclaimed as she marched determinedly toward Gideon, her attention focused exclusively on the baby. She extended her arms to the child. Janna was perfectly willing to be swallowed up in Elena's embrace.

"That beautiful curly red hair." She tickled the child affectionately under the chin, only then acknowledging the other people around her.

"Hello, everybody. Adam, Sheila, you have a beautiful granddaughter."

"We were just commenting on that," Adam agreed with a wide smile.

"I heard you have a fondness for sopaipillas," Elena commented to Adam.

He rubbed his belly. "Mmm."

"I brought the makings, so I can fix you some later. But here are a few samples for you to taste now." She turned to her granddaughter. "Teresita, please give the sack to Mr. First."

The brown paper bag was grease stained, and as soon as Adam opened it, they could smell the enticing aroma of cinnamon and sugar. Like a little boy in a candy store, he dipped his fingers into the bag and eagerly withdrew one. His face melted with pure pleasure when he bit into the puffy fried dough.

Sheila chuckled. "You've got a friend for life. I've tried making them, but I'm doing something wrong. Mine turn out like lead golf balls."

"Maybe you do not have the fat hot enough," Elena suggested.

Adam planted a kiss on his wife's cheek. "You're forgiven, sweetheart." He turned to the others. "Her Swedish pancakes are to die for."

"And at the rate he eats them, I'll find myself accused of murder."

Clare's son Dave appeared from around the side of the house. "We're getting a soccer game started," he told Miguelito. "Come on."

"Can I go now?" Miguelito asked eagerly.

Lupe had barely nodded before the boys ran off to join a group of other kids kicking a ball around an improvised playing field. A minute after that, Teresita wandered away with Clare's girls to find other friends among the crowd.

"I sat y'all at our table," Clare told Lupe, "since this farewell is as much for you as it is for Gideon."

Lupe tried to put on a smiley face, but Clare could see she wasn't particularly comfortable with the arrangement. "Thanks for all this. It really wasn't necessary."

"Ah, bonita," Elena said to Janna, who was squirming to get down. "Let us see what is going on." Holding the child's hand, she led her toward a group of women arranging the table in the food tent.

"Everything smells delicious," Lupe commented to Adam.

"It does, doesn't it," he agreed, then thumped the middle of his chest with the top of his rolled fist. "I guess I shouldn't have had that second sopaipilla. Where'd you put the antacids?" he asked Sheila.

Sheila gave him a long-suffering shake of the head. "They're in the medicine cabinet, where we always keep them." She snickered. "Come on, big guy. Since they'll be right in front of your nose, you probably won't be able to see them.'' Her grin was full of humor and affection. ''I'll help you.''

They turned to go inside. ''Does this mean you'll confine yourself to only one helping of hot links and tamales this afternoon?'' she asked.

That left Craig, Julie and Clare along with Gideon and Lupe.

''Give me a hand with the rest of the food from the spare refrigerator in the mud room,'' Clare said to Julie.

''You two take care of that while I go wake my blushing bride,'' Craig said. ''She's slept enough.'' He and Kerry had arrived late the previous evening and were staying in the guest house behind the main house.

Suddenly, Gideon and Lupe were alone.

''I'm glad you came today,'' he said.

''It was very generous of your family to invite us.''

He latched on to her hand and gave it a gentle tug. ''Let's go for a walk.''

Lupe hesitated, but only halfheartedly. The truth was that his touch had her blood racing, as it always did. It shouldn't feel so good, and the realization that it did disturbed her. Enough that she slipped her hand out of his grip.

Quietly he led her away from the picnic grounds, all the while wondering if the rippling pulse he'd felt had been hers or his. They climbed in silence among oak and elm, where the cool air was pine scented and the children's voices blended with the other sounds of nature. It was a peaceful place. One of contentment. A perfect spot for lovers. It was here that he had brought her to offer her his ring and his lifelong devotion. It was here that she had promised hers.

She bit her lip and remained silent.

"When do you leave for San Antonio?" he asked.

The question seemed a violation of the sanctity of this cloister. "Not until the end of the summer. I still have to decide what to do with the house. My brother-in-law, Jesse, suggests I rent it out rather than sell. But I'll need the cash for a down payment on another place in San Antone."

"Have you considered renting for a while down there yourself? That way, if you change your mind and decide to return to Coyote Springs, you won't have to lose money on a quick turnaround."

She was tempted to tell him there wouldn't be anyone here to come back to. He would be in Dallas.

"It's a thought," she agreed, "if I can find a decent house. I hate apartments. Besides, I wouldn't be able to afford a very big one. The kids are already mad enough at me without confining them in a place where they wouldn't even have a backyard."

They'd talked once of getting acreage, enough for dogs and a horse or two for the children. It all seemed so long ago now, and unreal somehow, as if they'd been talking about other people's lives.

A minute went by.

"How about you?" she asked. "When do you leave? Have you found a place to live yet?"

"They want me there by the end of next month." That was barely five weeks away. "I'm not sure what I'll do as far as living arrangements are concerned. Another town house or apartment would probably be best. They have a really nice gated community not far from the center. It would be a safe environment for Janna. But I'd like to have my own house, too.''

''Where is the center in relation to Janna's grandparents?''

''Clean over on the other side of town. Probably an hour's drive during rush hour. Not that I would ask them to mind her during the day.''

Lupe nodded. ''Especially if Vanessa isn't there. Have you heard from her?''

He smiled ruefully. ''Received a card a few days ago—from Juneau. She's on an Alaskan cruise.''

''Good for her.''

An empty silence followed.

''The truth is I don't really want to go,'' he confessed. ''I've stayed awake at night, thinking and rethinking this decision to move.'' *And thinking about you and the chance for happiness we've missed.* ''Yes, the center's a great opportunity, precisely the kind of facility we'd hoped to build for ourselves here one day. But it won't be the same. I feel like a salaried employee transitioning to a new assignment.'' *Which had also been Nick's complaint when Gideon had proposed building on his own.*

Needing to touch her, he placed his hand on hers and stroked it, tormented by what the feel of her skin was doing to him.

''Gideon, don't.'' She pulled away and stared at the babbling stream below. ''I'm not happy about this, either—''

''Then why—'' He at least had the satisfaction of seeing her take a deep breath. Her reaction to him went beyond anger, or maybe *around it* was a better description.

With closed eyes and shaking head, she waved her hand to stop him. "Because it's time for us to move on."

"Because of Janna," he mumbled.

Lupe wheeled to confront him. "Don't blame an innocent baby for this, Gideon."

"No, I'm not blaming her," he corrected himself, and stared across the gulch to the multilayered green of the forest on the other side.

"Let me ask you something," he continued after a moment. "If things had been different between us and this opportunity to take over the PT center in Dallas had come up, would you have turned it down?"

She didn't respond immediately. "If things had been different, Gideon, would you have ever considered it long enough to ask me?"

A sour knot formed in his stomach. She was right, of course. If things had gone the way they'd originally planned, he would have dismissed the Dallas offer in a heartbeat. It wasn't what they'd planned or envisioned. And he'd already admitted it wasn't what he wanted now.

"We can still open our center here," he said. "Maybe the personal rift between us will heal and maybe it won't. But that doesn't mean our professional ambitions have to suffer. Nick is staying here. You stay, too, Lupe, and so will I. We'll open our center."

She shook her head. "It won't work, Gideon."

"Of course it will. There are lots of businesses that

succeed even though the partners aren't close friends.''

Her dark eyes shone. ''Friends. Is that what we were, Gideon? Close friends?''

His blood heated. ''Lupe, I loved you. I still love you. I'll always love you.''

''Which is precisely why we can't be just friends and business partners. No, it's better for you to go your way and for me to go mine.''

''Tell me you don't love me first.'' He had no choice. He had to touch her arm. To force her to face him. He tried not to be affected by the warmth and smoothness of her skin or the pulse he could feel beating beneath its surface. ''Tell me you don't care, Lupe.''

She bit her lip, her eyes glistening. ''I care, Gideon,'' she said in a small, humble voice.

It wasn't exactly what he wanted to hear, but he was desperate. It was enough to give him hope.

She was about to say more when they heard a woman scream his name. Clare's voice, and there was panic in it. Clare never panicked. An adrenaline rush had him jumping. He grabbed Lupe's hand and started running in the direction of the commotion. ''Janna,'' Gideon huffed. ''Something must have happened to Janna.''

They bolted out of the woods toward the group of people clustered around someone on the ground. Unconsciously, Gideon's hand tightened around Lupe's. His presence of mind was clear enough for him to see Elena standing at the edge of the crowd holding Janna in her arms. It wasn't his baby, so who?

Before he realized it was happening, Lupe charged into the lead, dragging him with her through the babbling crowd that instantly parted for them. Adam First lay on the ground, his right arm thrown across his chest to his left arm. His face was pale white, his expression one of excruciating pain.

"Dad!"

Sheila was bent over him, crying his name. Michael was beside her, his fingers searching for a pulse in his father's left wrist. Craig was on his cell phone giving precise information in a voice that sounded too damned calm. Clare was holding back her children, her expression one of horrified shock.

"What happened?" Lupe asked as she crouched opposite Sheila.

"I...He was complaining of a pain in his chest, then he fell down."

Gideon knelt beside Lupe and placed his fingers at the carotid artery in his father's neck. The pulse was weak and erratic. "I think it's a heart attack," he announced.

"Oh, God," Sheila cried.

"Give us some room," Gideon commanded his brother.

Unhesitatingly, Michael rose swiftly to his feet. His hands were visibly shaking as he pulled Sheila from the prostrate form of her husband. Clare was instantly by her side to fold her in her arms.

Gideon rolled back one of his father's eyelids and saw only white. He checked the other. The same.

"Air-evac's on the way," Craig announced, as he

switched off his cell phone. "They should be here in a matter of minutes."

Adam had stopped breathing.

"I'm not sure we have that long." Gideon gave his father's chest a sharp blow with the base of his fist. Sheila gasped as if she had been the one struck.

"I'll pump his chest," Gideon declared curtly to Lupe. "You breathe for him."

He ran his fingers hurriedly down the center of his father's chest to the tip of the sternum, placed the palm of one hand on the spot and the other hand on top of it, fingers loosely interlaced. In a steady, forceful pumping motion, he began heart massage. "One, two, three…"

Lupe tilted Adam's head back and stuck her fingers in his mouth to make sure the passage was clear. At the count of fifteen, she placed her mouth over his and forced air into his lungs. Once. Twice.

Gideon continued to count out loud. At fifteen, Lupe repeated the ventilating process.

"Can you feel a pulse?" Gideon panted the words between compressions.

Lupe positioned her fingers on Adam's neck, on the carotid artery. "No," she murmured. "I can't feel…"

"Oh, God," Sheila wailed in agony, and tightened her hold on Clare. Michael wrapped them both in his arms. The children were crying. The crowd that had gathered around them was dead silent.

"Yes," Lupe shouted triumphantly. "Got it. It's thready. Keep pumping." She forced more air into the unconscious man's lungs and again felt for a pulse. "It's getting stronger."

People began to shuffle. Neither Gideon nor Lupe heard the *whop-whop-whop* of the helicopter. It was unimportant background noise in a world gone deaf with terror.

Gideon's first reaction when a man's hands tried to pull him away was to resist, then to lash out with his fists.

"Gideon." Lupe's soft voice implored him. "Gideon, step back. It's the medics. Let them get to him."

Only then did he recognize the brown-and-white uniform at his side. Another paramedic had taken Lupe's place and was putting an oxygen bag on Adam's mouth. Realizing he was in the way, Gideon backed away, but his eyes never left the sight of his father on the ground, unconscious.

The medic who replaced him had opened a black case and set it beside him. He adjusted some dials and removed two electrically wired paddles, which he pressed to either side of the patient's chest.

"Got a reading," he announced, "but he's in fib. I'll have to shock him. Stand back."

The crowd remained frozen in place, mesmerized.

The other medic ceased squeezing the oxygen bag. A jolt of current arched Adam's inert body. Gasps went up; then breaths were held. The medic checked the defibrillator's monitor. No change in reading. Another jolt. Another check.

"We've got a sinus rhythm. Keep bagging him while I get an IV started."

With an incredible efficiency of motion, the paramedics had an intravenous needle inserted into Adam's arm and had lifted the still-comatose patient onto a gurney.

Gideon felt as if he were watching a movie or a play as they popped the stretcher onto its legs and wheeled it to the waiting chopper. The crowd covered their eyes and held hats as the helicopter lifted off, bathing them in a blast of wind and dust.

"You go with your family," Elena said quietly to Gideon in Spanish. "Lupe and I will bring Janna."

Janna. God help him. For a minute, he'd forgotten her.

"Go on, now. We'll get the child's seat from your car, gather the rest of the kids and be right along."

"You don't mind?" It was a silly question, he supposed. The concern on Elena's face said this wasn't a matter of inconvenience. "*Muchas gracias, Doña* Elena. Thank you," he repeated.

"*Andale!*" she prompted.

He raised his hand and touched his daughter's cheek, then spun and followed the rest of the family. He was the last one into his brother's Suburban. He slammed the door, and Michael rolled cautiously over the uneven dirt road from the picnic area. Once on the main road he applied the gas more aggressively. No one said a word.

LUPE SAT beside Gideon—waiting. Over an hour had passed. No one spoke. There wasn't much to say. Only pray. Gideon had taken Janna from Elena as soon as they'd shown up. Lupe had stood by and watched him hug his child. She'd never doubted that he loved his little girl, but watching him hold her, she realized how thorough and abiding the bond was. Not just affection. Not duty toward his offspring, but a true devotion to the child.

The minutes slid by, and the room settled into a timeless pause in life. Gideon was being faced with the mortality of his father, a man he loved and respected very deeply. He might lose him forever.

And she was losing Gideon. Not through death. She shuddered. But because of pride. Pride they both had too much of.

He hadn't reacted the way she felt he should have. He hadn't passed a pop quiz he was in no way prepared for. Well, he should have been prepared. He'd made love to a woman. He should have anticipated the possible consequences. He should have been prepared for those consequences.

Not that he had a monopoly on foolish pride, however. She could see that now. He'd been with another woman. Never mind that it was before they met. The thought of him making love to someone else deeply offended her. She'd gone to her marriage with Miguel as a virgin. They'd both prized that gift. She'd also known he didn't come to her completely inexperienced. But she was willing to forgive him. Why then, wasn't she willing to accept Gideon on the same terms? Pride. Stupid, foolish pride.

She heard footsteps in the hallway and looked up to see a tall, gray-haired man wearing a white coat enter the room. Everyone rose as if on signal. Sheila took a step toward him, Michael and Clare at her side.

Lupe stopped breathing. Her heart pounded. Had Gideon's father survived?

"Mrs. First, I'm Dr. Fallbrook."

"What can you tell us, Doctor?" Sheila asked, frightened, her voice shaky.

"Let's sit down." The invitation, instead of relaxing tensions, served to increase them. The surgeon chose a seat in the corner so the family could sit at angles to him. When everyone was settled, he said, "We can tell from our initial cardiogram and enzyme tests that Mr. First has definitely suffered a mild heart attack."

Sheila squeezed her eyes shut. Her chin trembled. Michael, sitting beside her, reached over and took her hand. She grasped it like a lifeline.

"Mild?" Gideon's brows rose precipitously. His father had been sheet white and unconscious. His pulse had stopped, as had his breathing.

"While he's been here," the doctor continued, "he's experienced no complications such as heart failure or abnormal rhythms, but we need to do an arteriogram immediately to determine the degree of blockage in the coronary arteries supplying the heart muscle."

"What's the prognosis, Doctor?" Michael asked.

"We'll have to wait until we complete our tests. Then we can decide what our treatment will be. Medication. Dilating the affected arteries or possibly bypass surgery."

Adam First was still alive, but he was not out of danger.

CHAPTER FIFTEEN

ANOTHER TWO torturous hours went by before Fallbrook reappeared. Again he addressed himself primarily to his patient's wife.

"Your husband had a significant blockage, about ninety percent in one of the arteries leading to the heart. Fortunately, the area affected was not extensive, so bypass surgery is not necessary, but we have put in a stint to keep the passage open."

Everyone's breathing seemed to be shallow. Sheila, trying hard to be strong, accepted a tissue from Clare and held it to her nose.

"What now, Doctor?" Gideon asked.

Fallbrook smiled reassuringly. "Actually, your father's general physical condition is excellent for a man his age. He's not overweight or diabetic, which really helps. But his cholesterol is much too high, so we'll be prescribing some medication to bring it down. He'll have to watch his diet."

"He will," Sheila announced with a determination that made the people around her smile, including the physician.

"How long will he have to stay here?" Clare asked.

"Two to four days at least, to make sure we have

him stabilized, but unless there's another episode, we can probably release him Tuesday or Wednesday.''

"Can I see him?'' Sheila's voice was still shaky in spite of valiant efforts to control it.

"Yes, for a couple of minutes. He's in ICU right now. A little later, if everything stays normal, we'll move him to a private room. He's awake, but he's very tired. A brief visit will reassure him, and he'll be able to sleep more comfortably.''

"Go on,'' Michael urged her.

She surveyed the faces of the others, seeking permission.

"He needs you,'' Gideon told her. "We'll wait here until you're ready.''

Brushing back tears, she took his hand and thanked him, then followed the cardiac surgeon down the hall to where Adam First lay.

THE NEXT DAY was Sunday. Gideon had invited Sheila to stay with him and Janna at the town house so she wouldn't have to make the long trip in from the ranch. But his stepmother had declined. She had no change of clothes, no toiletries or nightgown, and in spite of Adam's not being there, she would be more comfortable in her own bed. Which was all just as well. Janna had decided that night to be a pill about going to bed and staying asleep.

At eight-thirty, Clare arrived at the town house with Sheila and insisted Gideon leave Janna with her so he could drive his stepmother to the hospital. Adam had been moved out of the intensive care unit into a private room, which was already crowded with bouquets of flowers, balloons and get-well cards.

"They won't give me a decent meal in this place," he complained with feigned exasperation. Gideon got the distinct feeling his father was enjoying the attention, if only for a little while. Unless a tiger could change its stripes, he'd be restless in no time at all.

"How do they expect a man to regain his strength without a hearty breakfast?" he grumbled. "Don't they realize it's the most important meal of the day?"

"I'd say he's on the mend," Gideon assured his stepmother. "He's almost as cantankerous now as he was when he broke his leg in the tornado."

"Don't remind me," Adam barked. He'd hated the time he'd spent in the hospital and had proved it by being the classic terrible patient, constantly complaining about everything. Yet, when he left, the staff gathered to fondly bid him farewell. It obviously hadn't taken them long to see through his act. Of course, the chocolates and pastries he had delivered regularly might have helped persuade them.

"How about running out and getting me a bacon-and-egg breakfast burrito?" Adam asked his son.

"Adam—" Sheila began in a chiding tone. Gideon realized she was still too vulnerable to appreciate the humor in her husband's request. He winked at her.

"Not a chance, Dad. In fact, your bacon-and-egg days are pretty much behind you. Cereal and yogurt from now on."

"Jesus wept and cried. You expect a man to run a ranch on that stuff?"

Gideon chuckled. "Yep." He could see his father

was putting on an act. Without a doubt, Adam would cheat once in a while when Sheila wasn't around to pull his ear, but it would be calculated cheating. His father would do what was good for him. "You'll learn to love granola."

"Speaking of which," Sheila said, "I need to talk to the nurse about diet and nutrition. Can I leave for a few minutes without the two of you sneaking out for a butter-pecan milk shake?"

Adam laughed. "She knows me too well. Go on, sweetheart, but if tofu is on the list, cross it off. I prefer my beans whole from a cast iron pot, not made into mushy paste."

"I'll remember that," she said as she leaned over and kissed him affectionately on the lips. "No more bean dip. Got it."

"I didn't mean that," he was quick to object, but not fast enough. His wife was already halfway out the door, a very pleased smirk on her lips.

Gideon observed his father's expression as his stepmother slipped out the door. And envied him. His old man had married the woman he'd fallen in love with. Their courtship had been rocky, to be sure, but in the end, they had recognized they were made for each other.

"She was scared to death yesterday, Dad. We all were."

Instead of dismissively scowling, his father remained solemn. "Scared me, too, son. I'm old enough to know I'm not immortal, but I'm not ready to find the hereafter yet."

"You've got plenty of good years left," Gideon

reassured him. "I expect you to be standing tall and popping your buttons at Janna's wedding."

Adam pulled back against the pillow, his eyes wide. "She's got a boyfriend already? I recognized that she was precocious..." He relaxed the bravado. "I'll be there, even if I have to eat tofu."

"Sans salt," Gideon added with a gleam of mischief.

"Ugh. How about pepper? Maybe I can put enough hot sauce on it to disguise its tastelessness."

Chuckling, Gideon said, "I bet you can. I guess we know what to get you for your birthday now. Black, white and red pepper, jalapeños and habaneros." It felt good to see his father's humor intact. "How do you feel?"

"Sore. I always imagined heart attacks were one-time shots. You had it and it was over. But I feel like someone's got a fist planted firmly in my rib cage."

Gideon knew from working with people in various forms of rehabilitation that injured muscles didn't heal overnight. The heart was a muscle, the one that never stopped working until... "Are they giving you anything for the pain?"

"Yeah. It's no big deal. Not nearly as bad as being kicked by a horse."

"Less embarrassing, too."

"I'm not so sure about that. These fancy duds—" he fingered the ill-pressed cotton of his hospital gown with disgust "—aren't designed to afford a man much dignity."

Adam grew serious. "This little episode has made me think, though. Time is the one thing we can never get back, son. Make the most of it. What's that fancy phrase? Carpe diem? Seize the day.''

Gideon resisted the urge to squirm. The conversation had somehow shifted from father to son.

''I've mulled over what's really important to me,'' his father continued. ''It comes down to one word. Family. I'll go on a permanent diet of bean sprouts and carrot sticks if that's what it'll take to be with my family.''

''I WAS AFRAID you'd abandoned me,'' Adam said Wednesday morning when Lupe entered his room. He was sitting in a metal-framed easy chair, fully dressed, a magazine open on his knees. His complexion had the healthy glow of the outdoorsman he was, and the sparkle was back in his eyes. Obviously he was on the mend.

''How are you feeling?'' she asked.

With a wide grin, he reached out and drew her close for a fatherly kiss on the cheek. ''Fit as a fiddle and anxious to get the hell out of here.''

He was being discharged.

''You saved my life the other day,'' he commented.

''It was Gideon,'' she replied. ''I just helped.''

''You make a good team. I owe you my life.''

She would have liked to wave the notion aside that she and Gideon somehow belonged together. After all, they'd told each other the exact opposite, that they needed to split. ''I'm glad I was there to help.''

''You just missed him, by the way.''

''Isn't he driving you home?''

''No, he's staying in town so he can visit Nick.''

She would have thought Gideon's father would take priority over his friend. But family would surround Adam. Nick was alone.

"Michael is bringing Sheila in from the ranch. They should be here any minute now. Can't be a minute too soon. This place is dangerous. All these sick people. Never know what germs might attack you. Give me the good clean smell of a horse barn any time."

One of those uncomfortable silences followed.

"He'll probably be out this weekend." No need to ask who "he" was. "Don't you be a stranger, either." Adam's face lit up as if he'd had a sudden brainstorm. "Say, why don't y'all, Elena and the kids, drive out for the weekend, too. You can sit around and giggle while I eat my oatmeal and carrot sticks."

She sympathized with him. He was a man who enjoyed food. "I don't think it'll be quite that bad. A low-fat diet doesn't have to be boring or tasteless. I bet Sheila will surprise you with her imagination and skill."

He chuckled softly, a mischievous gleam in his eye. "I'm sure she will. But you haven't answered my question. How about coming out for the weekend? Make up for the last one I spoiled. I have a couple of ponies that I know the kids will enjoy. I might even rustle one up for you."

She laughed. "No, thanks."

"To the pony or the weekend?" Before she could firmly turn him down, he added, "Won't you do this for a sick old man who needs company?"

"You're overplaying your hand, dear," Sheila said

as she walked in the door. She greeted Lupe with a
gentle hug. ''I haven't had a chance to thank you for
the lovely plant you brought yesterday. I'm adding it
to the garden at home.''

The potted mums Lupe had found at a nursery were
a deep mahogany with amber centers. They struck her
as more masculine than the pretty pinks, whites and
yellows she'd seen.

''Hi, Lupe.'' Michael strode into the room, all
smiles and chipper. ''Ready, Dad?''

''You bet.'' Adam stood up, then frowned when he
saw the orderly behind his son pushing a wheelchair.
''I don't need that,'' he declared emphatically.

''Hospital policy, sir,'' the corpulent man in the
green scrubs explained. He offered an ironic grin.
''It's not to protect you. It's to protect us. We don't
want to take a chance on you faking a fall and then
suing the hospital.''

''I wouldn't do that,'' Adam protested before he
realized he was being joshed. ''Oh, all right. But I
hate these things.''

''I'd say you're healthy, then,'' the orderly replied.

''The invitation stands,'' Adam called to Lupe as
he was wheeled out the door.

Sheila trailed behind. ''Do come. We'd like to see
you.''

Lupe thanked her but said she couldn't make any
promises and then excused herself. Nick had been admitted for knee surgery yesterday morning. He'd been
jovial and full of bad hospital jokes when she'd
stopped by his room. The operation had been per-
formed in the afternoon. He should be available to

receive visitors by now. She'd brought a card but no flowers. Nick wasn't the flowers type. Tomorrow, when he would no doubt be feeling better, she'd bring him some other kind of get-well present.

She took the elevator from the third floor to the fourth. Room 411 was at the end of the corridor, of course. As she approached, she heard male voices and knew instantly Gideon was with him.

More by happenstance than design, she'd managed to miss him on her visits to Adam the past three days. Missed him in more ways than one. But she wouldn't dwell on it. She'd told him at the ranch before Clare's terrified scream had interrupted them that it was best if they went their separate ways. She still believed it. Their breakup hadn't been all his fault, but it wouldn't be fair to him or to Janna to accept the marriage proposal she suspected he had been about to renew. She admitted caring for him, but it wasn't enough.

She debated with herself whether to enter the room. Going in would mean she'd have to spend time with Gideon and then say goodbye. Perhaps it would be better to leave now and return later. Coward, she chided herself. She was about to knock on the door frame when she heard Nick's voice.

"I'm still scared, Gid."

Lupe paused, then slowly dropped her hand. Nick afraid? Of what? Being frightened didn't match her mental image of Gideon's friend, her friend, the man they'd almost been partners with. Nick had always been so decisive, so determined, the stable guide of reason when Gideon's plans became unrealistic. Nick afraid? It didn't make sense.

"I would never have gone through with this if you hadn't been here for me, pushing, cajoling, persuading."

"I didn't say anything you weren't telling yourself, Nick."

"But I wasn't getting anywhere. You're the one who got me off dead center."

"Being afraid is nothing to be ashamed of," Gideon said. "Anyone who tells you he isn't afraid of surgery is a liar."

"Not afraid, Gid. Terrified. I was sure I was going to die. I guess I still am."

"That makes your going through with the surgery all the more courageous. That's what bravery is, my friend, doing what has to be done in the face of fear."

"Thank you for helping me see that."

"De nada, amigo. De nada."

Lupe backed away. Entering that room now would be to interrupt a very private moment between the two friends, and if they suspected she'd overheard them, they'd be deeply embarrassed. She took a step back and retreated the way she'd come.

Her mind tried to process what she'd learned. Nick had been avoiding the operation he needed because he was afraid of dying. He'd endured pain for months because of a phobia about surgery, and Gideon had talked him through that fear. Without judging or criticizing. As a sympathetic friend.

Lupe lay awake that night, thinking about Gideon, picturing him sitting at the bedside of his friend, comforting him, reassuring him, helping him maintain his dignity. The image was poignant, yet there was something redeeming about it, too. It brought back other memories. Gideon holding his daughter in his arms, pure joy radiant in his clear blue eyes. Him standing on the sidelines at a soccer game, becoming hoarse as he yelled coaching tips and encouragement, then counseling her troubled son on how to be a man. The way he'd assured Teresita on her first horseback ride, giving her tips and pointers on how to handle an animal twenty times her size. The polite deference with which he always addressed Elena as Doña Elena.

She recollected, too, the gleam when he asked her to marry him. There was a kind of rapture, a quality of pure happiness when she said yes that had melted her heart.

Most of all, she remembered his misery when he said they couldn't have sex. Once again she'd misinterpreted his motives. He hadn't been rejecting her. His refusal to consummate what they both wanted so desperately was proof of his respect for her values— values she would willingly have abandoned in the heat of passion. Instead of saying he didn't love her, he'd proved that he did, that he loved her enough not to let her make a mistake she might always regret. He'd been right when he said they would have hated each other and themselves in the morning.

Gideon First wasn't perfect. He didn't always make the right decision the first time. But more important, he made the right decision when it counted. She'd given up *good* in her quest for *better,* when for her there was no better man.

LUPE HAD just returned from the mall with Elena and the children when she heard a car pull into the driveway. Even before she peeked through the lace curtains over the sink, she knew who it was.

She watched him get out of his Explorer. He looked tired as he closed the vehicle door. He always seemed a little wrung out these days. Taking care of a baby wasn't easy, and the planning he'd been doing in addition to his job at the school had him burning the candle at both ends. Even the fatigue didn't disguise his determination, however, nor did it rob his step of a lightness she hadn't seen lately. Something had changed.

From behind her, Elena said, "The kids need to get busy cleaning up the front yard. That windstorm this afternoon blew trash all over the place."

Before Lupe could respond, her mother-in-law had fled through the living room and was gone.

Gideon's hand was raised to knock on the back door when Lupe opened it. For a heartbeat, they stared at each other.

"Hi," he said.

"Hi," she responded unimaginatively. "Uh, your dad—he's okay, isn't he?"

"He's fine. Giving Sheila a hard time, of course."

"Of course."

He chuckled. "Mind if I come in?"

"Oh, yeah." She stepped aside. "Sorry."

She swung open the screen door and stood with her arm extended. He brushed past her. There was no overt move to touch her, but she could feel the electricity between them. She barely controlled the urge to put out her hand to him.

"Coffee smells good." He glanced from her to the glass carafe on the coffeemaker.

In fact, the black brew was stale. She might have told him that, but he wasn't here for coffee.

"Let me make a fresh pot."

He leaned against the counter, observing her as she emptied the carafe, scrubbed it clean and refilled it with tap water. Her movements lacked the usual easy grace he'd learned to expect from her. He was making her nervous, giving her the same jitters she'd had after their first kiss in this very room almost two years earlier. A kiss that started off as friendly and quickly progressed to something a lot more passionate. It pleased him that he still had the power to elicit that reaction.

"I didn't get to see Nick today. How's he doing?" she asked over her shoulder.

"Great. They'll probably have him up and walking a few steps tomorrow," he replied.

"The surgery was no problem, then. That must have been a relief for him."

"He can handle anything."

No mention of helping him through a mortal fear of the operating table. Strange, Lupe thought, that she'd allowed his modesty to slip by her in all the acrimony of the past two months.

"Where's Janna?"

"Kerry's fallen in love with her new niece. She insisted on staying with her for a while."

"Janna's easy to fall in love with." Lupe's voice trembled with the words. She gripped the edge of the counter with both hands and took a deep breath, unwilling to turn around and let him see the tears brimming. "Did you come to say goodbye?" Her voice was thick. "Is that why you're here?"

To hold you in my arms, he wanted to shout. *To tell you I love you. To make you marry me.* "Please sit down."

She fought to control the shakes that suddenly racked her body, to hold back the tears that threatened to fall. Head lowered, she moved to the table and slipped into her accustomed seat.

He took the one opposite and reached for her fumbling hands. "What happened to Dad on Sunday," he said gently, "made me realize how short life is."

She had her lips pinched between her teeth. "I know." She closed her eyes. "I've been thinking the same thing."

"I told Craig a little while ago that I'm not taking the Dallas job," he murmured. "I'm staying here, Lupe. And I want you to stay here, too."

She raised her head and stared at him with watery eyes.

He went on before she could object. "I'm going to start a PT center here, Lupe. Our center. The one we planned. I want you to be a part of it. You might be right—working together could be uncomfortable for a while. But we're both professionals and damn good at what we do. Coyote Springs is our home. This is where we belong."

She said nothing, her eyes downcast. The coffeemaker sputtered. She intertwined her fingers and released them, then joined them again. Tears welled. "The center," she mumbled. "What about Nick?"

"He's willing if you are."

Without releasing her hands, Gideon rose from his chair and circled to her side of the table. He crouched beside her. "The center is important, but that's not really why I'm here, Lupe." He cupped her chin with his free hand and met her gaze with his. "I love you, Lupe. I love you with all my heart and soul, with every fiber of my being. I want to marry you and have children with you."

With her head bowed, she continued to bite her lip.

"But if I can't, I still need to be near you." His hand glided up her cheek. His fingers toyed with the delicate skin below her ear. Instinctively, she tilted her head into his gentle touch, savoring its warm strength. "I know I've disappointed you, that I'm not worthy of you. But I promise I'll do everything in my power to be the man you deserve. And then maybe someday you'll let me put my ring on your finger again."

The sputtering behind her stopped. The room fell uncomfortably silent.

"I was wrong," she finally said.

He waited, not sure what she was talking about, afraid to ask.

"I was wrong to judge you the way I did."

His hand curled behind her neck. "You were right, sweetheart. I should never have had any doubts about what to do. Janna is my daughter. I love her. But I didn't understand that yet. I was so afraid you would reject her—"

Lupe started to protest.

He pushed on. "I misjudged you. I believed you

would reject her because she was another woman's child, a reminder—"

"She's a baby," Lupe corrected him. "She deserves to be loved for her own sake."

His smile was rueful. "And I was so preoccupied with my own sense of guilt that I didn't see her as an individual human being and you as a loving mother."

"She's also your daughter, Gideon, which makes her all the more special."

"Forgive me, Lupe. For being such a blind fool."

"Maybe we've both been blind," she consoled him.

"Stay here, Lupe, and work with me."

"What about the ring?"

"The ring?" His heart pounded.

"You said you'd give it back to me. Is that part of the deal?"

Was she rejecting the notion—or embracing it?

"It's an offering. A pledge."

"Not good enough, Gideon." She watched his expression sag. "Either I get the ring back, or it's no deal. I pack my bags and leave."

She watched his face light up, the sadness and fear flee and turn to gladness.

"You want it back?"

She smiled and nodded.

He couldn't believe his good fortune, or that he'd had the sense to slip the ring into his pocket before leaving on his way over here. She wanted his ring back. She wanted to marry him, be his wife, the mother of his children. He tried to put his hand in his pocket, but he was on the wrong knee. Instead of standing up, he switched knees. Somehow, it seemed fitting that he be in that posture when he slipped it onto her finger.

He held her hand and looked into her black eyes. "Guadalupe Hernandez-Amorado, I promise to love, honor and cherish you for the rest of my life. Will you marry me?"

"Gideon First. I will be your wife and the mother of your babies—all of them."

He stalled, not quite sure how to interpret the last remark.

She laughed then and lunged forward to hug him. "I trust there aren't too many more."

"God, I hope not."

She pulled back, brows raised.

"I mean…"

"Shut up, you nitwit, and kiss me."

He rose to his feet and lifted her with him. "I really do love you." He brought his mouth to hers and possessed it.

She uttered a soft moan of pleasure. With her eyes closed, she luxuriated in the sensations racing through her. She'd missed his touch, the feel of his hard body pressed against her, the gentleness of his firm caress. Old longings, old urges racked her, and the sweet knowledge that they would make love overwhelmed her. She wanted him. Here and now.

The front door slammed. She almost didn't hear it or didn't let it register. With a shudder of regret, she squirmed out of his embrace. Breathless.

"Mommy, Mommy." Teresita's voice came from the living room. "Can I come in?"

Lupe glanced at Gideon, who seemed equally ill at ease. Not breathless exactly. Panting, like a hungry wolf. *Soon,* she yearned to tell him.

"Of course, sweetheart."

"Grandma said you wanted to be alone with Gideon. Are you still mad at him?"

Lupe shot him an amused grin, a come-hither leer. "No, honey. I'm not mad at him anymore."

Elena walked in behind her granddaughter, Miguelito a step behind her.

The older woman's face lit up. She dashed forward and took Lupe's left hand and stared at the ring on her finger. "You…"

Smiling at her mother-in-law, Lupe announced, "I've decided we're staying here in Coyote Springs."

"Yeah!" they both exclaimed.

"And marry Gideon."

"Really? He'll be our new papa?" Teresita asked.

"You mean it this time?" Miguelito challenged, not quite as trusting as his younger sister.

Lupe wrapped her arm around Gideon's waist and leaned into him. "You're going to have a baby sister."

"And maybe later a little brother, as well," Gideon added.

"Does that mean Mommy will get a big belly?" Teresita asked.

"Gross," her brother commented.

"It won't be gross," Gideon assured the boy. "It'll be beautiful." He gazed at Lupe with adoring eyes.

"Your mother will be beautiful with a big belly." He looked at her, wishing he could get started on the project immediately. "Very beautiful."

"I'm glad I'll have a baby sister to play with," Teresita noted. "And that someday Miguelito will have a baby brother to play with, too."

"I'm not going to play with him. That's what girls do."

Gideon chuckled. "You mean you won't teach him how to fish and play soccer?"

"That's not the same," the boy objected.

"We'll see." Gideon kissed the top of Lupe's head. "In the meantime, we have a wedding to plan."

EPILOGUE

"I DON'T LIKE the looks of this storm," Sheila said. She finished rolling out the dough and gently lifted it into one of the two pie pans she had on the counter. "Road conditions are going to be treacherous, and flying will be even worse."

Adam wrapped an arm around her shoulders. "You're a worrywart." He gave her an affectionate kiss on the temple.

She harrumphed. "As if you're not. Haven't you finished cutting up those apples yet?"

"Patience, woman."

He sliced the last of the dozen Granny Smiths and was sprinkling them with cinnamon and sugar, under his wife's careful supervision, when they heard the sound of a vehicle pulling up outside, its horn tooting merrily.

"They made it." Sheila breathed with relief.

"Of course they made it." Together they moved to the back door.

The cold air brought Michael and his sister Kerry blustering into the warm kitchen.

"Smells like heaven," she said, kissing her stepmother on her flour-dusted cheek.

Kerry's husband, Craig, and her son, Brian, followed a moment later with the hand luggage. More kissing, hugging and hand-shaking ensued.

"Mmm. Pumpkin pie baking."

"She already baked the mince," Adam told him.

"Where're Clare and the children?" Sheila asked Michael.

"Driving over separately. Figured there wouldn't be room for everyone in one vehicle. I felt like Santa, sandwiched in with all the presents, as it was."

"How's school?" Adam asked his grandson. The nineteen-year-old had filled out since he'd seen him last and looked like a man instead of a gangly teenager. College obviously agreed with him.

"Fantastic," Brian replied. "I'll be working on one of Craig's job sites this coming summer."

Adam was proud of the boy and pleased that Kerry's husband was helping him in his ambition to become an architect.

"The storm's moving in fast." Craig peeled off his leather jacket. "Where's the rest of the clan?"

"On their way," Adam assured him.

"How's Janna?" Kerry asked affectionately, and accepted a cup of tea from Sheila.

"Beautiful and getting big. She keeps her old grandpa hopping," he assured her proudly. "Wait till she gets here and starts leading the carols."

It was another thirty minutes before Clare's Suburban pulled into the yard behind the ranch house.

"No word from Gideon and Lupe yet?" Julie asked as she shucked her heavy parka. She'd spent the night on the Number One and come over with Clare and the four children.

"I tried to get them on their cell phone," Adam told her, "but no answer."

"It's snowing," Beth-Ann, the younger girl, announced happily.

Everyone went to a door or window to gaze out at the fluffy white dots drifting down.

"Isn't it lovely?" Sheila exclaimed, trying not to show her apprehension for the family members driving on unpaved roads.

"When was the last time we had a white Christmas, Dad?" Julie intertwined her arm with his as they watched the pristine flakes touch the winter-frosted ground.

"It's been years. We don't usually get snow until January, if we get any at all."

Over the next hour, the women busied themselves with cooking and baking, wrapping a few last-minute presents and supervising the men as they brought in more cordwood for the immense stone fireplace in the living room, rearranged furniture and maneuvered the huge potted fir in front of the picture window. The children wanted to decorate it immediately but were told they had to wait for Miguelito, Teresita and Janna.

"They should have been here by now," Sheila confided to Adam a little past two o'clock. "I hope nothing's happened to them. There's already more than an inch of snow on the ground."

"Relax, sweetheart. You know Gideon's always late."

"Not since he and Lupe got married, he hasn't

been," Sheila reminded him. "In fact, they were early the last three times they came for dinner."

"I'm sure they're fine," he reassured her. "You know there's always last-minute stuff to do this time of year. Besides, Gideon's a good driver."

"See if you can get him on his cell phone," she urged.

"I just did. It rings but no answer. Probably dead batteries."

Another hour went by.

"Still no word?" Michael asked.

Adam shook his head, clearly worried.

"I'll take the four-by-four and look for them."

"I'm going with you," Brian insisted. "If they slid off the road, you'll need a strong back."

"Call in every ten minutes," Adam instructed as he handed a cell phone to Brian.

The two men were climbing into Michael's truck when they heard a horn blaring. They all peered through the now-driving snow to see the headlights of Gideon's Explorer. It crunched gently to a stop.

Relief washed through Adam. He strode over to the vehicle. "Y'all okay?"

"We're fine, Dad." Gideon chuckled. "You order this white stuff just for us?"

Lupe crawled out of the passenger seat, looking miserable as the snow buffeted her face. She opened the back door of the van and accepted Janna from Elena. Miguelito and Teresita were already scurrying past her to make snowballs. Gideon joined Lupe and put a protective arm over her shoulders at the same time Adam shielded Elena from the storm.

"Have the kids help you unload the presents," Gideon said cheerfully to his brother as he escorted his wife and daughter to the back door of the ranch house.

After all the fluttering that inevitably followed the latecomers' arrival, the adults settled down in the large living room and sipped hot coffee, tea and spiced apple cider in front of the blazing fire while the children decorated the tree.

"What happened?" Adam finally asked. "Why didn't you call to say you'd be late? You had Sheila really worried sick."

Sheila drew back and peered at Adam while everybody else smiled into their cups. He wasn't fooling anyone.

"We had to stop for a few minutes," Gideon explained. "I tried to call you, but the battery on the cell phone was dead. Apparently, someone—" he raised an eyebrow in his wife's direction "—forgot to charge it this morning."

"Me," Lupe said contritely, smiling at him. She took a sip of her herb tea. "I was preoccupied."

Elena was grinning from ear to ear.

"Last-minute present wrapping?" Kerry asked.

"Not exactly," Lupe responded.

"Though it is a wonderful present," Gideon contributed.

Sheila gazed at her new daughter-in-law, caught Elena's eye and suddenly grinned mischievously. "What exactly did you have to stop for?"

"She got sick," Miguelito yelled from across the room. "Gross."

"Car sick?" Adam asked.

"Nope," Gideon said and wrapped his arm around his wife. "Morning sick."

Everyone froze, then started talking at the same time. "Morning sickness?"

"I just found out two days ago," Lupe explained.

The women laughed and cried. The men beamed and slapped one another on the back, as if they all deserved congratulations. The mood that had been quietly content blossomed into unbounded, exuberant joy.

"Every time I think Christmas can't get any better," Adam said, his eyes suddenly glassy, "it does."

It wasn't until much later that night, when everyone had retired, that Gideon lay under the covers with his wife in his arms and whispered in her ear. "You make me the happiest man in the world, Lupe. I love you."

"And I love you, Gideon. I always will."

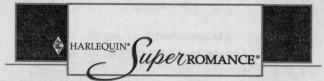